Angels Fly

by

Donna Simonetta

This is a work of fiction. Names, characters, places, and incidents are either the product of the author's imagination or are used fictitiously, and any resemblance to actual persons living or dead, business establishments, events, or locales, is entirely coincidental.

Angels Fly

COPYRIGHT © 2016 by Donna Stevens Simonetta

Cover Art by *Debbie Taylor*

The Wild Rose Press, Inc.
PO Box 708
Adams Basin, NY 14410-0708
Visit us at www.thewildrosepress.com

Publishing History
First Fantasy Rose Edition, 2016
Print ISBN 978-1-5092-0789-3
Digital ISBN 978-1-5092-0790-9

Published in the United States of America

Dedications

To Leo, the best husband in the world, for your unfailing support, love, and willingness to eat frozen pizza for dinner, so I could have time to write!

~*~

And to my wonderful mom and sisters—Mary, Judy, and Mary (aka Queen), who loved my writing from the start and are the best support system I could ever have!

~*~

And last but not least—to Joe, AJ, and Maryann, for being my earliest readers and cheerleaders, and providing excellent feedback to help me make *Angels Fly* the best it could be!

"Angels fly because they take themselves lightly."
~G.K. Chesterton

Chapter 1

"Are you sure cocktails are the traditional follow-up to yoga class?" Kelly asked from her perch on a tall bar stool at the tiny table. She tugged at her messy ponytail and looked around the bar. Her gaze drifted right past Zane and his boss Uriel, who watched from the bar, as if she hadn't seen them.

"I can't believe you'd question me on this, Kelly. It is an absolute must, post-yoga." her friend, Grace, replied with gravitas while Janie laughed.

Kelly shrugged and raised her margarita glass as she toasted with a chuckle. "Then here's to 'Downward Facing Dog'!"

Her two friends hoisted their own glasses and chirped in unison, "To 'Downward Facing Dog'!"

Kelly pulled the zipper on her pink hoodie a little higher over the gray tank top she wore underneath it. "I feel a little self-conscious being here in our yoga gear. This is one of the new hot spots in town; I feel like I should be more dressed up than this—heck, I should be more dressed up than this to go to the grocery store!"

"It is the place to see and be seen at night, but look around, it's the middle of the day, it's practically empty," Grace said.

A beam of bright mid-afternoon southern California sun shone through the wall of windows to the street, bounced off the jeweled pendant light over their table, and cast an amber glow on Grace's honey blonde hair. Dressed in low-slung yoga pants and layered black and white tank tops, she leaned back and languidly swung a mile-long leg off the tall stool as she twirled back and forth.

Janie pulled her gauzy over-sized shirt tighter across her plump bosom and replied, "I'm feeling a little underdressed, too."

Grace looked around the bar and shrugged. "The only person who's looked our way is the bartender—and he's been checking out Kelly since we got here, so I think the yoga pants are working for him."

Kelly leaned off the side of her chair to peek around Grace at the bartender in question. Her face flushed as pink as her hoodie as she squeaked, "Grace! He can't be looking at me that way! I'm old enough to be his…" She paused and finished with dignity, "…his moderately attractive older sister."

Grace snorted, and she even made the rude noise sound elegant. "His older sister's hot best friend, maybe." She looked to their companion for confirmation. "I'm right on this one, Janie, aren't I?"

Janie nodded. "Oh yeah. His older sister's hot best friend, for whom he's secretly lusted since junior high."

Kelly swatted Janie's arm. "You two are crazy—he's a child. And I'm…not."

Janie peered at the bartender over the rim of her glass. "Younger than you—yes—but not a baby. If he's serving drinks in a bar, he has to be over twenty-one, and he has a lovely aura—I think he might be an old soul."

Uriel looked at the bartender and frowned with an appraising nod. "She's right. Most humans are full of hooey when they talk about the metaphysical, but the bartender has a pure aura. Maybe when his time comes, he'll work for me."

Zane rolled his eyes, disinterested in the bartender and his potential career in the afterlife. He pushed the cowboy hat back on his head and asked, "What's the deal here, Uriel? This Kelly person is my new assignment?"

"Yes, she's Michael's widow."

"She seems happy enough to me."

The taller man waved one of his long-fingered hands dismissively. "Rookie mistake, Zane. You need to learn to listen for a little longer before you judge. Things are very rarely how they appear to be on the surface." He inclined his golden head toward the table.

Zane got the hint and directed his attention back to the women's conversation.

"In all fairness, Grace, if she wasn't always so buried in her work, our Kelly would know the rules of yoga cocktails," Janie said.

Kelly held up her hands defensively. "Hey, I'm not buried in my work. I've even been taking a vacation while my editor works on my manuscript."

She blushed at her friends' dubious expressions and confessed, "All right—I have been doing a little research on my next book, but mostly I'm footloose and fancy-free."

She paused and swiped at the salt on the rim of her glass with the tip of her tongue before taking a sip. "For a little while. At least until my editor sends it back to me for revisions."

Janie popped a handful of peanuts from a bowl on the table into her mouth and chewed as she studied her friend. She swallowed. "And what do you propose to do with all your free time? Hmm?"

Grace put her glass down with a thunk, flapped her hands, and opened her eyes wide. "Oh! I've got an idea. You can find a man and have a wild, passionate fling."

The smile vanished from Kelly's face and her voice was tight. "I'm not ready to start dating. I wish you guys would stop pushing me."

Grace reached across the tiny table to grasp her friend's hand. "But Michael's been gone two years, Kel. It's time."

She held up Kelly's left hand, which still sported a diamond solitaire and platinum wedding band. "At least take these off. No decent man would approach you while you're wearing them—they're a big, flashing neon 'hands-off' sign to everyone except the douchiest douche, and those are not the guys you want to attract."

Kelly pulled her hand back and blinked away tears. "I'm not trying to attract anyone! And I like wearing my rings. It makes me feel closer to Michael."

Janie put her arm around Kelly to give her a loving squeeze, and her voice was gentle when she spoke. "Michael didn't want you to be alone forever. He wanted you to be happy."

"I am happy! I love my work, I live in a great city, and I've got the best friends in the world." She narrowed her eyes and pointed between them. "Although, just between us, I have to admit sometimes they can be a little pushy."

"Okay. No passionate fling," Grace conceded. However the stubborn set of her delicate jaw indicated she wasn't about to back down. "But you could put yourself out there, just to make some male friends."

"I've got male friends." Kelly counted them off on her fingers as she spoke, "David, Bill, Greg."

Grace ticked the three off on her own fingers, and said, "Gay, my husband, Janie's husband. They don't count."

"See? You're still trying to get me to date, otherwise they would count."

"It never hurts to expand your circle of friends," Janie said. "You could try a social networking site."

"Online dating? Please. It's so not my thing, even if I was ready to date. Which I'm not."

"I don't mean online dating, although when you're ready to date, there's nothing wrong with it. I meant those sites where you can re-connect with old classmates—people like that. I'm all about online social networking lately, and it's been fun. All kinds of people have found me, and I've really enjoyed being in contact with them again."

With a waggle of his fingers, Uriel opened Kelly's thoughts to Zane. She was considering Janie's suggestion. She lived in San Diego now, but as she'd grown up in New Hampshire, and went to college in Boston, it seemed like a safe way to get her well-intentioned friends off her back. Most of her old school friends probably lived a safe three thousand miles away, so even Grace and Janie couldn't think it was a reasonable distance to carry on a relationship. What would they do—meet for dinner halfway? Say in Kansas?

She nodded sharply. "Okay. I'll do it. I'll mix and mingle on the Web, if it'll get you two sharks to back the heck off."

Janie held up her hand like she was making a

pledge. "Promise. If you give this an honest chance, I'll leave your non-existent dating life alone."

Grace lifted her martini glass. "Amen. To first steps."

They clinked glasses solemnly while Kelly opened her eyes wide and blinked in what she hoped was an innocent expression. She secretly hoped all her high school classmates, with the exception of her best friend David Taylor who lived just up the road in Los Angeles, were living a continent away in New England.

Uriel waved his hand, and Kelly's thoughts were once again closed to Zane.

"Still think all is well with her?"

The cowboy shrugged. "Maybe not. She's hanging onto Michael the same way he's hanging onto her." His dark blue eyes narrowed as he took in his boss' appearance. "Y'know, Uriel, if we're gonna make ourselves visible, you might want to blend in a little more with the locals."

Uriel fluttered his huge, snowy wings in irritation, and then slowly folded them against his back. The air around them shimmered the way heat rises off hot pavement, before they flickered one last time and vanished from sight. He also tamped down the glow of light that emanated from him before he made himself visible to the humans in the bar.

The bartender started, and the clean glasses he took out of the drying rack to stack behind the bar clanked as he bobbled them in his hands. He put the glasses down and then made his way down the bar to them. "Hey guys. Sorry, I didn't see you come in—hope you weren't waiting too long. What can I get you?"

"We just got here. No problem, man," Zane said in

his slow Western drawl. "I'll take whatever you have on tap, and my friend here will have a red wine."

As the bartender pulled the tap to pour beer into a frosty mug, his gaze followed theirs. He pulled a wine bottle out from beneath the bar and poured a glass. As he waited for the mug to fill with amber liquid, he looked pointedly at a loud group of business people from the nearby convention center as they came in and took the table next to Kelly and her friends. "Those three aren't too bad, huh? They seem like fun. Y'all better make your move before one of those guys does." He winked as he put their drinks on the bar. "Or before I do. I think the brunette's pretty cute."

Zane picked up his beer and took a long draw. "We're just looking."

The bartender shrugged and walked toward the waitress who waited at the other end of the bar with an order for him. He called over his shoulder as he went, "Suit yourself, man. It's just the good ones are few and far between in my experience; you gotta act fast."

Uriel swirled his Cabernet, inhaled the bouquet, and took a sip. "Kelly is a special person. I can see why Michael is reluctant to let go, but until he does, he can't move on to the next plane, and as long as he's hanging around Kelly, she feels his presence and won't let go of him and live her life. It's a vicious cycle."

"Without a doubt—but is Michael ready to let her go?"

Uriel nodded. "He is. He's a good soul, and he's realized Kelly is missing him too much to move on with her life. She's still a young woman at thirty-five; he knows if she opened her heart again she could find love and have a family."

"What's in it for Mike?" the cowboy asked with a raised eyebrow, his eyes still riveted on the women like a predator reluctant to let his prey out of his sights.

"He'll find joy in her happiness, and he can move on from this earthly plane. He's got a lot of loved ones waiting for him, both souls he knows, and those he's yet to meet. It's a win-win situation, really."

"Why me? I mean I like Mike and all, and I'm always glad to help out a buddy, but this whole love thing isn't really my gig."

Uriel acknowledged the truth of Zane's words with a curt nod of his head, but said, "Michael asked for you specifically. He likes you, and more importantly, he trusts you with this delicate mission."

The muscles in his square jaw worked as he said through clenched teeth, "But you said it yourself—I'm a rookie—I've only been in your Guardian Angel Corps for a hundred and thirty-one years."

"True," Uriel conceded, "but you mustn't be modest—you show great promise. You've helped a lot of troubled souls in that time."

Zane looked away from Uriel. A car horn honked, and he squinted in the bright sunlight as he gazed out the window to the street. California traffic was insane—give him a horse anytime. He rubbed the dimple in his chin. God, how he hated that thing—during his lifetime, his currency had been his toughness, and the damned cleft in his chin made him look like some ruffled shirt-velvet-waistcoat-wearing riverboat gambler. His pretty face made him work twice as hard to maintain his tough-guy image.

He nodded once before he finally spoke. "Yeah, but usually I'm helping guys like me, who got off on a bad path and need a little nudge to get back on the straight and narrow. I don't have a clue how to get a grieving widow woman to move on and find love again."

Uriel allowed a small smile to cross his classically handsome face, and Zane knew that even if his boss was amused by his arguments to be taken off the case, there was no chance he was getting out of this assignment.

"Michael has an idea that he's pursuing, which should help. Evidently there's a man from Kelly's past here in San Diego who he thinks might be the one to help her move forward with her life—his name is James Flynn—Michael is working that angle."

Zane looked away from Kelly and turned to Uriel. He decided to make one last-ditch effort to make this assignment a little more bearable. "If I have to work this case, can't I take the guy? I don't really understand women."

"What male does?" Uriel asked with a shrug, "But obviously, Kelly would recognize Michael, and this other fellow doesn't know him. Never fear, Zane, Michael has every confidence you'll figure out what to do."

Zane felt his words like a punch to the gut, but schooled his features to his trademark iciness, so his pain wouldn't show. "But you don't."

Uriel placed a fatherly hand on the younger angel's shoulder. "If I didn't trust you, you wouldn't be here right now. Just watch Kelly today. Make sure she signs up for that online thing. It's part of Michael's plan."

Zane raised an eyebrow. "So it wasn't just chance that her friends suggested it?"

"Leave nothing to chance," Uriel said sagely. "I just put the tiniest hint of a suggestion in her friend's mind. It's up to you and Michael now."

****

At the same time, a few blocks away, Michael was at a waterfront bar in Seaport Village waiting to put his part of the plan into action. He sat at the bar and nursed an Irish whiskey as he stared with open curiosity at the tall, gorgeous redhead yelling at James Flynn.

James watched her storm out, and flounce down the waterfront to the parking lot. He shrugged, brushed his sun-streaked dark blond hair out of his eyes, folded his long, lean frame onto the barstool next to Michael, and ordered a beer.

Michael said with sympathy, "That didn't end well, huh?"

"Nope, but she was too young for me, anyway." James winked, and his green eyes were alight with humor in spite of the situation.

One wall of the bar faced San Diego Bay and was completely open to the beautiful day. A breeze ruffled Michael's brown hair, and he smoothed it down with one hand as he replied, "Maybe, but a lot of guys would be crying in their beer to watch a hottie like her take off."

"She might be hot, but that's about all she has going for her." James rubbed his thumb and forefinger together. "And she was only interested in one thing— let's just say it wasn't my good looks or sparkling personality, and I'm not about to become her own personal ATM." He took a long draw on his beer and chuckled humorlessly. "Which is ironic, considering my ex-wife left me a few years back because I didn't make enough money for her. Guess she jumped ship a little too soon."

"Wow. Those grapes are sour."

"Possibly, but experience has been a harsh teacher. My best friend is married to a good woman, but most of the women I've known have been more like my ex-wife or my date tonight. They'll stick around as long as they think there's a payoff in it for them, but when someone with deeper pockets comes along they're off like a shot."

Michael sipped his drink and shook his head. "Not all women are like that. My wife's the greatest woman in the world—smart, funny, good-looking, and she makes plenty of her own money, so I'm more the dead weight financially in our relationship." He chuckled and then added as the weight of what he was doing hit him like a physical blow, "I'd do anything to make her happy."

"Good deal for her."

"For me, too. See, she feels the same way about me, so it all works out fine. If just one of you is trying, it won't work," Michael said.

"You're a lucky man. If I'm going to be honest about it, in my marriage neither of us really tried. I was too wrapped up in my work and she was too wrapped up in another man and his Swiss bank accounts. I've dated my fair share of women since my divorce, but none of them sound like your wife."

"None of them?" His drinking companion was incredulous. "Surely out of all the women you've known in your life, there's been one who was different?"

As the other man shook his head, Michael sipped

his whiskey, smacked his lips in satisfaction—being able to make himself corporeal had its advantages, and savoring a good Irish was one of them. He turned his attention back to his target. "Sounds like you've been picking the wrong women."

James laughed shortly, and then fell silent.

When he didn't show any signs of carrying on with their conversation, Michael was forced to peek into James' thoughts.

James was thinking that he liked this guy. He didn't usually talk like this with other men about relationships, but he figured what the hell, they'd probably never see each other again. The man had a distinct Boston accent and was probably in San Diego for business—this bar was near the convention center and always had a lot of out-of-towners. Also, he had obviously hit pay dirt with his wife. Maybe he knew something about meeting a good woman, and could pass it along to James, because he was sure as hell sick of the bad ones he'd been seeing lately. He'd made light of tonight's scene, but he was tired of women looking at him, and seeing only his wallet. He had so much more to offer, but he'd yet to meet a woman who was interested enough to look deeper than his black credit card. He was at a point in his life where he wanted more—wanted what this man seemed to have in his marriage, a partnership between two people who loved and respected each other. It could be the fault was in his choice, not in all women. Hell, they couldn't all be like his grasping ex, and that was the assumption he'd been operating on since his divorce.

Since James was coming around all on his own, Michael held his counsel and sipped his drink while the other man worked his way around to finally speaking.

"Okay, you could be right that I've been choosing the wrong women," James admitted. "How do I pick the right ones instead?"

Michael looked out at the water. "How about in your past? Before the ex—did you ever know a good woman, and it just didn't work out between you? Y'know what I mean—the one who got away."

James turned on his bar stool, and stared out at the boats in the bay. He picked at the label on his beer, loose from condensation. "Funny you should put it that way. There was a girl, back in the day, whom I've always thought of that way. Her name was Kelly Morrison; she was from my home town back east."

Michael felt his heart leap at Flynn's admission— pay dirt! He forced his voice to sound calm. "Sounds like there's a story there to me. Let's hear it."

James glanced at him out of the corner of his eyes and turned up the corners of his mouth. "It was right after I graduated college. I went back to my folks' house to figure out what the hell to do next. My kid sister had just finished high school, and had a huge graduation party."

He paused, and Michael prompted, "And this girl—Kelly, was that her name? She was there?"

He nodded. "Yep. I felt older and superior to my sister's friends." He winked and said facetiously, "I was twenty-two after all, the height of sophistication. I was trying to get away from the party—my parents' house overlooks the ocean, so I went out to the bluffs to get some peace and quiet, and Kelly was there. She was a little shy, and she wanted to be alone, too."

"So you decided to be alone together."

"Yeah. She was smart, funny, and cute, so I didn't mind the company. She seemed more mature to me than my sister's other friends."

"What happened?"

"We hung out that night, and then went out the next night. Then she got back together with an old boyfriend and dumped me."

"You never saw her again?"

"I saw her around town that summer, but she was always with the boyfriend. Then in the fall she went to college—Boston University, I think—and I moved to New York to focus on my art."

"You don't know what happened to her? Where she is now?"

One side of his mouth tilted up, "I imagine she's back east doing something with books—she loved reading—and raising a passel of kids with the guy she dumped me for."

"Could be," Michael shrugged nonchalantly, while he waged an internal struggle to not overplay his hand. "Or maybe this Kelly is on her own now, too. You could try to find her—there are lots of sites online to hook-up with people from your past, social networks."

James frowned, "I don't know about that. I was just a blip on her radar screen; she'd never remember me. She probably still lives in New England, and I live here in San Diego. What would be the point?"

Michael shrugged again, as if the other man's decision didn't matter to him one way or the other, when in reality, all of his plans for Kelly's happy future hinged on James finding Kelly through the social networks he'd oh-so-casually mentioned. Assuming, of course, that Zane could get Kelly to do the same. He tossed back the last of his Irish, and forced his voice to sound light and breezy. "Whatever. Only one way to find out, and that's to go online and see if she's on there." He rose and tossed a twenty on the bar. "I've got somewhere to be, but if I were you, I'd try to find this woman. You might be pleasantly surprised. Good luck, man."

****

Zane gave Kelly a little bit of a head start and then tossed some money on the bar to pay for his beer. Uriel had left a while ago, but Kelly and her friends had lingered over their yoga cocktails. He smiled as he thought about them. He could see why Michael was so crazy about Kelly. He just hoped the guy his friend had in mind for her would appreciate her quick wit and kind heart and snap her up fast, so this assignment would be over and he could move back to the street punks that up until now had been his work in the afterlife.

Kelly separated from her friends on the street. The other two women were going to a parking garage to get their cars and head out of the city center to their homes, but Kelly was within walking distance of her downtown condo. Zane decided invisibility was the way to go, after all he didn't want her thinking she had some kind of crazy cowboy stalker.

He pursed his lips and considered the idea. If she did think he was stalking her, it might drive her to this guy Michael had in mind for protection. He shook his head. That wouldn't work—modern women didn't turn to a man to protect them, like they had back in his day—they fought their own battles now. He had to figure out some other way to prod her. He wished he could just herd her toward the guy Michael had picked out for her, like he used to do with cattle when he was a working cowboy.

Kelly waited on the corner to wave good-bye to her friends, and then turned to walk home. As her friends drove out of sight, her bright smile faded, and her shoulders sagged.

"Why on earth did I agree to sign up for that stinking social network?" she muttered under her breath.

Zane trailed her onto the elevator in her bay-view condo building. An elderly lady got on with them, and he observed Kelly turn up the mega-watt smile again for the other woman's benefit. He leaned against the back of the elevator, looked closely at Kelly's eyes, and saw for the first time that the smile didn't reach them, even as she chatted and laughed with her neighbor.

When the woman got off a few floors up, Kelly slumped back against the elevator, as she waited for the top floor.

He followed her out, and drifted through the door to her penthouse condo while she fumbled for her keys in her large handbag.

He looked around with interest. The wall that faced the bay was all glass, and the view was incredible. In spite of being set in an urban environment, the condo was decorated in a way that made him feel like he was in a cottage by the shore. The kitchen was open to the living area and had cheery white cabinets, light-colored granite counters, and stainless steel appliances. Opposite the kitchen sat a desk with a laptop on it. Littered with papers, it was clearly where Kelly did her writing. The whole feel of the room was homey and airy—it said a lot about the woman who lived here.

There was a long table along the wall next to the front door with a pottery bowl sitting on it and Kelly's unopened mail tossed beside the bowl. But the focal point on the table was a large framed photograph of Kelly and Michael on a sailboat. Michael had his arm draped around Kelly's shoulders, and they both squinted into the sun and grinned widely for the camera. They looked so happy, so clearly oblivious to the pain that was ahead for them that Zane felt a catch in his heart. They'd suffered a great deal during Michael's illness, and Kelly had been grieving ever since his death. Zane decided if he could play a part in bringing some peace and happiness to them, he had to do it, no matter how much he hated the job.

He heard Kelly's keys rattle in the lock. She came in and tossed them into the bowl, where they landed with a clatter. She slipped out of her shoes and looked at the photo.

"Hey, Michael. I'm home," she whispered wistfully to the picture, "and you wouldn't believe what Grace and Janie have put me up to. Social networking—bah!"

She padded to the kitchen and pulled a diet soda out of the fridge. The soda hissed as she popped the top of the can. She leaned against the granite countertop, and took a sip, before continuing to talk out loud. "I mean really, if I wanted to be in touch with people from high school, I'd still live in New Hampshire."

She pushed off the counter and strolled over to the table with her computer on it in the living room. She stared at the machine as if it were a poisonous snake about to strike.

Zane rubbed a hand against his tanned neck as if to

ease tension and said, even though he knew Kelly couldn't hear him, "C'mon. Turn on the computer. You've got to sign up for this site if Michael's plan is going to work." He sighed at her obvious reluctance. "Looks like I've got to do a little herding." He locked his gaze onto her as he put an idea in her mind.

Kelly fought against his suggestion, and stuck her tongue out at the computer as she flopped on the sofa and sank into the soft blue and white striped cushions. She reached for the television remote, but looked guiltily back at her desk. Finally, she tossed the remote down and stood up. She exhaled loudly and muttered, "But a promise is a promise, and I promised them that I'd do this."

She stomped to the desk, yanked the chair out, and plopped down with a beleaguered sigh to turn on the computer.

****

The next night, James Flynn paced his penthouse like a caged tiger. The loft style condo took up the entire top floor of his building, and all the exterior walls were floor-to-ceiling glass to maximize the view of San Diego Bay. He picked this place because it provided great light for his work, but an added benefit was that the view didn't suck. Especially when he compared it to the rundown apartment in New York where he had lived with Tracy when they first got married. The only view they had was of the filthy alley, full of rats and garbage.

He opened the slider and stepped out onto the balcony that wrapped around his condo. He leaned on the railing and watched the lights on the cars as they passed over the bridge to Coronado.

This morning he'd finished getting the pieces off to the gallery for his upcoming charity exhibit, and he'd been antsy ever since. With too much time on his hands, he kept thinking about his conversation with the stranger in the bar the day before—he never even got the guy's name. It wasn't like him to talk so openly to anyone, let alone a stranger, but their honest conversation made him think about things he normally tried to push to the back of his mind.

Since his angry divorce, James closed himself off to women. The betrayal he felt, both from Tracy's infidelity and her openly money-hungry attitude, ate away at him. Tracy cheated on him with, and left him for, a rich man—purely for his money—it wasn't that the guy was smarter, funnier, kinder or a better lover than James. Arnold was none of those things; as a matter of fact, he was thirty years older than Tracy, and a nasty piece of work, but he was loaded, and that's all that mattered to his ex.

The irony was that as soon as their divorce was finalized, James' career took off. A lucky sale to a Manhattan society trendsetter, and suddenly his paintings were everywhere. His shrewd agent and business manager, Ellen Markowski, had marketed him aggressively, and within a couple of years, originals of his work hung in all the best homes and museums. Even more gratifying to James was that posters of his work hung on kids' walls and in college dorm rooms across the country.

He'd never given much thought to the financial aspects of his career, but he had to admit the cash made his life easier. He was able to leave cold New York City to move to sunny San Diego to be closer to his best friends, and he never had to worry about where his next meal was coming from now, or how he was going to pay the rent, in fact, he paid cash for this condo two years ago.

He mulled over his life, post-Tracy, and thought the stranger could be right; the women he chose to go out with after his divorce were all pretty shallow. Maybe he did pick them that way, so he wouldn't have to share himself emotionally, but there was no way he was going to set himself up for that kind of hurt again, so he saved his love for work, friends and family—the people and things he knew he could trust.

In all fairness, he couldn't blame the women he'd dated for just being who they were. Maybe the guy from the bar was right, and he should try to find a different type of woman. Did they even exist? And if they did—where would he find one?

He shook his head—now that was just cynical thinking. Good women had to be out there, after all, his best friends had a great marriage, and the stranger's wife sounded too good to be true.

And then there was Kelly Morrison.

She'd been chasing his thoughts around all day. Her eyes had drawn him in, and all these years later, he could still see them in his mind—a gold-flecked hazel, they had been filled with humor and intelligence even at eighteen. He hadn't thought about Kelly in a long while, but now that he had, he couldn't stop thinking about her; wondering where she lived, and what she was doing with her life.

He straightened his spine and strode back inside. He grabbed a beer from the fridge and his sleek laptop from the counter, and flopped on his overstuffed, charcoal gray sectional sofa, which faced a gas fireplace on an exposed brick wall. James pushed a button, and the laptop started with a loud musical chord. He decided to take the stranger's advice and went straight to a popular social networking website. He used the index fingers of both hands to peck in his registration information.

James frowned and ran his fingers through his hair. There was no reason to be so stressed—he'd see if Kelly was on here. No big deal. Even if she was, it didn't mean he had to contact her. He could just satisfy his curiosity about what she was up to—hell, she probably lived across the whole damn country.

He typed in her name and took a swig of his beer while he waited for her information to pop up on his screen. He leaned forward to place the brown bottle on the table with a *thunk* as he peered intently at Kelly's profile.

"Damn," he muttered when he saw there was no picture.

"Double damn," he said when he saw that her name was Kelly Morrison Lynch now, so she must be married. He tried to ignore the sharp pang in his gut at the thought. Wait—her relationship status was blank, so maybe there was hope she was single, too. He laughed to himself, and wondered why he cared so much about her marital status—he hadn't seen her in seventeen years, had he really thought she'd be frozen in time waiting for him?

Then, as he read where she lived, his jaw dropped, and he fumbled for his beer. He exhaled with a whoosh—so much for the safety net of three thousand miles making the decision for him about whether or not to contact her.

Ms. Kelly Morrison Lynch, relationship status unknown, lived right here in San Diego, California.

****

Kelly rushed into the living room from her bedroom where she'd hurriedly changed her clothes. She pulled on a pair of heels, as she scurried past David and Grace.

"I'm so sorry; I'm running late for dinner. Did you call? Will the restaurant hold the reservation?" She gratefully took the glass of wine David handed to her and gulped some down, "I was reading a book by the roof-top pool, and I totally lost track of time."

Her friends lounged in her living room and sipped white wine as they watched Kelly's frantic push to get ready with affectionate amusement. She was always getting lost in a book, her own work or someone else's, and they'd seen this mad dash to make a reservation on time before.

"I did and they will," said David with a smile. "So chill—we've got plenty of time."

Invisible to the others, Zane watched from his perch on the granite island, which separated the kitchen from the living area. He swung his legs and his cowboy boots hit the wooden cabinets with a *thunk* that only he could hear. Tonight would be the turning point—he only hoped he could get Kelly moving in the right direction.

"Don't worry about me—for a change I don't have to be home at a certain time for the sitter," Grace said as she stretched her long legs out in front of her. "Bill's piloting the red-eye from New York tonight, and Lydia's at a sleep-over, so I'm all by my lonesome. I feel free as a bird."

Kelly sat down at her desk. "Then you don't mind if I check my email quickly before we head out?" She turned to David and grimaced, "Grace and Janie bullied me into signing up on one of those social networks, and I'm wondering if anyone's tried to get in touch with me." She flashed a bright smile at her old friend. "I sent a friend request to Susie Davidson, and I want to see if she's responded."

"Susie Davidson," Grace's voice dripped with disdain. "We didn't badger you into doing this so you could reconnect with Susie Davidson."

"Hey, what've you got against old Susie? She was an integral part of our nerd squad in high school," David said. "Right, Kel?"

When she didn't reply, he glanced over at his old friend to see her frozen at her computer; all the color drained from her face. "Kel, what's wrong?"

"I didn't hear from Susie, but I did get a message from James Flynn," she whispered.

David jumped to his feet and peeked over her shoulder at the computer screen. "Yummy James Flynn from Rye?"

Grace snickered. "Sounds like a sandwich. I'll have a Yummy James Flynn on rye. Hold the mayo."

Kelly and David swung their heads in unison to stare at her.

"What? It's not my fault you two come from a town named after a bread."

David shook his head mournfully and intoned, "Californians."

"Native, baby." The blonde woman grinned playfully. "And don't you New England Yankees forget it."

"What does he say, Kel?" David asked with interest.

Kelly gulped. "He wants to get in touch and maybe meet for a drink." She twisted her head to look up at David, her eyes huge in her pale face. "He lives here, David. In San Diego."

"Oh. My. God. You have to meet him, and if you don't, I will," David said.

He managed to bring a small smile to Kelly's previously stunned face. "I don't think you're his type. Sorry."

"What do you mean? He prefers brunettes?" David winked. "A man can hope—you don't have to be such a dream dasher, Kel."

"Is there a picture?" Grace asked, as she strolled over with her wine. "I've got to see the man who's got David drooling, and you looking like you're about to pass out."

"I'm not drooling," David protested.

"Oh, please, darling." Grace pretended to wipe the corner of his mouth with a cocktail napkin.

"Okay. Maybe slight droolage, but James Flynn is totally drool-worthy. At least he used to be. Is there a picture of him now?"

Kelly shook her head. "Nope. Not much of anything on his profile, it looks like he just registered."

David raised his eyebrows. "And he contacted you right away? In-ter-es-ting."

Grace got the bottle of wine from the terra cotta bottle holder on the kitchen island, which separated Kelly's computer area from the kitchen in the large open living space. She topped off all of their glasses.

"Call me Nancy Drew, but I sense a mystery here. What's the story with Yummy James Flynn from Rye?"

As Kelly continued to stare at the message on the screen in silent amazement, David decided to answer. He settled onto the sofa and began as if it was storytime in nursery school. "Okay—seventeen years ago, Kelly and I had just graduated from high school. One of the popular kids, Becky Flynn…"

"Flynn? Sister of Yummy James?" Grace interrupted as she settled in a chair opposite David.

He nodded eagerly. "Yep. She was a cheerleader, not in our usual social orbit, but she invited the whole class to a bash at her house, so even our little nerd squad went. Yummy James was four years older than us, but he was home because he'd just graduated from art school…"

Grace interrupted again, "Ooo…Yummy James Flynn is an artist! This gets more and more interesting." She paused, her brow furrowed, "Wait. He's not *the* James Flynn is he? The artist? Lydia's got one of his posters in her room."

David shrugged. "I don't know. I never made the connection before. Do you know, Kel?"

When she just shook her head mutely, and continued to gape at her computer, David picked up his story. "Kelly was really shy then…"

"Still is," Grace observed sagely. "She can just cover it up better now."

"True, but if you keep interrupting, I'll never get to the good part."

"Sorry. Carry on." Grace took a sip of wine and waved her other hand regally.

"During the party, Shy Kelly wandered off by

herself, only to be found by Yummy James. They talked for hours, and then he planted one on her."

Kelly smiled, her eyes dreamy and unfocused. "My first kiss. It was magical."

"Wow," Grace breathed the words with awe. "My first kiss happened when I was playing Spin the Bottle in someone's musty basement in junior high. Yours is so much more romantic. Especially if it turns out he is *the* James Flynn; he's one of the most prominent artists of our generation. Anyway—what happened next?"

Kelly picked up the narrative, evidently recovered from her initial shock. "He called me the next morning to ask me out. I couldn't believe it."

"Did you go?"

Kelly laughed. "You better believe I went! I'd been crushing on him since I was a kid. I couldn't believe my first date was going to be with James Flynn."

"Where'd you go?"

"He took me to Portsmouth, and we had dinner at a fancy restaurant. I felt so grown-up. Then after..." She paused.

David interjected, "Here's where it all begins to fall to shit."

Kelly stuck her tongue out at him and went on with the story. "His parents had taken his sister away as a graduation present, so his house was empty. He took me back there after dinner."

"I imagine some serious necking ensued," Grace suggested hopefully.

"Oh, yeah." Kelly conceded with feeling. "But I was so naïve back then. After all, the night before had been my first kiss, after spending my high school years invisible to any male except David. It all seemed to be happening so fast. He was kissing me, and touching me, and in the heat of the moment he guided my hand to his…y'know…manhood." She blushed to the roots of her hair.

David exploded with laughter. "How do you still manage to be such an innocent after all these years? I really love you, kid."

"Stay on topic. I'm interested in Yummy James' manhood." Grace leaned forward in her chair, eager to hear the rest of the story.

Kelly's blush deepened, and David gave a knowing smile. "I still remember what our girl said about his 'manhood' when she got home and called me that night." He paused dramatically. "We came to refer to it as the Three H's. Hot. Huge. Hard."

"Scared the crap out of me," Kelly remembered with a rueful smile. "I froze and made an excuse to leave." She shrugged. "So he took me home."

"Where Miss Kelly promptly called me to discuss, and I imagine Yummy James went home to take a cold shower." David once again took up the tale. "I was so intrigued by the Three H's, I almost hung up on her to head over to see if Yummy James was interested in exploring an alternative lifestyle with me."

"If only you had, then maybe you and I wouldn't have cooked up the ridiculous plan we did." Kelly gnawed on her bottom lip.

Grace laughed. "Oh no! What did Lucy and Ethel do next?"

"I was so inexperienced, and so very flipped out. I didn't know what to do, and my parents were less than thrilled that my first date was with a twenty-two year old unemployed art school grad. I'd always been such a good girl; it was the first time I'd defied them to do something they didn't like. The whole thing had me terrified."

"I told her if she wanted out of whatever was happening with James, to call him up and say she'd gotten back together with her boyfriend." David pointed to his chest with a flourish. "Moi."

Grace rolled her eyes. "And he believed that? I'm starting to see why you call him 'Yummy James' and not 'Brainy James'."

"James never met David." Kelly defended the man she hadn't thought about in ages. "He didn't know David was gay. I hated to do it, but I lied, and told him that David and I had fought, but we'd made up and I was back with him, so I couldn't see James again."

"That's it? You ended it and didn't see him again?"

"We saw each other around town that summer, but then I went away to college, and I heard he moved to New York. I really liked him, and I always felt terrible about lying to him. I was just so young and out of my depth."

"And now he's back. And in San Diego," Grace observed. "It seems like kismet."

"Does his profile give his relationship status?" David asked hopefully.

"Uh huh. He's divorced."

"You're both single. And both transplanted to San Diego. Kismet," Grace repeated with a sharp nod of her head.

"I don't know about that, Grace. I'm not even sure if I'm going to meet him for drinks."

Zane huffed and jumped off the counter. This woman was not going to make his afterlife easy. She was going to back out of getting in touch with this guy—not acceptable. Flynn was the man Michael had chosen for her. She had to do it; otherwise all their good work was in vain. The friends were the weak link; he had to use them to get to Kelly. He folded his arms across his chest and focused his attention on Grace.

"You have to!" Grace exclaimed.

Zane's smile was smug as Grace took his suggestion and said, "You said you felt bad about lying to him. You could just meet him for one little drink, and apologize—it might ease your conscience."

Sensing Kelly's resolve weaken, Zane turned his attention to the man. They couldn't steamroll her. One thing he'd learned about Kelly from watching her for this assignment was that she could dig in her heels and be stubborn as a mule if she thought she was being pushed. He urged the man to back off a bit, but to still encourage her.

David stuck in his two cents' worth. "It's just a drink, Kel. No one's saying you have to run off to Vegas and marry the guy, but aren't you the least bit curious about him?"

"Well…yeah," she admitted reluctantly and looked at her friends' imploring expressions. "Oh, God. Stop with the puppy dog eyes, both of you! I'll do it. I'll meet him for a drink."

Zane was afraid she agreed just to shut her friends up, but wouldn't follow through with her promise after they were gone. He needn't have worried, David understood Kelly all too well and didn't need any angelic suggestion this time. He knew just what to do and acted before Zane could intervene.

Good man. The cowboy nodded as David got up

and swung Kelly's chair around so she faced the computer. "Right now. While we can see you do it. Get typing, missy."

With a deep, fortifying breath, Kelly hit the button to respond. "Here goes nothing."

Chapter 2

Zane and Michael leaned against the concrete wall, which separated Seaport Village from the waters of the bay. Zane managed to look casual, yet vaguely menacing, in his faded jeans, black T-shirt, and worn boots. His cowboy hat pulled low over his icy blue eyes. On the other hand, Michael bounced in place with excitement. The sun caught auburn highlights in his brown hair, and in his polo shirt and khaki pants, he blended in with the summer convention and tourist crowd better than Zane did.

James walked up the steps to the same restaurant where Michael had met him a few days before. He was dressed in a crisp, white shirt and dark jeans. He approached the young woman at the hostess stand, and with his charming crooked grin managed to obtain a table for two in the shade with a view of the water. When he took off his sunglasses and tossed them on the table, James anxiously scanned the strolling hordes.

"He seems nervous. That's a good sign, right, like he wants to impress her?"

Zane shrugged at Michael's words spoken at hyper speed and in his Boston accent. He might be an angel now, but at heart Zane was a nineteenth century cowboy from the Arizona territory, and he moved at a much slower pace than his friend. Except when he drew his gun, he remembered—he'd been known for his speed on the draw.

"Maybe." He straightened a little and whistled low under his breath. "Look who's here."

Michael looked from Zane back to the restaurant steps to see a small, plain woman being seated at the table next to James. To everyone but the two of them, she looked like a non-descript, middle-aged human, with tightly permed hair, and dressed in a light blue knit pantsuit.

"Another angel? What's another angel doing here? Doesn't Uriel trust us to get this job done? I mean, this is my wife we're talking about. I'm going to do everything possible to—"

"Fallen." Zane cut him off with the one cryptic word.

"Fallen? Fallen what?" Light dawned on Michael's face—he had been a high school English teacher in life, after all.

"A fallen angel? Like in *Paradise Lost*? No freakin' way."

"Way," Zane drawled.

"She looks so average. Not at all the way I'd pictured a fallen angel looking."

Zane allowed his friend one of his rare smiles. "Evil doesn't always come in an easy to recognize package."

Michael's smile was sheepish. "You got me. I would've thought she'd look like a silent movie vamp, with black hair, red lips, and a long cigarette in an even longer holder." He shook his head in disbelief. "Not looking like Mildred from Accounting."

"Lesson learned for you, Mike. Evil can look pretty darned banal." Zane paused, looked intently at his companion. "But that doesn't make her any less dangerous."

Michael frowned. "I'll be on my guard. Don't worry."

The fallen angel saw them looking at her, and a half-smile played around her mouth. She waggled her fingers at them in a sarcastic greeting.

"It's not a coincidence she's here, is it, Zane? What could she possibly want with Kelly?" Michael's voice sounded desperate.

Zane nudged him with his shoulder, in what passed for a consoling manner from the rough-mannered cowboy. "We'll keep Kelly safe, my friend. No fears on that account."

***

James took a draw on his beer and drummed his fingers on the colorful tile table. Glancing at the crowd, he didn't see anyone who looked like she might be a thirty-five-year-old Kelly. He glanced at his watch, and reminded himself—he was early, she wasn't late. He needed to get a grip and stop being so impatient. He felt like a teenager waiting for his first date. Kelly was just an acquaintance from his hometown, right? No reason for him to get all tied up in knots about meeting her for a drink.

He surveyed the other tables to make sure he hadn't missed her and she was seated somewhere else. Nope, just the usual tourists, happy hour crowd enjoying the daily drink specials, and one middle-aged woman sitting alone. She met his eyes with interest, and he quickly looked away and hoped she hadn't recognized him. He managed to fly under the radar most of the time here in San Diego, but the occasional

33

rabid fan did hunt him down. He hoped this woman wasn't one of them.

He looked back toward the street and saw her as she strolled along the walkway—Kelly. She looked a little older. Hell, who didn't? But she looked great. In white jeans and a lavender sleeveless top, with sandals on her feet, she swung her straw bag as she walked and looked around with interest. Her brown hair was a little longer than shoulder length and was cut in stylish layers. James had spent enough time around women to know that kind of casual disarray didn't happen by chance. It took an expensive haircut, and a lot of those mysterious products women used, to achieve the look. The bright sunshine brought out a myriad of highlights in her hair. He was sorry the big, round sunglasses obscured her eyes. He used to love her eyes.

A family with several excited children approached her from the opposite direction, and she laughed as the kids swarmed around her, like the water in a stream flowing around a rock.

James felt his heart stutter at that smile. It lit her up from within. Man, he had been a young, stupid jerk to let her get away all those years ago.

She walked up the three steps to the outdoor bar and approached the hostess with some hesitation, as if she were shy.

James stood and cleared his throat a little nervously before he asked, "Kelly?"

****

Kelly heard her name being called and turned. When she saw the man who had done the calling, her stomach did somersaults. It was James, and wow did the name "Yummy James" still apply. He looked even better with a few years on him than he had at twenty-two. His face had weathered some, but it had always been a good, strong-boned New England face, not classically handsome, but striking. It was the kind of face that would only improve with age. There were lines around his eyes that suggested a lot of time spent in the sun, or smiling, or maybe both.

He shoved a lock of hair out of his eyes, and the gesture made Kelly realize he was just as nervous as she was about this meeting, which surprised her.

"James," she replied with a smile, and met him halfway to his table.

He grinned, which deepened the creases around his eyes and made Kelly's heart pound the same way it had when she was a teenager.

She held out her hand, and he took it in both of his, rather than shake it as she'd clearly intended for him to do.

"Hi Kelly, I got us a table." His voice was deep, and the combination of it and her smaller hand in his two large, work-roughened ones did nothing to slow her racing pulse. He jerked his head to indicate the table for two behind him.

Okay. It was her turn to talk again, and her nerves made the words come in a rush, "Great. I was so glad you suggested this place. I love their Mai Tai special at happy hour." She felt her face flush. "Okay. Not the most sophisticated admission. I probably should order a dry martini, or something, anything but the fruity tourista cocktail."

He smiled, and it transformed his face. The rather intimidating look softened and he picked up his bottle of beer by the neck and waved it. "Yeah, like I'd care.

I'm having a beer. Domestic, even."

They sat across from each other, and Kelly pushed her sunglasses up on her head like a hair band.

A waitress came to take her order. After she left, there was a brief, uncomfortable silence, and then they both spoke at the same time.

"I was so surprised to hear from you."

"I couldn't believe it when I saw you live in San Diego now, too."

They laughed awkwardly, and the waitress came back with Kelly's Mai Tai. She reached for the glass, and James looked at the diamond rings on her left hand. He gestured toward the jewelry with a sharp movement of his head. "Married, huh?"

The question made Kelly's palms sweat, and she took a fortifying swig of her drink before she answered. "I'm widowed. My husband passed away."

He reached across the table to cover her hand with his. "I'm so sorry. When did it happen?"

She attempted to clear the lump in her throat. "Two years ago. Cancer."

He winced and squeezed her hand, his gaze locked on to hers as he said, "That's tough. We lost my mom to cancer eight years ago. It's brutal to watch someone you love suffer so much and be able to do nothing. You feel so helpless."

She felt the muscles work in her throat, as she fought to maintain her composure. She blinked rapidly and cleared her throat. "You really understand. I don't talk to many people about that time, because no one really seems to get it, but you do. Helpless was exactly how I felt, like I was on an out-of-control roller coaster, and I couldn't do anything to stop it."

His eyes held only sympathy—not pity. It was a distinction Kelly appreciated.

"It was like that with my mom, too. I would've done anything to make her well again, but there was nothing I could do." He paused, and then added, "He must've been a helluva guy for you to still be wearing these two years later." He ran the pad of his thumb over her wedding rings.

She felt a jolt of awareness at his touch, and snatched her hand back. It felt like a betrayal of Michael.

"He was. Michael was more than my husband. He was my love and my best friend—we were a good team."

"Michael?" James looked puzzled. "So you didn't end up with David? I'd assumed you had."

Her eyes grew wide and she almost had a Mai Tai noser as a short burst of laughter erupted mid-sip. "David?"

"Yeah—David. You two seemed so crazy about each other that summer. You know...when we..." His voice faded.

Her eyes grew soft. "David and I are still crazy about each other. As friends. He was even my 'Man of Honor' when I married Michael."

James furrowed his brow. "Man of Honor? What's that?"

"Like a Maid of Honor, only a man. I couldn't imagine anyone else standing up for me at my wedding. But, David's gay, James."

"Wow. Did he come out when you were dating? That must've been hard on you."

She knew this conversation had to happen, but

she'd been dreading it, and guilt about her teenaged self's lie hit her like a sledgehammer.

"No. I've known that David is gay since we were kids. I knew that summer."

James shook his head, as if to clear it. "But you threw me over for him—even though he's gay and you know it?"

She watched as realization dawned. Hurt and then anger showed in his eyes. He laughed, but the sound was devoid of humor. "Oh. I get it. You just wanted to get rid of me. You guys were never together. Do I ever feel like an ass. I'm sorry I bothered you again." He reached for his wallet in the back pocket of his jeans as if he meant to pay and leave.

Kelly reached out to stop him and again there was that frisson of awareness when their skin touched. "Please, James. Don't go. It's not what you think. I was just so young and totally out of my depth romantically with you. I got scared, and David and I cooked up that ridiculous story. I'm so sorry."

"But that doesn't make sense. I know you were only eighteen, but you were so much more mature than my sister, and as much as I love her, I've got to say she'd been around the block once or twice by that time."

Kelly rolled her eyes. "Well, not me. You were my first kiss, James. When things got so heated between us, I just freaked out." Her eyes searched his. "Do you think you can forgive me?"

He studied her face, and huffed out a breath, as he seemed to come to a conclusion. "Of course I can. That was a long time ago, right? And I'm sorry too, Kelly. If I'd known you weren't that experienced, I would've behaved differently."

He caught the waitress's eye and made a circular gesture over their drinks, "Another round, please."

Kelly felt relief wash over her at his words, and now that her nerves had settled she realized she was starving. "Oh—and I'd love a fish taco. I didn't have time for lunch."

He held up two fingers. "And two fish taco platters, please."

The waitress walked away, and he said with a happy grin, "It's nice to hear you say you're hungry— most of the women I meet seem to survive on lettuce and the occasional splurge on a stalk of celery. It's fun to be able to share a good meal with you."

****

The fallen angel looked pointedly from James and Kelly's smiling faces to Michael. She lifted her hands and made a circle with the thumb and forefinger of her right hand and slid the index finger of her left hand in and out in a suggestive manner.

Zane growled low in his throat. "Ignore her, man."

Michael waved his hand in a dismissive gesture. "She's just trying to get my goat. It's not going to work."

Zane looked surprised. "Still...it must be hard to see Kelly on a date with another guy."

Michael shrugged. "It's not the easiest thing I've ever done, but two years ago it would've been worse. Now I just want her to be happy and the two of us holding onto each other, and the memory of what we had, isn't going to do it. She needs to move on—and so do I."

He beamed at the man who sat with his wife. "And

look at the expression on his face. He'll treasure her, and if I've got to let her go to another man I want it to be to someone who'll appreciate what a special person she is." His voice broke a little, and he shook his head briskly as if to clear it. "So, Mildred from Accounting can make all the obscene gestures she wants, and it won't get to me."

"You're a better man than me, Mike."

"And this is news to you, cowboy?" Michael teased.

Zane laughed and it was a rusty sound, as if he hadn't done it for a long time.

"Well, Mildred's getting to me. I can't figure out what she's doing here. Why would the fallen angels take an interest in this particular case?"

Michael looked thoughtful. "Maybe because Uriel has taken a personal interest in it?"

Zane pursed his lips and nodded. "That could be."

They watched as the fallen angel paid her tab and walked across the sidewalk to them. Both angels stood a little straighter, and their posture instinctively became more defensive. A faint odor of sulfur hung about her like a fog.

"Geez, Mildred, you stink like rotten eggs." Michael held his nose in distaste.

"Mildred?" She shrugged. "It's as good a name as any. You may call me Mildred."

"Okay…Mildred," Zane said with disdain, "what's your game?"

"Believe me, cowpoke, I don't play games."

She turned to Michael, and the slow smile that oozed across her face made him shiver. Her next words chilled him to the bone. "As your lovely widow is about to learn, to her sorrow."

"What I'm asking myself, Mildred," Zane drawled, "is why a hot-shot fallen angel could possibly care about these two inconsequential humans?"

She shrugged, which caused her foul odor to waft across to them. "I don't per se, but my boss really hates Uriel, and Mr. Big-Shot-Archangel seems to care about what happens to these two goody-two shoes. Voila! Here I am."

Michael was incredulous. "You're willing to ruin two people's lives just to score brownie points with your boss?"

"Well—duh! I'm a fallen angel, moron, ruining human lives is what I do. Getting on the big guy's good side is just the icing on the cake." She paused and cocked her head before she corrected herself, "Not the big *big* guy. My boss is more like his first lieutenant."

Zane pushed his cowboy hat back on his head and looked straight into Mildred's eyes before he spoke through clenched teeth. "I'm not big on repeating myself, so listen real close, lady. If you harm Kelly Lynch in any way, you'll be bringing a world of hurt down on yourself. Now that might be how a fallen angel like you gets your jollies, but I don't think so. The one you call 'the Big Guy' is inconsequential compared to the Big Guy we've got on our team, and you'll be squashed like a bug, and I have to admit, I'll enjoy seeing it."

Michael nodded knowingly and wagged his finger at Zane. "See—that's why you're not moving on to the next plane with me, buddy. Your joy in another's suffering, even a stinky old evil broad like this one, isn't what gets you ascending."

Zane shrugged. "I can wait a little longer. Especially if it means keeping Mildred from hurting Kelly."

Mildred looked into Zane's cold eyes, and swallowed hard. "I have to say, I'm used to the good guys being more—well—good, but the truth is, whether it's me or somebody else on the case, my boss isn't going to let this woman find happiness without a fight."

Zane looked out over the bay. "Then a fight's what you're going to have, Mildred." He turned his head back and locked his gaze onto hers. "Brace yourself."

She gulped, backed away and the air closed in around her as she vanished in a blink of darkness.

"You really can be one scary s.o.b. when you put your mind to it," Michael said in awe.

"Possibly the only true thing she said is that they'll keep coming for Kelly and James. So she'll be back— or another one even worse than her—they'll just keep coming, and we've got to be ready for 'em." He narrowed his eyes, as he looked in James and Kelly's direction. "Shit. Flynn's spotted you. Get invisible. Pronto."

****

James pointed at the two men by the water's edge. "Over there—it's the guy who talked me into contacting you!"

Kelly turned around to look. "Who? The cowboy? I've been seeing him around the neighborhood a lot lately, and I was wondering what his story is." She smiled over her shoulder at James. "Occupational hazard—I'm always interested in other people's stories. You never know what'll give you an idea for a plot."

James shook his head. "Not the cowboy. There was

42

another guy there with him a minute ago. Where could he have gone?" The guy had vanished the same way the other night, too. He looked back at Kelly, and all thoughts but her left his head. He shrugged with a grin on his face. "Speaking of your occupation, I still can't believe you're K.M. Lynch. I love your books."

She blushed. "I can't believe you read them. You must be one of the fifty people who do."

"You're being too modest. You're not Agatha Christie, no, but your mysteries are popular. I love your detectives—Tony and Tessa—they're like a modern-day Nick and Nora Charles."

She looked pleased. "That's what I was shooting for with them! An homage to Hammett, but a lot of people don't get it. I'm impressed, Flynn."

He held up his hands as if to ward off an attack. "Hey, I've been known to read a book now and again."

Before Kelly could shoot a quip back at James, a weathered man bellowed his name from the sidewalk. He bounded up the steps and strode over to their table. His gray hair was in a military style buzz cut. He wasted no time on small talk. "Hey, Flynn, any chance you can crew for me tomorrow in the Beer Can Races?"

"Hello, Floyd. Nice to see you, too. Let me introduce you to my friend, Kelly Lynch. Kelly, this is Floyd Lester."

A wide grin split Floyd's face. "Sorry, folks. I didn't mean to be rude. It's just all the usual suspects have bailed on me for tomorrow's race, and I really need people to crew for me." He narrowed his already squinty eyes at Kelly. "You look outdoorsy—any chance you know how to sail?"

Kelly leaned back with one arm over the back of

her chair, clearly amused by the man's brusque manner. "I used to sail back in the day, but it's been a while."

"Still—you could be rail meat?" He referred to the person who leaned off one side of the boat in a race to keep it from tipping keel too far on one side and slowing it down. It was a task that didn't require much skill, but could prove vital in a race.

Her slow smile started a fire in James' belly. "Sure, I could be rail meat. What time do you need me, and where do you dock your boat?"

"Kelly, you don't have to give in to this steamroller." James laughed.

"It's okay. It's been a long time since I've been out on the water. As long as you swear I won't have to do anything more complicated than rail meat duty, I'm in."

"If you're sure, I'll pick you up on my way," James replied with a casualness he was far from feeling. He was usually pretty smooth with the ladies, but Kelly was throwing him off his game, and he was grateful for an excuse to see her again the next day.

"Great!" bellowed Floyd. "I knew I could count on you, Flynn. See you both tomorrow."

He turned and left the deck of the bar as suddenly as he had appeared.

"He's quite the character," Kelly observed with a happy grin.

"Sure is. He's retired Navy, and he runs a tight ship—brace yourself."

"As long as he's not expecting too much from me. I haven't been on a sailboat in at least three years. Maybe four."

Her lips turned down and the sparkle went out of her eyes, which made James guess her husband's illness was what put an end to her sailing fun.

He watched her in awe, as she blinked, swallowed, and pasted a smile on her face—no question, Kelly Morrison Lynch was as tough as they came.

"The Beer Can Races. I remember the first time Michael and I visited San Diego. We were staying at a hotel with a view of the bay. On Wednesday, suddenly it was filled with sailboats—it was almost as if they appeared out of nowhere, like a flash mob for sailors. It was quite a sight!"

"It's a lot of fun. Floyd's pretty competitive in the Beer Can Races, but it's usually a good time. Do you know where the name comes from?"

Kelly shook her head. "I don't, and I've always been curious about it."

"Supposedly, you can tell the course of the race by following the beer cans the crew throw off their boats. But I've never seen anyone drinking, certainly not on Floyd's boat." He winked at her. "At least not until after the race, and then all bets are off."

****

Kelly felt a jolt of pleasure at his sexy wink, and was flooded with uncomfortable feelings of guilt mixed in with the lust. She didn't think she should be feeling this kind of down low thrill with any man but Michael. Time for her to get home. Alone.

She looked at her watch. "Wow. We've been here longer than I thought—the time's flown! I better get going."

She was flattered by the way his face fell, but that feeling just made her all the more anxious to get away. She shouldn't care that he was disappointed to have their evening together end so early. It felt like she was being disloyal to her husband's memory.

"Can I walk you to your car?"

She shook her head, as she gathered up her things and he paid the tab. "I walked. I live just across the way."

"Me too! Where do you live?"

His eyes opened wide when Kelly gave her address. "That's on the opposite corner from my building!"

He told her where he lived, and her jaw dropped. "How long have you lived there? I can't believe we haven't seen each other before now."

"I've been there about two years," he replied and placed his hand lightly on her back to guide her down the steps to the sidewalk. "You?"

"Seven years. Michael and I bought the condo when we first moved here. He taught English at a public high school in the city, and I work from home, so we could live anywhere, and we liked being downtown and on the water."

His hand brushed hers as they walked side by side, and he took her hand in his as if it were the most natural thing in the world. Kelly stiffened slightly at the touch, but didn't pull away.

The handholding made this all feel more like a date and less like two old friends meeting for a drink. Kelly had to admit the warmth of his large hand on hers felt good. It had been a long time since she had held hands with a man, and she remembered now it was one of life's small pleasures. But the enjoyment filled her with guilt. She knew Michael was dead. She wasn't about to go all Miss Havisham, and float around her condo in her wedding dress waiting for him to come home, but she still felt guilty. Like she was cheating on him by holding hands with another man.

And they were supposed to see each other again the next day for the Beer Can Race. Driving to the marina tomorrow with James would make it all seem even more date-like than the handholding. As they approached her building, she used the excuse of digging through her big straw bag for the keycard to the entrance to pull her hand from the comfort of his. Not looking up as she pawed through the cavernous purse, she said in a rush, "About tomorrow—there's no need for you to give me a ride—I can get there myself, if you just tell me where Floyd keeps his boat."

James shoved his hands in his pockets and jerked his head to indicate the building on the opposite corner. "I live right there, Kel, it seems silly for us to take two cars."

Her laugh was nervous as she triumphantly pulled the key card out of her bag and stuck it in the slot. The loud, harsh buzz of the door as it unlocked caused her to raise her voice to respond, "Far be it from me to be silly. I'll meet you out here tomorrow."

Kelly pulled a slip of paper and a pen from her bag and jotted down her number. She handed it to James. "Just call as you're leaving, and I'll meet you down here. No need for you to come up."

****

James watched until Kelly got in the elevator. They waved to each other as the doors shut, and he turned and walked across the street to his building.

As he disappeared through the doors, Zane and Michael made themselves visible.

"Man! That wife of yours is like a skittish colt.

Who woulda guessed you'd be such a tough act to follow?" Zane teased.

Michael puffed out his chest. "I was a man of hidden depths and talents."

One corner of Zane's mouth tilted up. "Evidently. Guess I better head up there and make sure she doesn't try to weasel out of meeting him tomorrow for this sailing thing."

"Thanks, man. You're a good friend."

Before he vanished, Zane replied with a slow wink, "Don't let it get around. I've got that whole bad boy rep to maintain."

He got to the condo before Kelly. Like every other time he'd seen her come in, she looked at the framed photograph of Michael and her, but tonight she picked it up and held it to her chest as she slumped to the sofa. Tears trickled down her cheeks.

"I'm so sorry, Michael. I didn't mean for that to be a date, but it sure felt like one." She sniffed loudly. "And the worst part is I liked it. I really enjoyed myself, and I'm seeing him again tomorrow."

She looked at the picture of them sailing together in happier days. "And sailing was our thing. I feel like a heartless hussy—maybe I should just cancel. Pretend I got sick or something."

"Uh oh," Zane said out loud since he knew she couldn't hear him in his present non-corporeal state, "red alert. She's winding up to back out." He concentrated and sent a quick suggestion up to David in Los Angeles. Within seconds the phone rang.

"Hi, David." She snuffled. "No, I'm fine. Yep. He's the famous artist. Pretty cool, huh?"

She tried to keep her voice light, but David clearly

wasn't fooled.

"Spill it, Kel, what happened? Why are you so flipped out?"

"I'm a horrible person, David," she wailed. "I had fun."

Silence greeted her admission. Finally David spoke, "Fun? Like jumping his bones fun?"

She rolled her eyes. "No, you sex maniac. Like drinks, tacos, laughing fun. And I'm going to crew in the Beer Can Races tomorrow with him," she said as if she were admitting to multiple homicides.

"Oh horrors! And you might actually laugh and have fun again then. Whatever am I going to do with you, sweetie?"

"But I'm married, David. I shouldn't be having fun with a man—especially if he's got this great smile that makes a girl think of bone-jumping fun."

David's voice was gentle. "You're not married, Kelly. You're widowed. It's okay to have fun with a man, even the bone-jumping kind of fun. Listen to me, please; you're not cheating on Michael."

She swiped at the tears on her face. "Really, David? Because it sure as hell feels like it!"

"Michael was the best male friend I ever had, at least of the non-bone-jumping variety, and he was one of the kindest people I ever knew, always so generous with his spirit. He wouldn't want you to be alone. You're still young, Kel, Michael wouldn't want you to spend the next sixty years by yourself, married to his ghost. He loved life, and he loved you. God, did the man love you! He'd want you to live every moment of your life to the fullest."

She met his statement with watery sniffles. "You

know I'm right, Kel."

"I guess," she said grudgingly.

"Promise me you'll do the sailing thing with James tomorrow."

She hesitated, and he added, "If I was there, I'd make you pinky-swear."

Ever since they were kids, Kelly's honorable nature made the silly, childish action an inviolate trust. If he could get her to pinky-swear, he knew she'd keep her date with James no matter how much she wanted to get out of it.

She sniffed and crooked her little finger in the air. "All right. I virtually pinky-swear that I won't back out of the race tomorrow."

Chapter 3

James and Kelly walked on the dock toward Floyd's sailboat, which was an anthill of activity as sailors prepared for the race. There was no handholding today, but at least Kelly hadn't backed out the way he'd been afraid she would. However, she was much more subdued than she'd been the night before. They'd had a great time together, he knew it, but something had her running scared now. Usually a fairly commitment-phobic man himself, James recognized the signs in his companion, and felt a newly discovered sympathy for the women he'd run from after his marriage. It didn't feel good to be on the receiving end of the cold shoulder from someone you liked, even if you suspected fear was the driving factor, and not lack of attraction.

As they got to Floyd's berth, James squinted into the sun, and shaded his eyes with his hand as he looked up to try and find his friend among all the people on board.

Floyd's familiar bellow could be heard as he spotted them on the dock. "Shit, Flynn, don't you ever answer your phone or check your voice mail?"

James called back, "Good to see you, too, Floyd. I'm just fine, thanks. And you?"

Laughter rang out from the other sailors at his good-natured ribbing of Floyd's notorious lack of social skills. The old salt glared at his crew, who all busied themselves to try and keep him from seeing their amusement.

James grinned at the older man and explained, "I've got that charity exhibit this weekend and my manager's in hyperactive chipmunk mode. Calling me from New York every five minutes, so I turned my phone off, and I'm trying very hard to pretend it doesn't exist. I'm here now—talk to me—what's up?"

Floyd jerked his thumb at the bustling activity behind him. "I managed to get a hold of all my usual crew after all. I called to let you know that I didn't need you or your girlfriend today."

Girlfriend—oh no. James snuck a look at Kelly out of the corner of his eye, and saw that the word had her poised like a gazelle ready to flee from a hungry lion. *Not helping here, Floyd.*

He glared at his old friend, who misinterpreted the look and said, "Sorry you came all the way here for nothing. I guess we could find something for you to do…"

Kelly laughed, and held up her hands. "That's okay. I'm sort of relieved to be off the hook. It's been a long time since I crewed for anyone."

James felt his heart warm at the sound of her laughter. He didn't just want this woman physically— although, oh man, did he want her physically—he also really liked her as a person. Her humor, intelligence, loyalty, and kindness all warmed his soul. It'd been a long time since he felt this way. Like maybe seventeen years? The last time Kelly and he had gone down this road together. Of course, back then it had ended pretty badly for him. He was hoping for a more positive outcome this time around.

"What do you say, Kel, want to head over to Harbor Island Drive and cheer them on?" He mentioned a spot on the bay where they could pull over and get a fabulous view of the races.

He braced himself to hear Kelly say "no thanks, take me home", but she looked at his face thoughtfully, and he feared she could see the anxiety he was feeling about her answer, but she surprised him with her response. "Sure. Sounds great!"

"You are full of surprises, Kelly Morrison Lynch. Let's go!" He held out his hand, and grinned when she reached out shyly and he felt her soft hand in his.

Floyd hollered down, "Meet us at the usual spot after for the post-race celebration. I appreciate the fact you were both willing to help me out when I was in a bind, even if it didn't turn out to be necessary. You've earned your berth at the party."

****

Unseen by the humans at the marina below them, Zane and Michael hovered on snowy, white wings.

Michael's brow furrowed in confusion. "Did you do that? Arrange for the crew to miraculously appear, but not let James know until he already had Kelly here? Because a maneuver like that has angel written all over it."

Zane shook his head once, slowly. "Nope. Not me. I thought it was your doing, but I couldn't figure out what you were up to."

There was a brief shimmer in the air beside them, and Uriel appeared to the two angels, although not to the humans. He looked larger than life, as usual, his wingspan was easily twice the size of theirs, and he seemed to be lit from within.

"It was I. I arranged for his usual crew to be available after all."

"But why?" Michael asked. "I thought sailing was a great thing for them to do together. Kelly used to love it when we went sailing."

Uriel's smile was kind, and his voice gentle, "And that's one reason right there. It was your thing to do together. We don't want Kelly thinking too much about happy times with you at the moment."

Michael conceded the point with a terse nod. This setting up your widow with another man had moments of extreme suckitude. He did want her to be happy, and knew that she could be with James, but sometimes he felt a brief, very un-angelic, pang of jealousy, which he quickly quashed. It was time for Kelly and him both to move on to the next stage.

Uriel wrapped one massive wing around Michael. "I'm sorry, my friend. Kelly will never forget you, and the love you shared, but if we allow her to focus too much on it right now, the guilt will paralyze her."

"I know. I'm back with the program now. Just a little blip. I want what's best for her, and I'm willing to do what it takes to get her there."

Zane still looked puzzled. "So, that's the only reason you didn't want them on Floyd's boat today, Chief?"

A scowl marred Uriel's features. "Not the only reason, no." He looked at the cowboy with approval. "Very astute of you, Zane; you're coming along nicely. The fallen angel you call Mildred had planned an accident for James and Kelly, if they sailed today. When the air horn sounded Kelly would have been startled, jumped, and been knocked overboard. I couldn't allow it to happen, but I'm sorry to interfere. I know this is your show."

"No problem. I appreciate the save," Zane drawled.

"Just be aware that you may not always see Mildred, but she's up to no good all the time. Right now she's preparing to come at James and Kelly from another angle, so be prepared." And with those words, there was another shimmer in the air, and Uriel was gone.

"Cryptic much?" Michael said.

"Always with the cryptic. That's Uriel for you," Zane scoffed, before he imitated their boss's deep voice. "'Be prepared. I won't tell y'all for what, just be prepared.' Very helpful."

Michael chuckled. "Oh well. I guess you stick to Kelly, I'll stick to James, and we'll help them dodge whatever Mildred throws their way."

Zane spat. "Defense. I hate it. I still believe the best defense is a good offense. So, while Mildred's off stirring up trouble in her cauldron, whaddya say we get these two a little closer? Make it harder for the fallen ones to tear them apart?"

****

Mildred flapped along the streets of Manhattan on dingy wings. Her prey was a woman who was clearly trying to look a decade younger than she was. Cosmetic surgery had made her breasts improbably large for her small frame, and her lips puffed up to unrealistic proportions. A bad Botox experience had frozen her face into a perpetually startled expression, under a crown of bleached blonde hair. She tripped down the sidewalk on heels so high it was obvious they were designed for sitting and posing more than for walking.

She entered the chic restaurant of the moment in the city, and regarded the maître d' with annoyance. At least Mildred thought it was annoyance. The woman's face seemed incapable of movement, but her blue eyes flashed in a way that indicated anger.

"I'm sorry Mrs. Blackburn, but your husband's secretary called a little while ago to cancel your reservation for lunch today. She said he wouldn't be able to make it."

"That son of a bitch," she growled. "So, I came all this way for nothing?"

"I'm afraid so, ma'am. We're full, but if you would care to sit in the bar…"

She cut off the man's offer with an impatient wave of one well-manicured hand, as she pulled her state-of-the-art cell phone out of her oversized designer bag with her other hand, and stepped outside to make her call.

Mrs. Blackburn snapped into her phone. "Debbie, I want to speak to him. Now. What do you mean—'he's unavailable'? He's always available to me."

She deflated like a balloon popped by a pin at the secretary's response, but her voice was still sharp when she replied, "Fine. Have him call me as soon as he's free."

Mildred folded her gray wings, and they vanished with a puff of dust. She made herself corporeal next to Mrs. Blackburn.

"Oh dear, sounds like he's getting ready to trade you in for a newer model." She tsked with a sympathetic shake of her head.

Mrs. Blackburn almost got whiplash from the

angry twist of her head to glare at Mildred. "What? No. My husband is a very important man. He's just busy."

The fallen angel stuck out her hand, and jerked her head at the entrance to the restaurant, "I'm Mildred. I've got a reservation here for lunch, and no one to share it. I heard I had to try this place when I was in town, but no one else from the accounting convention was able to come with me. You look like you could use a little company. Care to join me?"

She hesitated for just a moment, and then shook Mildred's hand. "I'm Tracy, and I'd like that. Thanks."

Mildred took a peep into the woman's thoughts, since she couldn't get any read off of her frozen face. Mildred fought back a satisfied grin at what she heard.

The old broad seemed intuitive, and Tracy really needed advice. Also, Mildred was from out of town, which was another point in her favor. Tracy didn't want any of the vicious cats in her social circle to get wind of her marital problems.

As Mildred followed the other woman to their table, Tracy's calculating mind raced. Mildred had struck on her secret fear. Arnold had been acting different lately. And forty was pulling up on her with alarming speed. She'd been in her twenties when she met Arnold, and she'd fought time every minute since then, fearing the moment when he got old enough that even thirty years younger than him wasn't enough to keep his raging ego satisfied.

She never should've left James way back when. If she'd just held on for a little longer, she would've been able to share in the fame and fortune he enjoyed now. Instead, she was about to get unceremoniously dumped for a young chippie. She just knew it. And Arnold had insisted on a pre-nup, to which she'd foolishly agreed. Her ego had kept her from ever believing this day would come.

Trailing behind Tracy, Mildred felt evil ooze throughout her being. She could work with this kind of fear and greed.

****

Michael and Zane hovered above James' car as he parallel parked alongside the bay, where the sailboats had gathered to wait for the races to begin.

"Nice manners," Michael said with a nod of approval when he saw James hustle around the car to open Kelly's door. However, when the artist took her hand to help her out of the car, Zane perceived a brief flash of pain in the other angel's eyes.

As the couple stood next to the car, James was apologetic. "Sorry I don't have chairs, or even a blanket, to sit on. I thought we'd be sailing, so I didn't think to throw anything to sit on in the trunk."

Kelly smiled, and leaned back against the car. "This is fine." She arched an eyebrow at him. "Unless you're one of those people who are weird about their cars being touched. This *is* a pretty snazzy car."

He joined her against the classic red and white Corvette convertible, with his shoulder touching hers. "Nope. This is good for me."

Michael fluttered his wings and gulped. "Wow, do you think he's making his move already? He's a fast worker. Look at how close he's standing to her."

Zane took pity on his friend. Despite all the best intentions, it couldn't be easy to watch another man put the moves on your wife. He looked, and saw the way James leaned down into Kelly as he spoke to her. Yeah.

This guy was getting ready to make a move, and there was no reason for Michael to have to watch.

"Y'know what, buddy? I got this covered. Why don't you see if you can track down Mildred and find out what she's plotting now?"

He watched as Michael heaved a sigh of relief. "Are you sure?"

"I'm positive. Uriel told us to be prepared for Mildred's next move. If you can figure out what she's up to, we'll be ahead of the game."

"Well…if you really think I'd be better used doing that…"

Zane pursed his lips and nodded as he pretended to consider the matter. He lowered himself to a seated position on the hood of James' car. "I really do. Not much happening here, so both of us don't need to sit around and twiddle our thumbs while they watch the races. You go find Mildred."

Michael heaved a sigh of relief. "Thanks, Zane. We'll meet up later."

He vanished in a blink of light, and Zane focused his attention on James and Kelly.

An air horn blasted, and Kelly, whose nerves were already strung taut by James' physical proximity, almost jumped out of her skin.

James wrapped an arm around her shoulder, and pulled her to his side. "Easy, Kel. It's just signaling the start of the first race. Good thing we aren't crewing for Floyd. You would've jumped overboard before we even got started, and you drowning would've put a serious damper on the evening."

Zane pumped his fist as Kelly leaned against James, but his feeling of triumph quickly gave way to frustration as he saw a guilty expression flicker across Kelly's face before she gently disengaged and moved slightly, so James either had to take his arm from her or move to keep it there.

In the little time they'd been observing James, Zane had learned he wasn't the sort of man to force his attentions on a woman. He could tell that James felt a little hurt by Kelly's retreat, but pulled his arm from her shoulders, and disguised the motion by using it to point out Floyd's boat to her.

Zane scowled at the space that existed now between Kelly and James. He knew deep down that James was taking the right approach with Kelly; they couldn't rush her into this relationship. She needed to be gentled along until she could overcome this misplaced guilt about Michael. He understood, but he really wanted this assignment to be over—this whole love thing really wasn't his gig. He tucked his wings away, and settled back on his elbows to watch the races. At the rate things were going, it was going to be a long night.

****

A few martinis later, and Tracy had poured her life story out to Mildred.

Mildred downed the last of her boilermaker, and signaled the waiter to bring another round.

"I've seen it happen so many times, Tracy, these rich, old fools keep going for younger and younger women." She snorted in derision. "And they even convince themselves the girls aren't with them for their money."

Tracy's laugh was brief and humorless as she snatched her martini from the waiter's tray. "As if I never should've left James for Arnold. It turned out to be the biggest mistake of my life."

Mildred shook her head in feigned amazement, since she knew Tracy's whole story before she met her, and her first marriage to James was the only reason the fallen angel was sitting across the table from this self-centered bore, forced to listen to her trite tale of woe. She forced a smile to her face. "I still can't believe your ex is the artist James Flynn. I'm living in San Diego at the moment for an assignment, and I've seen him on the news and around town. What a hunk."

Tracy would have wrinkled her brow if the Botox allowed her to do so. "Assignment? I thought you were an accountant." Her glazed eyes narrowed in suspicion. "You're not a reporter are you? Trying to get the scoop on Arnold and my marital troubles, or digging up dirt on James?"

Mildred laughed mid-swig of her drink. "Me? A reporter? No, I've got to move around a lot for my work. Right now I'm doing an audit of a company that's based in San Diego. I'll be there for about two more months," she lied with ease.

Tracy's martini-fuzzed brain accepted Mildred's explanation without question, and her thoughts turned right back to herself, the way they were wont to do.

"James is still a hunk, huh?"

"Is he *ever*," Mildred said. "I was actually seated near him in a restaurant a few days ago. He looked way more delish than anything on the menu. He was there with some mousy thing. She wasn't nearly as glamorous as you. He's certainly traded down—why'd you ever let a catch like him go?"

Tracy sighed, slumped in her chair and whined,

"He was broke! We both worked waiting tables. We lived in a dump, and it was still a struggle for us to not get evicted. I didn't think his art would take him anywhere but the poorhouse. Then I met Arnold, and all his lovely money. I didn't want to be cold and hungry anymore, and I thought Arnold adored me."

Which Mildred suspected the woman knew wasn't the case with James, but Tracy wasn't about to admit to anyone that she didn't think her first husband loved her.

Mildred sensed it was the time to make her move. Luckily for her, Tracy was too soused to see the calculating gleam in her narrowed eyes as she said, "You seem to regret your choice. It's never too late to fix things, you know."

Tracy's drunk was taking a turn down Maudlin Street, and she sniffed loudly. "I don't know about that, Millie. I think the James boat sailed a long time ago."

"I disagree. From what I've read about him, he's never married again. Maybe he's been pining for you for all these years." Mildred bounced a little in her seat, as if an idea had just come to her. She waved her now empty glass around in her excitement to punctuate her words. "I know! You should see him again. You could run into him somewhere all casual-like. I bet he'd love to see you. Especially since you're still looking so fabulous."

Tracy pursed her lips and dug the olive out of her martini glass. "I do look great, don't I?" She popped the olive in her mouth and munched it with a thoughtful air. "But he lives across the whole country. How could I just run into him?"

The fallen angel tapped her finger on her jaw as she pretended to give the matter serious thought.

"Before I left San Diego for this conference, I saw on the news that he's having an exhibit to benefit some charity this weekend, and there's a big shindig for it, too. You could visit me in San Diego, and we could go to it. I'm sure I could get tickets from the company I'm auditing." She winked. "They want to get on my good side, if you know what I mean."

Interest flared in Tracy's eyes. "I like it. I could get all dolled up for that kind of event."

"You'll knock him off his feet. He'll be begging for you to come back to him when he sees what he's been missing."

Mildred glanced toward the window as she spoke, and saw Michael peering in at her, his eyes narrowed with suspicion.

"What is he doing here?" She spat the words out in disgust.

Tracy followed her gaze, and shrugged. Mildred suspected since it didn't involve Tracy, her interest in the man at the window was non-existent.

As Michael moved to come into the restaurant, Mildred threw a wad of cash on the table, and hustled Tracy out to the sidewalk. The fallen angel grasped her companion's elbow and rushed her in the opposite direction from Michael. She spoke with a casual good cheer that she was far from feeling.

"I've got to get back to my conference now, or I'll be late for the afternoon sessions, and you've got some shopping to do if you want to blow your ex away this weekend."

At the mention of shopping, Tracy was eager to get going. She struggled to keep up with the brisk pace Mildred set, but was hindered by her stiletto heels and tight skirt.

Mildred pressed a business card into Tracy's hands. "I'll be back in Cali tomorrow. Call me when you have your travel arrangements. I can't wait to help you on your mission." She winked.

"I will." Tracy hiccupped, in what she hoped was a discreet manner. "Thanks for everything, Millie. I feel so much better now I've got a plan. I'll call you when I've booked my flight."

As Michael gained on them, Mildred beat a hasty retreat.

****

Michael got to the socialite just in time to see her hop into a taxi. How did she manage to get a cab in Manhattan so fast? She really must have dark forces on her side.

He decided to follow her, rather than Mildred. He was curious to find out who she was, and to try to figure out how the fallen angel might be using her to hurt Kelly and James.

Chapter 4

"Where are you calling from, Kel? It sounds all echo-y."

"That's because I'm in the ladies' room, David," she whispered into the phone.

"And loud music, too." David paused then laughed. "Oh my God! You're calling me from the ladies' room in a bar. I feel like we're back in college."

Kelly rolled her eyes. "I'm so glad I could help you recapture your lost youth. Now, would you please focus? I don't know how long I've got before someone else comes in here."

David stopped laughing, but Kelly could still hear the smile in his voice. "I'm sorry, sweetie. What's up? I thought you were doing that sailing race thingy with Yummy James tonight."

"His friend didn't need us to crew after all, so we went to watch the races together, and now all the participants are at this tiki bar for a post-race celebration. The boat's owner asked us to join them, so here we are," she whispered rapid-fire into the phone as she leaned against the sink and kept a wary eye on the door.

"Okay…" David drew the word out. "Tiki bar, huh? Sounds like fun, so what's got my best girl running so scared she's calling me for a consult from the bathroom?"

"James is acting all date-like," she announced.

A long pause ensued, and she opened her eyes wide and shook the phone as she waited for David's response.

Finally, he spoke in a measured voice. "To the untrained eye, a man might perceive watching a sailing race together on a summer night, and then going for drinks as a date."

"Not helping, David."

"What? Is he being a creep? Did he hurt you? Do I need to come down there and kick his ass?"

"No. It's just when we were watching the race, he leaned against me."

David gasped. "The cad!"

"I'm serious, David. And since we've been here, he's bought my drinks, and if any of the guys come up to us he does that oh-so-casual drape of his arms around my shoulders. You know what I mean?"

"Sure, I've done it myself. It's the guy trick for letting other men know, 'hands off, this one's mine'."

She nodded. "Exactly."

"So you want the other guys to hit on you?"

She waved her free hand in frustration, and said through gritted teeth, "No, David. I do not want the other guys hitting on me."

"Not seeing the problem then, Kel. A man you like and have fun with, is clearly feeling the same way about you. That's a good thing. Not cause for a frantic ladies' room call to your best friend. He's single, and I know this is hard for you to come to terms with, but you're single. Hang up the damn phone and go have fun, woman."

She sighed. "I guess you're right. I'm sorry I

bothered you."

"You're never a bother, kiddo," he replied with affection.

"Hey—I just remembered. James is having an exhibit of his work for charity this weekend—he invited me and said I could bring some friends. I'm going to see if Grace and Janie and their spousal units can come. Do you want in?"

"Hell, yeah. Sounds fun. When is it?"

"Saturday night."

An outdoorsy older woman, with skin so tan it looked like leather, entered the ladies' room and stood at the mirror next to Kelly. She ran her fingers through her short, gray hair as if to style it, but she looked at Kelly in the mirror with open interest as she fluffed, and Kelly turned partially away from her to finish her call.

Zane slouched unseen against the wall. *I knew I could count on David to calm her down. Glad I gave her the nudge to call him. Phase one of my plan went okay. Now on to phase two.*

He stared intently at the older woman as Kelly put her cell phone back in her purse and pulled out her lip-gloss. As she turned back to face the mirror, the older woman said, "Hi. I'm Betsy Lester—Floyd's wife. You're here tonight with Jamie Flynn, aren't you? I've known him since he was born."

Kelly hesitated and then nodded. "Yeah. I guess I am here with him. I'm Kelly Lynch."

Betsy raised her eyebrows. "You're not at all his usual type."

"What do you mean?"

The woman gestured at Kelly's left hand in the

mirror. "Well, for one thing you're married. I guess because his ex-wife left him for another man, that's always been one line I've never known Jamie to cross before."

They walked out of the ladies' room, back into the bar, where the after-race party was in full swing.

Kelly felt insulted this woman thought she was some sort of adulteress, and her reply was curt. "That's a line I feel pretty strongly about, too."

"Really?" Betsy asked with a hearty dose of skepticism in her voice.

"Really." Kelly's answer was firm. "I'm a widow. And I never cheated on my husband."

Betsy's shoulders relaxed, and her smile reached her steely gray eyes for the first time. "A widow. Oh, I'm so happy to hear that."

At Kelly's shocked expression, Betsy was quick to clarify, "I'm not happy that you're a widow. I'm really sorry for your loss. I'm just relieved that Jamie isn't dallying with another man's wife."

Kelly frowned. She still felt like she was another man's wife, but maybe everyone else was right, maybe it was time to let go and start living her life again. She wasn't immune to James' charms now any more than she was when she was eighteen. But Betsy's words made her feel a little insecure and she wanted some clarification, before she put herself out there with James.

"You said 'for one thing' before. Is there some other way I'm not James' usual type?"

Betsy laughed. "Quite a few, from what I've seen of you so far. For starters, you've got a brain and you're age-appropriate." She looked at the bar, where James had a bottle blonde hanging off of him. "Unfortunately, that's the kind of woman I usually see him with. I think he chooses the young, shallow ones deliberately because they won't expect too much from him."

Kelly was surprised by the sharp pang of jealousy and hurt she felt as she watched the girl paw at James, and laugh a little too loudly at something he said. This had to be a record, she'd just decided to give James a chance, and within two minutes she was being thrown over for a younger woman.

She swallowed hard. "Wow. I was only in the ladies' room for like five minutes. I guess out of sight, out of mind, huh?"

Betsy's smile was maternal. "Don't be so sure about that. She approached him as soon as you walked away. And for the record, he's never brought a woman to the Beer Can Races before you. Plus, I've never seen him look at another woman the way he's been looking at you tonight. And I'm including his ex-wife."

She gave a sharp bark of laughter and gestured at James with her head. "Besides, look at him now."

Kelly looked over to where James was sitting at the bar under a fish net filled with colorful glass balls. He was desperately trying to catch Kelly's eye, and when he finally had her attention he mouthed, *Help. Me. Now.*

Betsy gave her a little push in his direction. "You saw the man. Go bail him out."

Kelly smiled at the older woman. "Thanks, Betsy. It was good talking with you."

"You too, Kelly. I'm hoping we'll be seeing a lot more of you." She made a shooing motion with her hands. "Now, go. Before Jamie pops a gasket."

As Kelly wended her way through the crowded bar to James, Zane patted himself on the back for a job well done. Earlier, Kelly had been ready to crawl out of the ladies' room window to escape. Now she was on her way back to James' side, and if Zane wasn't mistaken, and he didn't think he was, she was about to kick some bleached blonde ass.

He decided to make himself corporeal and have a celebratory beer. He settled at the bar to watch the show.

****

James thought Kelly would never make it through the crowd, but finally she was here. Her smile was grim as she took in the sight of the bimbo, attached to him like a limpet.

"Kelly," James said with obvious relief, "you're back. At last."

He tried to stand at her approach, but the girl wouldn't release the vise-like grip she had on his arm. He doggedly stood and dragged her to her feet with him.

She eyed Kelly with disfavor, but didn't loosen her grip. If anything, it got tighter.

"We're busy here, lady."

"Mmm...I can see that," Kelly said with a half-smile as she moved the little, paper umbrella out of the way and sipped her drink from the novelty glass shaped like an Easter Island head.

With extraordinary effort, James managed to shake the girl loose and gestured to his barstool. "Please, take my seat, Kelly, since yours is occupied."

The girl radiated frustration as Kelly and James traded places and she found herself next to the other woman rather than her prey.

"There." James said with such deep satisfaction that he noticed Kelly had to smother a laugh.

The girl narrowed her eyes, and looked with suspicion from James to Kelly. She appeared to decide to be friendly in an attempt to win points with James. Her hand hung limply from her wrist as she extended it to Kelly.

"Hi. I'm Brandi." She added by way of explanation, "With an 'i'."

Kelly took her hand and shook it. "I'm Kelly. With a 'y'."

James had been bringing his beer to his lips, but an explosion of laughter at Kelly's quip forced him to pull it away from his mouth.

"Ever the traditionalist, aren't you?" He chuckled and waved a playful finger at Kelly, as he brought the longneck bottle back to his lips. "See—our New England upbringing always tells. No self-respecting woman from New Hampshire would spell Kelly with anything but a 'y'."

Kelly nodded seriously. "I am way too bound by convention." She looked across the bar, and saw Betsy wink broadly at her before turning to talk to Floyd, who looked in their direction with interest.

Brandi looked between them with narrowed eyes and a moue of displeasure "So are you two from, like, the same town?"

"Mm hm," Kelly murmured in agreement.

"Were you his babysitter, ma'am?" Brandi asked with feigned innocence.

Kelly's eyes widened, and she choked a little on her drink. James pounded her back, and jumped in to answer with the air of a shipwrecked man who'd just spotted a life raft.

"Oh no, she couldn't have been my babysitter. I'm way older than Kelly. If you think she's old," he continued to pound her back, as his words caused another round of coughing from an indignant Kelly, "than you must think I'm positively ancient. An old man, that's me."

"Practically doddering," a recovering Kelly gasped the words.

Brandi leaned across Kelly to grasp James' arm, and he had to take evasive action to keep from getting caught in her clutches again.

Brandi purred her response. "You might be more...mature...than me, but you're such a famous art guy. I saw your picture on the news the other night, and they said you might be reclusive or something, but your paintings sell for a bundle. I'm your biggest fan, even if you are reclusive." She wrinkled her nose in confusion and asked, "Does that mean old?"

"No, it means I like my privacy."

She flashed him a mega-watt smile. "We could definitely go somewhere more private if you want. I just love your painting."

James felt like a cornered animal, and fortunately Kelly took pity on him. She asked Brandi cheerfully, "Which one?"

"Which one, what?" Brandi snapped.

"Which painting do you like best? You said you love his work—which piece is your favorite?" Kelly felt pretty certain Brandi had never heard of James before she saw him on the local news being described as rich and famous, and her answer proved her right.

"The, um, one with the flowers?" It came out more like a question than a statement.

James ignored her and looked at Kelly, "What about you? Have you seen my work?"

She flushed delicately. "I'm sorry, but I haven't. I didn't realize you were the same James Flynn I used to know, so I didn't pay much attention to your work."

Brandi crowed triumphantly, "You've never even seen the one with the flowers?"

James grimaced, and turned his attention back to Kelly. "I've got some pieces in my loft that I'm working on, and I'd love your opinion on them. Maybe you can come see them sometime?"

Kelly looked at him over her silly tiki glass, and waggled her brows. "Come up and see my etchings, little girl."

James grin was sheepish. "Something like that...did it work?"

Brandi interrupted, "I'm sure Kelly has to make curfew at the old folk's home, but I'd love to see your place."

"You know what, James? I think we've missed the early bird special that people our age enjoy so much, but if we hurry we can still grab dinner somewhere."

James practically threw money at the bartender in his eagerness to get away. "Good thinking. Maybe we can find some place that serves tapioca pudding for dessert. You know how geezers like me love it."

He grabbed Kelly's elbow and steered her outside, as Brandi sputtered and huffed at their retreating forms. He didn't stop until they were at his car.

****

He opened Kelly's car door for her with a flourish.

"How does Italian sound to my knight in shining armor?"

Kelly laughed. "I was glad to provide a knightly save, but we don't really have to go out to dinner. I was getting tired of the cracks about my age, and used it as an excuse to make a break for it."

She slid into the car. James leaned one arm on the roof and one on the door as he leaned in to ask her, "Don't you like Italian food? We could go somewhere else, or are you just anti-dinner in general?"

"I'm not anti-dinner. I would describe myself as strongly pro-dinner, even. I just don't want you to feel obligated to keep the evening going."

His voice was low, and he never broke eye contact as he said, "As far as I'm concerned, this night can go on forever."

At that, he shut her car door, and loped around to the driver's side. He got in and looked at Kelly as he buckled up. He smiled in the charming way that made her heart flutter and her legs squeeze together.

"So—Italian? I know a great place in Little Italy."

Kelly gulped. She knew she'd told herself she needed to start living again, but she'd been thinking of a quiet, Sunday drive to living. This man was making her feel like she was on the Autobahn back to life, but maybe that was the best way to do it. Jump in with both feet, like you would jump into a cold New Hampshire lake—it was just torture to go in slowly.

Her mind made up, she nodded and said, "Italian would be great."

****

"A tiki bar?" Michael's Boston accent pronounced the last word as "bah". "Really, Zane? I find you in a freakin' tiki bar? Got to hand it to you, man, you always do the unexpected."

Zane turned his head at the sound of his friend's voice, and spared him a brief smile. "Yeah. That's me—the cowboy Don Ho. I just can't stay away from the danged little paper umbrellas."

Michael laughed, and signaled the bartender to order a beer. He settled on a stool next to Zane. "Somehow, this isn't what I expected the afterlife to be. Sitting in a tiki bar with a stoic cowboy while we try to hook my wife up with another guy."

"What? You were expecting something more sordid?" Zane deadpanned.

"Where are the harps and clouds? That's what I want to know. We were promised harps and clouds."

"That's why we're hooking up your wife. I think the next plane will be harps and clouds, and that's where you'll be headed once we get Kelly all set with James. Now me—I'm happy with bars and beers." He tilted his bottle in Michael's direction, and took a swig.

Michael looked around. "Is Kelly here? Should I make myself invisible?"

Zane gave a slow shake of his head. "Nope. You're cool. James and she are on their way out to dinner. I just thought I'd finish up my beer, and then catch up with them at the restaurant."

"They must be having fun together tonight, huh?"

"Yep," Zane replied. After a brief silence he asked, "Did you find out anything about Mildred?"

I was able to track her, but I'm still not sure what she's up to. She was in Manhattan having a liquid lunch with some society broad. You know the type—made completely of peroxide and plastic. Name's Tracy

Blackburn."

Zane grunted. "Whatever she's doing with this woman it can't be good for our team. At least we know who to look out for now."

Chapter 5

Kelly felt woefully underdressed at the small, elegant Italian restaurant. They were both dressed for sailing in khakis, polo shirts, and windbreakers, while the other patrons were in suits, ties, and cocktail dresses. She fiddled self-consciously with her ponytail, and watched the owner chat with James. They clearly knew each other, and the man was treating them like royalty. She told herself to quit worrying, loosen up, and enjoy the meal.

Of course, butterflies seemed to have set up permanent residence in her stomach since their romantically charged car ride from the tiki bar. James had cast so many smoldering glances her way she was amazed her hair wasn't singed, but now they were back among other people, and her guilt about Michael and insecurities began to raise its ugly little head.

With one last beaming smile, the owner left them alone at the table. Kelly could feel James' gaze burn into her as she began to twirl her water goblet by the stem.

She kept her eyes cast down as she asked, "Does that kind of thing happen to you often?"

"What kind of thing?"

"The girl at the tiki bar."

Kelly heard the creak as he leaned back in his chair. "Ah. You mean Barnacle Brandi?"

She glanced up with a smile. "With an 'i'. Yeah, that's what I meant." Her gaze drifted back to the glass she continued to spin.

He shrugged. "I guess it does. A lot of women—heck a lot of people, men and women—seem to be drawn to fame. With the publicity for the charity thing this weekend, my face has been out there more than normal."

Kelly tried to keep her voice disinterested and casual, but didn't quite succeed. "She was very pretty."

"And dumb as a brick." He leaned forward, the corners of his mouth tilted up, as he winked. "I prefer smart, spunky brunettes."

Kelly couldn't keep the blush from flooding her cheeks. "That's not what I hear, Jamie. Word around the tiki bar is that Brandi is much more your type than I am."

"Let me guess who told you that—Betsy?"

Kelly nodded, but still stared at her glass of water, which kept her nervous fingers occupied spinning it.

"Calling me 'Jamie' was the giveaway. No one else has called me that since junior high school. Floyd and Betsy have been friends with my family forever, and I've managed to break Floyd of the habit, but she insists I'll always be 'Jamie' to her, and there's no moving Betsy once she's made up her mind."

Kelly glanced up to see him searching her face before lowering her eyes again. He must have sensed her insecurity, because he reached across the table and stilled her hand. He pulled it away from her glass and clasped it with his own.

"Maybe I have dated a lot of women like Brandi, but it was starting to feel really empty. That's one of the reasons I got in touch with you. I remembered you as being smart and funny, on top of being beautiful and sexy as hell."

He stared at her intently until she had no choice but to look up and meet his gaze. "You're someone I can see being my best friend as well as my lover, and that's what I want now. To tell you the truth, you're the only woman in my life I ever imagined that happening with—when you were eighteen and again now."

Kelly wrinkled her brow. "What about your wife? You must have felt that way about her?"

He chuckled humorlessly. "She was a lot like Brandi. My marriage wasn't like yours was, Kel, we were young and it was a very hormone-driven relationship. There was no friendship between us."

"Why did you marry her then?"

He squinted and frowned as he considered her question. "She seemed to really want to get married, and I just sort of let myself get swept along. How dumb is that? Looking back with twenty-twenty hindsight, I don't think I ever really loved her. Lust—we had that in spades." He shook his head and sadness clouded his bright green eyes. "But love? No."

The waiter interrupted to set a dish on the table between them. "Compliments of the owner. Enjoy."

James released Kelly's hand, and picked up a piece of rolled salami from the antipasti platter. "You've got to try this, it's the best I've ever had outside of Italy."

Rather than hand it to her, he held it out for her take a bite. As her lips closed around the meat, she fluttered her eyelids shut and moaned softly. "You're right. That is so yummy."

****

His pulse pounded as his blood raced through his body, in a southerly direction. He couldn't help but imagine Kelly making those little yummy sounds in an entirely different situation. A more naked situation.

Kelly looked at him, and he knew his eyes were dark with hunger—and not for the antipasti. She quickly looked away and took a sip of water. Okay, she wasn't ready for the steamy repartee yet; he needed to slow things down before he scared her away. He took a deep breath and tried to get his body's reactions under control.

"I'm sorry, Kelly, I don't want to push you. I'm trying to go slow. Really, I am," he lowered his voice and continued roughly. "I just want you so damn much."

Kelly rolled her eyes, not a response he'd ever gotten from a woman before after that kind of declaration. If he could win her over, she'd certainly keep him on his toes with her unexpected reactions. He couldn't believe she didn't know how desirable a woman she was. He saw the way the other guys from Floyd's boat were checking her out at the tiki bar after the race; why did she think he kept putting his arm around her? It was to stake a claim to get them to back off, so how did she not see it?

"You don't believe me?"

"It's kind of hard to believe that given the choice between a young, blonde bombshell like Brandi, and a thirty-five-year-old widow, you'd pick the widow."

He raised an eyebrow. "And yet, which one of them is sitting across the table from me? You sell yourself way too short, Kelly with a 'y'."

He thought long and hard before he continued. He

didn't want to scare her off, but he felt like he needed to confess something to her that would either send her running into the night, or help boost her confidence in herself and his feelings toward her.

"You've been my dream woman since that night we met when I was twenty-two. You were everything I wanted in a girlfriend, and when you dumped me for David"—he laughed and shook his head in disbelief—"or so I thought at the time. Anyway—I was shook up when you left. When I moved to New York, the women I chose were all the exact opposite of you. Dumb, shallow bimbos. I realize now that I thought they wouldn't be able to touch me enough to hurt me, because I sure as hell didn't want to feel anything again remotely like what I felt when I saw you with David that summer."

Kelly's voice was little more than a whisper. "James, I'm so sorry. I never dreamed you were hurt—I just assumed I was one girl in a long conga line of girls to your bedroom."

"I'm not denying there were girls before or since, but you were different. Special." He hit the table with his hand and the silverware rattled. "If I'd only known back then that you were just scared, I would've slowed things down, and I never would have lost you. Never married Tracy. Never been divorced. Things could have been so different for us."

Kelly covered his hand on the table with hers, and her voice was gentle. "I can't be sorry about the way things worked out, James. If we had stayed together, I never would have met Michael, and I loved him so much. We were really happy together, even if I lost him too soon. I can't even imagine my life without him in it."

"I get that, Kel, but my marriage was a train wreck. I realize now that I picked a woman as different from you as night from day to try and protect myself, but I still ended up hurt."

Kelly looked a little sheepish. "Betsy mentioned your wife left you for another man. That kind of betrayal would hurt no matter what the circumstances."

"Betsy's got kind of a big mouth."

Kelly held up her left hand and waggled her ring finger. "She didn't mean any harm. She saw my rings and wanted to protect you from the married vixen." She chuckled. "When she found out I was a widow, she actually said to me 'I'm so glad'."

James threw back his head and laughed. "Subtlety, thy name is not Betsy Lester. She's been protective of me since my mom died."

"I think it's sweet."

"Yeah," he admitted. "Floyd and Betsy are good people. They really helped me get through my mom's illness and death. They never had any of their own kids, so they've taken me under their wings since I moved out here."

He grew thoughtful and added after a pause. "At least Tracy and I didn't have any kids to drag through our marital minefield. Tracy said that being pregnant would ruin her figure."

Kelly's face was wistful. "I wish Michael and I had kids. We wanted to spend some time alone together before we started our family." Her voice broke and she shut her eyes and took a deep breath. "And then he got sick."

James squeezed her hand. "That's enough soul-searching stuff for one night." The waiter approached their table with a tray. "Here come our meals. I say we enjoy them and try to figure out which painting of mine Barnacle Brandi meant when she said 'the one with the flowers'. I don't think I've ever painted anything with flowers. Who do I look like—Georgia freaking O'Keefe?"

Kelly laughed as she picked up her silverware and dug into her eggplant parmigiana. "Nah. You're way prettier than Georgia O'Keefe was."

****

Zane was non-corporeal at the moment, as he didn't want to risk them seeing him again tonight in case they had caught a glimpse of him at the tiki bar.

Michael had chosen well when he decided to bring James back into Kelly's life. The man had handled her so well tonight—soothing her nerves and making her feel special and at ease. Hell, he even got her to laugh after she'd thought of Michael and their lack of children. No easy task, yet here she was—enjoying a delicious meal and the company of a man who was crazy about her.

He was a little tired of being a voyeur and decided to give them some privacy. With a longing look at their dinner, he made a promise to come back here sometime when he was corporeal. The food looked too good to miss.

Right now, he wanted to find Michael and discuss the possibility that the Tracy Mildred had buddied up to in New York was James' ex-wife. It didn't seem as though James had strong feelings for her anymore, so he couldn't figure out how the fallen angel expected to use her to bust up James and Kelly's budding relationship. Michael was a mighty smart guy, though, maybe he could see something Zane was missing.

****

James held Kelly's hand as he walked her to her apartment building from his car. While they were still in shadows, before they reached the bright light of the entrance, James stopped and turned to face Kelly. He cupped her face in one of his big, rough hands and rested the other lightly on her waist. He traced her cheekbone with a feather light touch of his thumb, and Kelly couldn't help but turn her face into his hand like a kitten. She did manage to stop herself before she purred, and was pretty darned proud of that achievement.

She felt his hand at her waist tighten, and he dropped his forehead down to rest against hers. When he spoke his voice was low and gruff with emotion.

"Tell me to leave right now, Kel, or all my good intentions to go slow this time are flying out the window, and I'm going to ask you to invite me up to your condo."

Kelly's voice was quiet. "I'm not ready for that yet."

He left his forehead resting against hers, but rubbed his head slowly back and forth. "I know. I should just go, but I can't bring myself to leave."

Kelly swallowed, and extended an olive branch, since she wasn't ready to call it a night yet either. "I think I'm ready for a kiss, though."

He lifted his head away from hers, and the happiness and blatant hope in his voice made her smile. "Yeah? Really?"

"Yeah," she replied and stood on the tips of her

canvas deck shoes to bring her mouth closer to his.

James bent his head and pressed his lips gently to hers.

Her heart pounded and her blood heated in her veins. It had been such a long time since a man had kissed her—and this was James Flynn. Her first love. She snaked her arms up around his neck and pressed her body closer to his.

Oh boy, he wasn't lying when he said he wanted to go back to her place. In this position she could feel the infamous Three H's in evidence against her belly. This time, though, it didn't make her want to run away from him. She wanted to grab his hand and drag him upstairs to have her wicked way with him.

James moved his hips sinuously and ground the Three H's against her body. She loved the way he felt against her, so hard where she was soft. He deepened the kiss, and Kelly responded with enthusiasm, almost oblivious to the fact they were making out on a street corner like teenagers. She remained aware of their location, but as long as his warm, velvety tongue continued to mimic what she wanted the Three H's to do a little lower on her body, she didn't think she could bring herself to stop even if they were on the infield at PETCO Park.

He pulled away from her, but his breath was still a little ragged when he asked, "Can I see you tomorrow?"

Kelly slowly opened her eyes and blinked them in an owlish manner. What had she been about to do? Gah! One kiss from this man and she was acting like a hormonal teenager. She was grateful for his phenomenal display of self-control, because she was one step away from acting on her earlier impulse to drag him upstairs, and she wasn't ready to take their relationship to that level yet.

If just one kiss in public had her feeling like this, it was not wise to go anywhere in private with James. Okay, in her defense it was a rock-em sock-em kind of kiss, but still. Acting like some kind of harlot wasn't the way to be true to Michael's memory.

A little voice in her head whispered, "Michael knows you love him, and living your life with passion is what he'd want you to do."

That thought stopped Kelly from fleeing the way she had when she was eighteen. She could keep her raging hormones under control and keep seeing James until she decided she was ready to take it to the next level. Right?

"I'd like that." She nodded and then blurted out, "But I can't!"

James looked stricken, but she saw determination in the set of his jaw. This man was not going to let her run scared again, the way she had when she was eighteen.

Before she could explain, he asked. "Do you have to work? I thought you were taking a little break until you heard back from your editor about your manuscript?"

"I am, but I promised my friend Grace that I'd hang out with her daughter tomorrow while Grace meets with a potential client. She's trying to start up an interior design firm, and this appointment could be a big break for her."

James chuckled. "You're babysitting?"

She returned his smile. "To protect Lydia's eleven-year old sensibilities we don't call it babysitting—we just say we're hanging out together. Helps her to save face. Having a babysitter is deeply uncool."

He hit his forehead with the heel of his hand. "I just remembered that I have to pick up my manager at the airport tomorrow anyway. She's flying in for the charity exhibit Saturday night. So, I'm not free during the day either, but how about dinner?"

She looked regretful. "I'm having dinner at Grace's after I'm done babysit...er...hanging out."

"All right then—Friday. And I'm not taking no for an answer."

"Friday is clear for me. Lunch?"

He kissed her forehead gently. "Wild horses couldn't keep me away. I'll call you tomorrow to set it all up."

****

James waited until Kelly was safely in the elevator before he got back into his car and drove across the street to the underground parking garage of his building.

Once they were both out of sight, Zane made himself corporeal. He leaned against the building, his hat low over his eyes and a toothpick clenched between his strong, white teeth. His casual pose belied the tumult of his emotions. That was a close one. He should have known better than to leave such a skittish filly alone for too long. He had, and sure enough, Kelly's nerves and guilt had her pulling away from love with James.

He'd gotten here just in the nick of time to plant the thought in her head that Michael would want her to keep on living her life. Luckily it worked. She'd agreed to see James again on Friday.

But he was her guardian angel, right? Maybe he'd arrange things so Kelly and James could see each other tomorrow in spite of their previous commitments. The fallen angel had something up her dirty sleeve with that Tracy woman from New York City, and the tighter he could weld Kelly and James together before Mildred's shit hit the fan, the better it would be for them.

He didn't dare leave Kelly alone for too long up in her condo, though. She'd get to feeling guilty again. He decided to find Michael and peek in on Kelly and James one more time tonight, just to be on the safe side.

****

The two angels got to Kelly's condo in time to see her emerge from her bedroom in the tight sleep T-shirt and boxer shorts she slept in, with her hair up in a loose bun and wearing her tortoise-shell eyeglasses. She went to the kitchen where the kettle whistled and made a cup of chamomile tea to help her sleep. She was feeling all charged up after her evening with James. She scoffed. *Evening.* Why not call it what it was? A date. Her date with James.

She picked up her mug and looked at the photo of Michael and her on the sailboat.

"Oh, honey. I'm so sorry. I kissed another man tonight, and I've got to be honest with you, I kind of enjoyed it. Okay. I really enjoyed it."

Michael sighed. "Oh, baby. It's all right. I want you to be happy."

Zane looked at his friend with sympathy. "Do you want me to put that thought in her head?"

"Nah. Deep down, I know she knows it."

She blew on her tea to cool it off and took a small sip. "Everyone keeps saying you'd want me to move on. To be happy. I wish you could give me some kind of sign if it's all right with you for me to date James."

Michael opened his eyes wide and smacked Zane on the arm.

"Hey. What the hell was that for?" the cowboy asked indignantly.

"I've got an idea for the sign she wants. I'm going to head over and work on James. You get her out on the balcony in a couple of minutes."

Zane squinted as he concentrated on getting Kelly outside.

She stood at the granite island and flipped through her mail, until she suddenly looked out to the balcony.

"Maybe I'll go drink my tea on the balcony—it's a warm night, and maybe looking at the water will help me settle down. Great. Now I'm talking to myself. I'm one step away from becoming a crazy cat lady."

Zane punched his fist in the air as she slid the door open. Yes! She was taking his suggestion.

Traffic noise from the street drifted in through the open door. He followed her out onto the breezy balcony. He had no idea what Michael was up to, but did his part and got Kelly outside, and now he was going to stick around to see what his buddy had planned.

He nodded with approval when a movement on the balcony in the building across the street caught his eye and he saw James step out and lean on the railing to look out at the bay.

James and Kelly still hadn't seen each other though. He wondered what else Michael had in mind— they could stand here all night and never see each other. Suddenly a bright light flashed over the building James was in. He nodded in approval. For someone who'd only been an angel a couple of years, that Michael had some good moves.

****

Kelly started at the brightness and looked over to see what caused it, and spotted James on his balcony in nothing but a pair of flannel sleep pants. His damp hair made her think he'd just gotten out of the shower. And she would so not think about him in the shower—naked, with the water sluicing over his delicious chest and abs. He looked pretty good shirtless for a thirty-nine year old guy. She couldn't help but notice; she wasn't made of stone after all.

She could tell when he finally noticed her on the balcony, because a smile lit up his face. She waved shyly. He put his hands over his heart and Kelly scrunched her nose in confusion. She shook her head and held her hands palm side up to indicate she didn't understand what he meant.

He held up his index finger to indicate he wanted her to wait a minute and ran into his loft. He came back out a moment later with his phone in hand and Kelly heard hers ring through the open door. She went in to grab it and returned to the balcony as she picked up.

In reply to her tentative "Hello", she heard James say. "You're killing me here, Kel."

Truly baffled by his words she asked. "What?"

"You really can rock the naughty librarian look, and you wouldn't know it, but you've hit on one of my secret fantasies."

"Naughty librarian? I'm in my pj's. I've never seen a librarian in her pj's before. What are you talking about?"

"The bun and the glasses. I didn't know you wore glasses." He gave a low growl.

"I usually wear my contacts. Glasses really do it for you, huh?" she asked in amazement.

"You have no idea."

She blushed at the intensity of his answer and changed the subject. "What was that bright light over your building a couple of minutes ago?"

"I don't know. I was wondering about it, too."

"Huh," Kelly pondered the matter. She'd just asked for a sign if it was okay with Michael if she dated James, and then she felt drawn to go outside. Right after she did, a flash of light made her look over and then she saw James. Now they were talking about naughty librarians. Could it be the sign she wanted?

She smiled. "You know my husband was an English teacher and he always had that naughty librarian fixation, too."

"Obviously, he was a man of fine taste and discernment," James quipped. "Seriously, though, I think most guys do. It's something about being the one to know what the woman looks like when the bun comes down and the glasses come off. And the little shirt and short-shorts, don't hurt either."

She shivered a little at the clear desire in his voice. James noticed and misinterpreted its meaning. "Speaking of which, you should probably head inside. With the breeze off the bay it's kind of cool out here, and I don't want you to get sick before the exhibit this weekend. I hate these things and I'm really counting on you being there to support me."

Glad for the cover story, Kelly agreed with alacrity. "You're right; it is pretty chilly out tonight. I'll see you on Friday."

"You can bet on it." His voice took on a devilish tone. "And, Kel, wear the glasses."

Chapter 6

"Are you sure you don't want me to take you to your hotel first?" James asked his manager as he maneuvered his car through airport traffic.

"No. I've been up since before dawn New York time, and I'm dying for a cup of coffee. There's a place I like near your condo. We can go there and then swing by your place and I can see what you're working on."

"Yes!" Unseen and unheard in the back seat, Michael smacked his hand on the armrest with satisfaction before he flashed to Zane's side outside the coffee shop.

"Hey, Mike. I got her here, just like you asked me to." He jerked his head to one of the outside café tables where Kelly sat with her friends Grace and Lydia.

"Good job, man. James and his manager are on their way. I made her have a major coffee jones and she insisted on coming here right away."

*****

Grace turned to her daughter. "Lydia, I think we need more napkins. Would you run inside and get them for us, please?"

Lydia folded her arms across her chest and rolled her eyes. "Puh-leeze, Mother, I'm not an infant. I know you're just trying to get rid of me so you can pump Aunt Kelly about her date last night."

"Aren't you clever?" Grace's voice was mild.

"Since you know what I'm doing, why don't you go get the napkins like a good kid?"

"Fine." Lydia stomped inside, leaving Grace and Kelly at one of the tables set up in front of the shop.

"Sheesh. She's not even a teenager yet and so much attitude. I've got a lot to look forward to." She turned to Kelly with an anticipatory air. "We don't have much time before she gets back—tell me all about last night, and before you ask—no detail is too small. Spill."

Kelly blew on her cappuccino before taking a sip to stall for time. She knew Grace would pounce on the news of her kiss with James like a coyote on road kill, and she wasn't ready to share these new feelings with the world yet. As Grace drummed her fingers on the glass top of the wrought iron table, Kelly knew she had to say something. "We ended up not having to crew for his friend…"

Grace interrupted, "Boring. And Lydia's already coming back, so let's cut to the chase. Did you sleep with him?"

"Grace!" Kelly could feel the flush spread from her neck up to the top of her head. "Of course I didn't sleep with him."

"Fine. Did you kiss? Please tell me you at least kissed him."

Kelly huffed in exasperation. "You're like a pit bull of gossip. Yes. I kissed him. Happy now? I kissed James Flynn."

Heads whipped in their direction at her too loud exclamation, and Lydia thumped a pile of napkins on the table and squealed. "Ooo…Aunt Kelly! You really kissed James Flynn? How was it?"

"Good question. I am so raising you properly." Grace beamed at her daughter and then turned to her friend and prompted, "Answer the child. How was it?"

Kelly became aware of the audience she'd inadvertently attracted. She put her mug down and leaned across the table to whisper. "It was darned good. Okay?"

A shadow fell over their table and all three looked up to see who was there. Kelly had thought she couldn't get any redder, but when she saw James standing there she could even feel her toes blushing. She really hoped he hadn't heard what they'd been talking about when he came up to the table.

The woman with him looked bemused. This must be his manager in from New York for the charity exhibit. She looked like an illustration of a sophisticated Manhattanite. Kelly couldn't tell how old she was, she could have been anywhere from thirty-five to sixty. With her improbably black hair pulled back in a sleek chignon, dressed in an elegant red business suit, and wearing designer shoes that probably cost more than a used car, she looked like some kind of hothouse flower transplanted in the West Coast sunshine.

Kelly smiled shyly at James and said, "Hey."

He leaned down and kissed the top of her head lightly, which caused one of Grace's eyebrows to arch all the way up to her hairline.

"Hey, yourself. I'd like you to meet my friend and manager, Ellen Markowitz. Ellen this is Kelly Lynch."

Ellen's curiosity about Kelly and James showed just as clearly in her expression as it did on Grace's open, tanned California girl face.

"Nice to meet you," Ellen snuck a peek at James.

"This one's never introduced me to one of his...friends...before. You must be something special, doll."

Kelly was afraid the blush on her face was about to become a permanent feature. James and she replied at the same time:

"I don't know how special I am."

"She sure is something special."

Grace looked at James with open interest. "Hi. I'm Grace Miller, and this is my daughter, Lydia."

"Nice to meet you both. Kelly's got nothing but nice things to say about the two of you." James flashed his crooked grin at Lydia, whose open-mouthed gape pegged her as being totally star-struck by him. "Lydia. Kelly tells me you like my work."

She nodded and her eyes were like saucers.

James' cheeks grew ruddy in light of her open adoration, but he gamely forged on in his attempt to talk to the girl. "She said you've got one of my posters in your room. Which one is it?"

She continued to stare at him wordlessly, until her mother nudged her under the table.

"Um." Her voice was breathless. "Brooklyn Bridge at Dawn."

"Good choice," Ellen gave a sharp nod of approval. "One of his finest pieces, in my opinion."

"I think so, too!" Lydia leaned forward in her seat and gushed. "The grandeur of the bridge compared to the homeless man living under it really makes a real statement."

Grace widened her eyes and mouthed to Kelly. "Grandeur?"

Kelly quickly lifted her mug to her lips to hide her

smile. She was crazy about Lydia and didn't want the child to think she was laughing at her hero worship of James. She didn't have to worry—Lydia had eyes for no one but her idol.

"Very powerful," Ellen agreed with gravity.

Grace looked at her watch and gulped the last of her green tea. "Look at the time. I've got to run to my meeting." She kissed her daughter's cheek. "I'll get you at Aunt Kelly's in a couple of hours." She swung her head pointedly at James as she spoke. "Call me if you guys are going to be somewhere else."

Clearly, she wouldn't mind if Kelly and Lydia spent the afternoon with James.

Kelly answered, since Lydia still sat transfixed by a sheepish James. "We will. Good luck, Gracie. I know you're going to knock 'em dead with your designs."

Grace crossed her fingers and raised her eyes to heaven, before she grabbed her portfolio case and rushed off.

"I'm going to grab a cup of joe. For some reason, I've been dying for one ever since the airport. Will you be here for a few?" Ellen asked Kelly, who nodded in reply.

As she walked inside to place her order, James pulled up a chair next to Kelly and sat. Kelly's apparently new permanent blush deepened when she felt the warmth of his muscular thigh pressed deliberately against hers.

"I've been taking a drawing class this summer," Lydia blurted out.

"That's great. If I can help you out with it, let me know." James' smile was warm as he unfolded one of the large napkins, and asked if either of them had a pen or pencil. Kelly dug around in her big straw bag and held up a black Sharpie in triumph.

"Perfect. Thanks." James took the pen and began to sketch with sure strokes.

Ellen came back with her coffee and sat in the seat Grace had vacated. She took a deep, fortifying sip and exhaled with satisfaction. She looked at Kelly through squinted eyes. "I'm sorry I keep staring at you, but you look so familiar to me. We've never met before, have we?"

Kelly shook her head. "No. I don't think we have."

James didn't look up from his sketch as he said. "Kelly's a published author, Ellen. She writes mysteries under the name K.M. Lynch, maybe you've seen her picture on one of her books."

Ellen heaved a sigh of what looked like relief to Kelly before bestowing a beaming smile upon her. "You're successful in your own right. Good, good."

James rolled his eyes. "Ellen thinks it's her job to protect me from gold diggers."

Kelly looked between them with wide eyes. "No one's ever thought I was a gold digger before. I'm not sure if I should be insulted or flattered."

James snorted with laughter, before lowering his head back to continue sketching on the napkin.

"I just look out for your best interests, James, nothing wrong with that." She looked back at Kelly. "No insult intended."

"None taken."

Ellen gave a short nod. "I was just reading your latest book on the plane. I picked it up at the airport. Good stuff. That must be why you look so familiar."

"I'm glad you liked the book. If you've got it on

you, I'd be happy to sign it for you." Kelly's cheeks turned pink, and she lowered her eyes modestly when she made the offer. She loved writing, but her shyness made her uncomfortable with the public profile that went along with it.

"Great! Thanks." Ellen pulled the paperback out of her briefcase and handed it to Kelly with a pen.

Lydia tore her fascinated eyes from James and announced in her clear, child's voice. "That can't be why you recognize her—Aunt Kelly never has her picture in her books."

Ellen raised her perfectly arched, thin eyebrows. "Why not? You're a great looking girl."

Lydia chimed in before Kelly could answer. "Mom says it's because she's 'a very private person'."

"Nothing wrong with that," James said without looking up as he continued to sketch.

"Originally, I think my publisher didn't want people to know if K.M. Lynch was a man or a woman, but Lydia's right, I've kept it up because I like my privacy." She rolled her eyes. "It's not like I'm some big star or something, I don't mean to come across like a conceited jerk. I just don't think I'd like being recognized at the grocery store."

"Believe me, in my line of work I've become an expert on conceited jerks, and you're definitely not one." Ellen patted Kelly's hand.

"Thank you." Kelly handed the book and pen back to Ellen.

"Thank *you*," Ellen replied, as she tucked the book back in her briefcase.

"Ta da!" James signed the napkin with a flourish and presented it to Lydia with a smile and a bow. "Just a little something for you to remember our first meeting by." He looked at Kelly and added with meaning, "Hopefully, it won't be our last."

Lydia turned as red as Kelly as she read aloud. "'To Lydia, in admiration and friendship, James Flynn.' Oh, look Aunt Kelly. It's you and me!"

Kelly looked at his quickly drawn sketch. It was rough, but his talent was immediately recognizable. Lydia and she sat at the café table. Their heads were pressed together, and they smiled as if they shared a private joke.

"You both looked so beautiful sitting there, I had to try and capture the moment. A Sharpie and a paper napkin don't really do you justice, but..." He shrugged and grinned sheepishly.

Ellen nodded. "He doesn't do stuff like this very often, kid. Take good care of that napkin. It'll be worth something someday."

Lydia held it with reverence. "Oh, I'd never sell it, Ms. Markowski."

"We could get it framed," Kelly suggested. "It's such a nice drawing of us. I'll have it framed for your birthday gift."

"Thanks, Aunt Kelly! That would be great."

Ellen tapped the side of her nose twice and then pointed the finger at Kelly. "A word to the wise. Spring for professional, archival framing to be sure that flimsy napkin is preserved properly. I know collectors who'd pay five figures for it, and an original, signed sketch by James Flynn is only going to increase in value. Even if it is on a coffee shop napkin."

Now it was James' turn to blush to the roots of his hair. "Jeez, Ellen, I'm sitting right here."

His manager held up her hands in mock submission. "I'm so sorry. I didn't mean to offend the sensibilities of the temperamental artist. I just want to be sure Lydia understands the value of her gift."

She finished her coffee and plunked the mug on the table. "Okay. I'm fully caffeinated. Let's go take a look at what you're working on. Care to join us, ladies?"

****

Zane looked at Michael with something akin to awe in his eyes. "Oh you're good for an East Coast city boy. I just hoped they'd run into each other, and you've got 'em spending the afternoon together."

Michael grinned. "You ain't seen nothing yet. Wait until they get to his loft."

The two angels flashed to James' penthouse loft with just a brief disturbance of the air to indicate they'd ever been there.

A few minutes later they heard Lydia's excited voice in the hallway as James' key turned in the lock.

****

"I can't believe I'm going to see a real artist's studio. My drawing teacher is going to flip! This has been the best day ever."

James stepped back to let the ladies enter first, "I hope you won't be too disappointed. You've got to remember these are works in progress, so don't expect too much."

Ellen patted his cheek with a maternal fondness that made Kelly wonder if the polished woman was older than she'd previously guessed, then swept into the room, followed by Lydia who looked as excited as if Mickey Mouse was personally escorting her into Disneyland. James put his hand on the small of Kelly's back and guided her in behind them.

She felt the warmth of his hand penetrate her thin, cotton shirt. Her thrill at that small contact distracted Kelly, and she didn't notice Ellen as she moved like a woman in a trance to stand in front of the gas fireplace.

"Ah ha!" Ellen shouted. "I knew you looked familiar! You're *Love Awakens.*"

"Ellen," James said with warning in his tone, but if he wanted to stop her, it was too late, Kelly already stood next to his manager and stared at the painting in front of her.

She blinked a few times and leaned in for a closer look.

It was her.

Well, it was eighteen-year-old her. She sat on a bluff overlooking the ocean in the moonlight. Her face was in profile as she looked out over the water. The colors and composition of the painting gave it a dreamlike quality and there seemed something otherworldly about her appearance. As if she were some sort of sprite or water nymph caught unawares by the artist.

"It's me. The night we met." She breathed the words.

James stuffed his hands in the pockets of his faded jeans and stared at his feet. "Yep."

"Wow, Aunt Kelly, you look beautiful. Magical. Almost like a fairy."

James nodded in approval. "You're good, Lydia. That's how she looked to me that night. It's what I tried to capture in my painting."

Kelly turned to Ellen. "What did you call this painting?"

She took a breath to answer, but James cut her off. "I think I should be the one to tell her, Ellen. It's called *Love Awakens*, because I think a part of me fell in love with you the moment I saw you sitting there. It was a big moment in my life, and I wanted to capture it on canvas. I started this painting that night, after you went home."

Ellen and Lydia exchanged a glance and the woman gently steered the child away to give James and Kelly some privacy—or at least to give them the illusion of privacy. Since his condo was a loft, it was basically one big open space with screens to separate his studio, and a wall of glass bricks to define his bedroom.

Kelly gaped at the painting. She felt flattered and scared in almost equal measures. "You've kept this for yourself. You didn't sell it."

Ellen called out. "Or exhibit it. It's always been just for him, and he could sell it for a pretty penny, believe you me."

James pointed to the corner of the massive room where his studio space was screened off with Japanese screens. "The stuff I'm working on is in the studio, Ellen. Why don't you take Lydia in to look at it?"

"Fine. I can take a hint. C'mon, kid, let's leave these lovebirds alone to work through their issues."

"I couldn't bring myself to part with it." He kept his voice low at first, but raised it now so Ellen could hear. "For any price."

"Hey, Aunt Kelly, there are some more sketches of you back here, but you're old in these," Lydia's voice rang through the loft.

Kelly raised an eyebrow at James, who still had his

hands in pockets. He cocked his head at the balcony. "Can we discuss this out there, please?"

Kelly nodded and went through the sliding glass door he opened to the outside.

****

James followed her, and leaned with his backside against the railing. Kelly faced him with her arms crossed in a defensive way and confusion clear in her gaze. James spared a quick glance into his studio, where Ellen and Lydia both rather pointedly tried to ignore the couple on the balcony.

He brushed a lock of hair out of his eyes and gave her a tentative smile. "I know this all probably seems kind of stalker-like, but it's not. I swear. I had trouble sleeping last night, and I did some sketches of you watching the sailing. It's not like I've been drawing pictures of you for seventeen years. I swear I haven't been. There's just the one painting in there and the sketches from last night."

She nodded. "Okay. If the sketches are of me last night then I'm more concerned about Lydia calling me 'old' in them." A half smile played at the corners of her mouth.

James grinned back. "It's all relative. When I was eleven, I thought twenty-five was old."

"Not to beat a dead horse, but I really need to know—the painting—why have you kept it?"

He shrugged. "Partly because of you, I admit it. You were the first girl to ever make me think the 'L' word and the first one to break my heart. Being a writer, you've got to know those are both emotions that get the creative juices flowing."

"And you've kept it all this time?"

"Yes, it means a lot to me. I don't know if this makes it better or worse for you, but I also keep it because it reminds me of home. That was my parents' backyard. Hell, it was the view from my childhood bedroom."

"Then I'm only part of the reason you didn't sell it?"

He nodded and watched her as she considered the matter. In spite of his nerves about her reaction to the painting, he couldn't help but smile at the little furrow in her brow as she thought.

She took a deep breath as she came to a conclusion. "Actually, that does make it better. Now that Ellen's given me some idea of what your work is worth, I'd hate for you to have lost out on all that cash just because of me."

"Ever the practical Yankee. So...we're good?"

She took a deep breath. "We're good. I don't want to turn around, so tell me. Are Ellen and Lydia gawking at us like they're at the theater and we're the star performers?"

He chuckled. "Nope. They're showing admirable restraint and both are standing with their backs to us. Shall we join them? I'd really love the chance to prove I'm not some kind of sociopathic stalker and show you all my non-Kelly related work."

****

"I can't believe you invited him to dinner," Kelly griped in the sunny kitchen of Grace's seaside home. She picked a piece of cheese off a platter and nibbled it in a distracted way.

"And I can't believe you didn't know I would." Grace laughed as she stood at the kitchen island and sliced vegetables for a fresh salad. "I mean, you have met me before, right? My daughter calls to tell me that y'all are at a hunky artist's loft and for me to pick her up there, you've got to know I'm going to ask him to join us for dinner."

Kelly narrowed her eyes at Grace in displeasure and then went back to staring out the window over the kitchen sink, to the patio where James sat with Grace's husband, Bill.

Bill fussed with the barbecue, and Lydia sat nearby on the grass lawn and sketched in a large pad. James reclined on a lounge chair. His long, denim-clad legs were stretched out on the chaise and drew Kelly's appreciative eyes to the way the soft, worn fabric stretched over his body in the most interesting places. He was so comfortable in his own skin, in a way her shy, nerdy adolescence kept her from understanding. All her adult success had never completely erased that youthful insecurity from Kelly's subconscious. It was what made it hard for her to believe that James Flynn was here with her now, and if she wasn't mistaken, he was very interested in getting to know her in the biblical sense. It was all too surreal. She was jolted out of her reflections by Grace's voice.

"And I've got to say, Kel, the man's a keeper. He was so kind and patient with all of Lydia's questions about drawing. And to arrange for her whole art class to go to a special preview of his exhibit was unbelievable!" She shook her head as she tossed the salad.

Kelly rolled her eyes. "Since the exhibit benefits a charity that supports youth art programs, it would seem pretty strange if he didn't invite a kids' drawing class to go."

Grace stopped tossing the salad and tossed her hair instead. With her hands on her hips she said, "Kelly Morrison Lynch, I'm running out of patience with you."

"You've been patient so far?" Kelly interrupted her friend's exasperated tirade with a chuckle.

"For me—yes—I've been patient, but now you're just looking for things to criticize about the man. And from where I stand, I don't see much to pick on about James. He's smart, funny, good-looking, successful, kind to children…" Grace ticked off his attributes on her fingers.

"In that case, I'll expect the announcement of his sainthood any day now."

"I'm not saying he's Mother freakin' Theresa; I'm just suggesting you give him a chance."

Kelly's attention wandered back to the window. "I wonder what Bill and he are talking about. It looks serious."

Grace moved around the island to stand at her side and cocked her head as she observed the men. "Boys and barbecue," she said by way of explanation. "My guess is they're debating the merits of gas grills versus charcoal."

****

James watched as Bill turned from the grill, picked up his beer from the round patio table and cleared his throat. His brows were drawn together and he frowned; he looked like a man with something serious on his mind. James was puzzled, as he thought they'd been getting along really well.

"You seem like a good guy, James."

James looked at him quizzically. "Thanks, man.

Why do I sense a 'but' coming?"

"Very astute—but…" Bill took a deep breath before he continued. "You seem to be getting close to Kelly. And with her father on the other side of the country, something has to be said, and I guess it's up to me to say it."

James took a sip of his beer to hide his half-smile as he realized what Bill was leading up to saying. He was well versed in the guy code, so he had a pretty good idea of what was coming. "Okay. Let me have it."

"Hurt Kelly, and I'll kick your ass all the way back to New Hampshire."

Yep. Just what James had expected Bill to say. He respected the man for standing up for Kelly. He knew how much her friends meant to her and wanted to be clear with Bill about how he felt about her.

His expression was serious as he held Bill's gaze and said steadily. "If I hurt Kelly, I'll hire someone to help you kick my ass."

Bill nodded curtly and turned back to the grill, a satisfied smile on his face.

"Just as long as we're clear."

****

Zane and Michael perched on the roof of Bill and Grace's sprawling ranch style house. They basked in the rays of the setting sun as it glinted off the Pacific. Their snowy white wings glowed softly in the light.

"You've got good friends, Mike. You were a lucky man during your life," Zane observed as Bill threatened James with a good old-fashioned ass kicking.

A wide grin split Michael's face. "Bill's good people. I knew I could count on him. Before I died, I made him promise to watch out for Kelly after I was gone, and damned if he isn't doing it." He paused and said wistfully, "I never dreamed that two years later I'd still be here looking out for her myself."

Zane radiated quiet confidence. "You'll be on your way to the next plane soon. Things are going good between these two."

The two angels looked down on the patio where Grace and Kelly had joined the two men, bringing with them a cheese platter and a bottle of wine.

"From your lips to you-know-who's ears," Michael said like a prayer.

"Uriel as good as told me there's good stuff waiting for you when you move on."

Michael nodded. "My folks will be there. It'll be good to see them again." He beamed down at the jovial quartet below. "And someday they'll all join us—and maybe Kelly's kids. Man, I hope Kelly and James have kids. She'd be the best mom."

Zane shook his head thoughtfully. "You're worth ten of me, Mike. I don't know if I could be so giving if I was in your place."

Michael waved his hands in dismissal. "Aw, sure you would. The dying puts things into perspective— you know it as well as I do. It makes your soul bigger or something."

A corner of Zane's mouth turned up. "And maybe there's some kind of angelic 'Afterlife Delight' waiting for you on the other side. Uriel hinted there might be. Then you won't have to be alone."

Michael looked hopeful. "You know I love Kelly, but I can't say I'd mind that. It would be nice to share things with someone besides a cranky, dead cowboy, but in the meantime, we've got to get Kelly settled in this world first."

Zane chuckled. "I trust Grace to keep things under control here. She's on our side. What do you say we head out and see if Mildred's back in town. Maybe we can get her to spill what she's up to with James' ex-wife."

Chapter 7

Grace had shooed Kelly out of the kitchen while Bill and she did the dishes, and Lydia had ambushed James again for drawing tips, so the two of them sat at the dining room table and poured over the girl's sketchpad.

Kelly found herself outside alone. She enjoyed the peace of the night and the sound of the surf as it hit the shore below her, where she stood on a bluff at the edge of her friends' property and looked out at the Pacific bathed in the moonlight.

She still had reservations about the wisdom of starting a relationship with James, but she loved how good he was with Lydia. There was something about a strong man who could be so gentle and patient with a child that turned her to mush.

Muscular arms wrapped around her from behind, and even before he spoke she knew it was James from the woodsy scent of his soap, and the aroma of oil paint and turpentine that always seemed to cling to his hands.

He reminded her of the night they met as he rested his chin on top of her head. "Different decade. Different ocean. Same girl."

"Always gazing out to sea, that's me. My grandfather used to call me his little dreamer."

"Nothing wrong with dreams, as long as you don't let life pass you by while you're dreaming them."

She tensed in his arms. "You've been talking to Grace about me needing to get on with my life."

"Nope. It was just a general observation."

She relaxed against him.

"Although, she is a smart woman. I like her a lot. You've got terrific friends."

"They're the best. I don't know what I would've done without them these past couple of years. You'll meet Janie and her husband Saturday night, she's different than Grace, more of an earth mother sort—she's a sweetheart."

They stood in silence for a few moments and looked at the water. Finally, James spoke. "I could stay here like this with you all night, but Grace sent me to tell you coffee's on, so I guess we should head back in."

Kelly turned her head to smile up at him and confessed bashfully. "I'd rather stay here with you, too, but Grace is a force of nature, so if she says it's time for coffee, then we'd better go inside and drink coffee."

He released her from his embrace, but clasped her hand in his as they strolled back to the house across the moonlit lawn.

"Speaking of meeting friends, tomorrow it's your turn to be in the hot seat, if you're free. I thought we could have lunch with my buddy Steve and his wife Daphne. They live out on Coronado, and I thought we could meet them at a restaurant there for our lunch date tomorrow."

Kelly loved Coronado, and wouldn't mind a trip to the island on the other side of the bay, but the notion of meeting his friends had her heart pounding. She gulped. "Well. Turnabout is fair play…I guess."

****

"Of all the places in this city she could be, Mildred had to be in a karaoke bar." Zane's words came out in a growl.

"She's evil, all right. No question about it." Michael winced as the fallen angel stretched for a high note as she belted out "My Heart Will Go On."

She finally came to the end of the song and waved at them. "That song was for two special guys in the audience tonight—a cowboy and a teacher—if they play their cards right, later on I'll dedicate 'Save a Horse, Ride a Cowboy' and 'Don't Stand So Close To Me' to them."

""Lucky us." Michael snorted as Mildred snaked her way through the crowded bar, to their small round table in the back of the room. The usually cool and collected Zane looked a little green around the gills at the notion of smelly Mildred riding him.

"Hiya, fellas!" She greeted them cheerfully as she flopped in a chair and signaled the waitress. "Boilermaker, hon. Anything for you boys?"

Zane tapped his beer bottle and shook his head at the cocktail waitress, "No thanks. We're all set."

"How was New York, Millie?" Michael asked. "I tried to talk to you there, but you just vanished. Don't worry, I didn't take it personally, and besides, it gave me the opportunity to follow the blonde instead of you."

The waitress came back with Mildred's order and a small bowl of pretzels. Michael waited until she left before he went on. "James' ex-wife? Really, Millie? Is that the best you can do?"

Mildred's smile was sly before she slammed back

the shot and chased it with a noisy slurp of beer. "I don't know, Mikey. She's very glamorous. Way more so than your mousey little widow."

Michael gave a quick laugh. "If you think any man would touch her when he could have Kelly, you're nuts."

Zane took a long draw on his beer before he agreed. "Certifiable, even."

Mildred waved her hand in a dismissive gesture, before she said through a mouthful of pretzels. "Oh, I don't think he'll go for her sexually, but you never know. I doubt your precious Kelly has put out yet, he might be all churned up and ready for a quickie with the ex."

"Doubtful," Zane said with quiet menace. "Why don't you cut the crap and tell us what you're really up to with Tracy."

"Nice language for a freakin' angel," she said with mock disapproval and popped another handful of pretzels in her mouth, following them up with a swig of beer.

"I wasn't a nice man when I was alive. My foul mouth is the least of the sins I need to atone for, Mildred. You'd do well to remember that about me."

He leaned back in his chair, his long legs stretched out. The sleeves of his T-shirt pulled tight across his muscular biceps. He looked at the fallen angel with icy eyes.

She shivered slightly in the face of his frozen glare, in spite of her obvious attempt at bravado.

Mildred batted her beady eyes. "I want my plans to be a surprise for you two, and for Uriel, of course. You wouldn't want to spoil my fun, would you?"

Zane continued his hard stare while a drunken group of women on a girls' night out took the karaoke stage and began a giggly rendition of "Love Shack". Mildred squirmed in her seat under his threatening gaze and then downed the rest of her beer in one swallow.

"Look at the time. James and Kelly are probably going to be home soon. A fallen angel's work is never done." With that, she vanished.

"Shit. What's that bitch doing now?" Zane asked with irritation.

"She does have a point about your language, man," Michael observed.

Zane signaled the waitress for their check. "Oh yeah? You do realize in her hurry to get to Kelly and cause trouble, she just stiffed us for her drink? Try and tell me you don't think she's a bitch."

Michael's eyes widened, and he sputtered. "That b…"

Zane looked at him expectantly, with rare humor shining in his blue eyes. When Michael realized he was about to curse also, he rapidly amended. "…harridan."

A slow smile spread across Zane's face. "That's what she is, all right. A low down, rotten…harridan." He looked at the bill and pulled out his wallet to pay. "And we better get to Kelly and James before she does."

****

Mildred cackled to herself with unholy glee, both unseen and unheard in the backseat of Kelly's ridiculous vehicle. She'd really tricked those two do-gooder angels. First, she'd stuck them with the bar tab, and then she'd misdirected them. She had no doubt they'd be waiting for Kelly and James outside of their condominiums, on the sidewalk where the couple usually said good night. Yet here she sat with her prey as they tooled down the road in this ridiculously cutesy vehicle. It was like a little, round, yellow ball of sunshine. Bah! It even came equipped with a bud vase, and—of course—Kelly kept gerbera daisies in it. All that was evil in Mildred churned at the idea of riding in the cheerful-mobile.

They were almost back to town now, where Kelly would park this kiddy car in the garage for her building. If Mildred could get them up to Kelly's place without going outside, where she suspected Zane and Michael would be waiting, her plan would be well on the way to success.

She knew Kelly had been very deliberate in her attempts to keep James out of her condo. She also knew there was a picture of Kelly and Michael prominently displayed there. If she could use her powers to will Kelly to invite James up, he'd surely see it and know Michael was the man whom he'd talked to in the bar. Being an honest, upfront man, Mildred shuddered in distaste at the notion, he'd tell Kelly, and she'd think he was crazy. Or better yet, from Mildred's point of view, she'd think he was trying to trick her and hurt her. Either option would work for Mildred's nefarious purposes. It would drive a wedge between these two, and de-rail the train to happily-ever-after they were currently riding.

The couple in the front seat talked and laughed together as they pulled into the garage. "Do you remember that old junker I had when I got out of college?"

"Of course I do, that's what you drove the time we

went out."

"I can't believe you remember."

Kelly grinned as she pulled into her designated parking space. "Don't be too flattered. I mainly remember because the passenger seat didn't lock into place, and you couldn't turn the heater off."

He laughed. "That's right. I'd forgotten about that."

"I haven't. I remember I was trying to look so cool on our date, but the floor was roasting from the heat, and I couldn't put my feet down, which wouldn't have been so bad if the seat wasn't rolling back and forth on its tracks. I had to sit there, all dressed up with my feet elevated, and the seat sliding like it was some kind of amusement park ride."

He grinned at the memory. "I'm sorry."

"No you're not."

"No. I'm not. It was a great little car—I loved it, but I am sorry you got the hotfoot."

Kelly laughed as she unbuckled her seat belt and turned to face James. Mildred concentrated her efforts on bending Kelly's will.

It seemed to have worked as Kelly said in a vaguely startled way, as if she didn't know where the words were coming from. "Would you like to come up for a night cap?"

James couldn't have been more surprised if she'd started to do a striptease for him. He didn't know what had brought on this unexpected offer. She'd been really anxious to get rid of him outside her building the past couple of nights.

But James wasn't one to look a gift horse in the mouth. "Sure." He replied with alacrity, before she could change her mind and retract her offer.

****

At the front entrance to Kelly's building, Zane and Michael both paced restlessly. Michael stopped to peer down the darkened street, "No sign of Mildred," he said with relief. "But no sign of Kelly and James, either."

Zane frowned. "What is that smelly bitch up to?"

Michael ran his hands through his hair. "Uriel said she'd been planning an accident for Kelly last night. He was able to avert it, but what if she's planned some kind of car wreck for them tonight?"

Zane made himself invisible to humans and unfurled his wings. "Damn it all, you could be right. I should've thought of that—it's just Mildred's miserable style. Let's follow the road back to Grace's house and see if we can find them."

As the two male angels flew away, Mildred emerged from the shadows where she'd been hidden. She had stayed upwind of them, so they wouldn't smell her distinctive sulfur odor.

She chuckled. "It's like shooting fish in a barrel. I swear they're making it too easy for me. Their little field trip should buy me some time for James to get to Kelly's place and see the photograph of Michael."

****

Kelly fiddled nervously with her keys as she opened the door to her condo. She really didn't want to bring James here. She'd intended to tell him that she'd had a lovely day and say goodnight, but instead she'd blurted out an invitation to come up to her place. Where in the Sam Hill had that come from? She didn't think it was a good idea to bring James into her home yet. She wasn't sure she was ready to move things to the next level, and James could curl her toes with just a look from those bright green eyes, and make her blood boil with his kiss.

She tossed her keys in the bowl on the table next to the front door, and looked at the picture of Michael and her with a mixture of guilt and sorrow on her face. Kelly kept her back to James and went to the open kitchen.

"What can I get you?" When he didn't respond, she turned around to face the living room over the granite-topped island. "James, what do you want to drink?"

Her eyes widened. James stood in her living room with the framed photo of Michael and her in his hands. He studied it with a concentration so deep he didn't hear either of her questions.

He tore his eyes away from it and looked at Kelly. There was urgency in his tone when he asked. "Who is this man in the picture with you?"

Kelly didn't know why the picture would upset him so much. He knew she'd been married. It's not like she kept it a secret—heck, she still wore her wedding rings. Was James jealous?

She was torn between relief and disappointment at the thought. Relief, because it would give her an out from this budding relationship, and let her return to her normal life. She could never be with someone who'd be jealous of her late husband, someone who'd expect her not to have photos from the ten years she'd been married to Michael. It was a part of her. It was part of what made her...well...her. She'd never hide it, not for anyone. Not even for James.

But there was disappointment, too. Her normal life might have been comfortable, but it was lonely, and she'd been starting to loosen up and enjoy her time with James, and to hope that he'd be around for a while. She really thought he was a better man than his behavior at the moment seemed to indicate.

She frowned at him, and her tumult of emotions caused her reply to be acerbic. "It's Michael. You know—my husband? I'm sorry the fact I keep pictures of him is a source of disapproval for you. Or maybe you thought it was another man, and I'd been pulling your leg with the whole widow thing."

She was on a roll now and laughed without humor as she continued her rant. "Oh right—and I got all my friends, even a little girl like Lydia, to pretend I have a dead husband just to punk you, because that's just the kind of woman I am."

He shook his head in confusion. "Hold on a minute, Kel, I never thought any of that stuff—where's all this coming from?"

At his reasonable tone, she deflated a little, and realized her response had been over the top. "Okay, that was probably a little extreme."

His smile was gentle, but he teased a bit. "Ya think?"

She rolled her eyes. "It's just—who did you think was in the picture with me? One of my stable of men?"

"No, I didn't think it was one of your many stallions." He looked back at the picture with interest and asked, "Did Michael have a twin brother?"

Kelly scrunched her forehead at the randomness of the question. "No. He was an only child. Why do you ask?"

He looked up slowly, his brow furrowed, and frowning, "Because I had drinks with this guy last week. He's the one who encouraged me to get back in touch with you."

Chapter 8

"Son of a…" Zane growled as he kicked the wall of the garage in front of Kelly's parked car.

"Harridan?" Michael suggested with false helpfulness.

"Bitch," Zane corrected.

"What's got your panties in such a twist, buddy? Sure, we wasted some time looking for them, but from the glass-half-full side of things, at least they got home safely."

"But Mildred tricked us. From the more realistic glass-half-empty scenario, I've got to ask myself—why?"

"Why does the pessimistic view have to be the more realistic one?" Michael snapped.

Zane sensed his friend's annoyance and knocked his temper back a few notches. Michael was good, and he hated to disillusion him, but a fact was a fact. "Because we're dealing with a fallen angel here, Mike. One of the bad guys. She didn't just send us on a wild goose chase for shits and giggles—she's been up to something while we've been out of her way—I'd stake my wings on it."

Michael nodded once in acknowledgment. "Valid point. We should check on them to make sure everything is all right—why don't we head out to the street? Maybe they're in front of the building saying their good-byes like they did last night after their date."

Zane nodded tersely and flashed out to the sidewalk opposite their two apartment buildings. Michael joined him a moment later and looked around.

"I don't see them, do you?"

"Nope," Zane gestured up with a jerk of his head. "But there are lights on in Kelly's place."

"Good. Good. So we know Kelly got home safe and sound." Michael nodded as if to reassure himself.

Zane felt guilty that his words had worried his friend about Mildred's evil doings, but he couldn't allow himself to protect Michael's sensibilities at the expense of their mission.

Zane watched as Michael's eyes drifted over to the top floor of James' building and realized what he'd already noticed. The loft was in total darkness, which probably meant James was in Kelly's condo. And Mildred was still on the loose and out to make trouble.

"It doesn't look like James is home yet," Michael observed, "Maybe he's on his way up now."

A slight movement on Kelly's balcony caught Zane's sharp eyes. Mildred. The fallen angel was up there, watching whatever was going on in Kelly's apartment. Silently, he pointed her out to the angel at his side.

"Son of a…" Michael hissed the words.

"Harridan?" Zane suggested with the hint of a smile.

"Bitch," Michael amended in a harsh rasp. "What's she doing up there?"

Zane spread his snowy white wings and gave them a flutter. "Only one way to find out."

****

Kelly's face lost all its color, and she sank into the over-stuffed armchair behind her. She stared up at James and blinked once.

Twice.

Three times.

"You're saying my late husband's ghost joined you for cocktails?"

James shook his head and lowered himself onto the sofa opposite Kelly. He still clutched the framed photograph, and he studied it once more before he answered in a puzzled voice. "No, he was as solid as you or me. He wasn't a ghost."

Kelly's eyes flashed in her pale face; her voice shook. "Now you're trying to tell me Michael's still alive? To make me think he faked his death to get away from me? What kind of sick, cruel game are you playing, James?"

He sprang to his feet and placed the photo back where it belonged. He sat on the ottoman in front of Kelly's chair and took her hands in his. They felt like ice, so he chafed them between his hands. "No games, Kelly. I would never, ever hurt you that way."

Her eyes softened a little at the obvious heartfelt sincerity of his words. "So, if you're telling the truth…"

"And I am," James interrupted with a squeeze of her hands.

She looked at him searchingly. "Okay—let's say you're telling the truth—then you met a man who looked like my late husband last week, and he convinced you to contact me."

James nodded, but didn't say anything more.

"What else can you tell me about him?" she prompted.

James took a deep breath as he tried to remember every detail of his encounter with Mystery Michael. "He was drinking whiskey. What did Michael drink?"

She hesitated and then answered in a small voice. "Jameson."

"Irish whiskey! There's no way I could've known that, Kel," he said in an attempt to convince her that he wasn't playing a cruel joke on her.

"Unless Bill told you tonight," she responded through tight lips.

James huffed in frustration. "He didn't." He raked his hands through his hair, which was already tousled from their drive home with the top down on her car. "What else? What else did I notice about him?" He asked out loud as he racked his brain for more details. "He had a wicked Boston accent," he finally said.

"You know Michael's from Boston."

He pounced on her words and waved a finger in the air to emphasize his point. "No. No, I didn't. I knew you met at college in Boston, but I had no idea where he was from originally. People from all over the place go to school in Boston."

Kelly inclined her head. "All right. That's true. This guy didn't tell you his name?"

"No, but I didn't tell him mine either. We were just shooting the breeze."

She raised an eyebrow. "About me?"

He flushed. "Yes. No. I don't know. My date was pissed at me, and she slapped my face and left. We started talking after that, and he said I was dating the wrong women."

Two points of color on her pale cheeks showed her irritation at his words. "My, my, my. What a colorful dating life you have. Going out with me must seem positively boring to you."

He rolled his eyes, as he felt his own irritation rise. Her lack of trust in him stung. Sure, his story was wild, but he'd never lie to her and was hurt she thought he would.

"Yeah. Having a shallow bitch slap me in public because I wouldn't buy her 'the most darling diamond earrings' was so much fun."

Kelly's jaw dropped. "She expected you to buy her diamonds? You guys must have been serious."

"Nope, it was just our second date."

"Wow. That's shocking."

He pointed to her in triumph. "And that's why I'd rather be with you! Because you think it's shocking to expect a man you're dating to exchange material goods for your physical favors. Especially one you've only been out with twice."

****

His eyes glittered like emeralds as he looked at her. "And believe me, Kel, you've got a much better shot at getting diamonds from me. Hell, if it would get you to trust me again, I'd shower you with the damned things."

A brief, uncomfortable silence followed his heated declaration. Kelly pursed her lips as she thought over his words and the depth of the feeling that was clearly behind them.

"I want to be able to trust you, and I don't need precious gems as bribery. It's all just so unbelievable. Don't you remember anything else about him?"

James' reply was sheepish. "I feel funny admitting I noticed this about another guy, but he smelled really good. Not overpowering cologne, but clean, kind of like the beach. I noticed because I always smell like turpentine. Occupational hazard."

Kelly patted his hand. "I like the way you smell, but Michael did always smell nice." She sat back in the chair as she thought and then jumped to her feet. "Wait right here!"

She ran to the master bathroom and opened the medicine chest. She took out a blue bottle of men's cologne and clutched it to her chest for a second before she hurried back to James.

"I've never thrown this away." She didn't want to admit to James that in the days after Michael's death, when she was lost in her grief and loneliness, she would sniff it to remind herself of him.

She uncapped the bottle and shoved it under his nose. "Did he smell like this?"

His eyes grew wide as he inhaled the aroma and nodded enthusiastically. "Yeah! That's it."

She took a brief whiff and closed her eyes as she inhaled her late husband's scent, and was startled when she opened them and saw the jealousy clear in James' expression.

"Ghosts can't wear cologne. Maybe someone's playing a prank on both of us," he said tersely.

"Who would do that? No one out here had any idea we even knew each other."

"Right." He exhaled in defeat and then snapped his fingers as he remembered something else. "I saw him again. The night you and I met in Seaport Village. He was with that cowboy you've been seeing around the neighborhood. I tried to point him out to you, but by the time you turned around he'd just vanished."

"People solid enough to wear cologne don't just vanish." She leaned her head against the back of her chair and closed her eyes.

She opened them slowly. "Unless…"

"Unless?" he prompted with curiosity.

She waved her hand and slumped back. "Forget it. It's too crazy."

"At this point, I don't think we can rule anything out as too crazy. I mean, our options are a ghost, or an evil mastermind out to punk us."

She laughed shortly. "Good point."

"What's your 'too crazy' idea?"

She leaned forward in excitement. "My friend Janie is really into New Age stuff. Especially…angels."

He propped his elbow on the arm of the sofa and leaned his forehead on his hand as he asked in amazement. "You think Michael and the cowboy are angels?"

"It's just a theory, and I told you it was nuts." She knew she sounded defensive, but was afraid her idea would scare James off and that wasn't her goal—she just wanted to get to the bottom of the mystery.

His next words made her heave an internal sigh of relief. "Hey, given our other possibilities, let's think about it. What has Janie told you that made you think they might be angels?"

"She believes we all have guardian angels to look after us. She says that the little voice in your head—the one that tells you not to go to the bank one day and later on you find out it was held up when you would've been there—is really your guardian angel steering you away from harm."

He looked skeptical. "But little voices can't drink

whiskey. Or wear cologne."

"Janie's read some stuff that suggests angels can become corporeal if necessary."

"And hang around in bars drinking whiskey? You'd think the guy upstairs would frown on that," he teased.

Kelly screwed up her mouth and rolled her eyes. "Fine. It was just an idea."

"And it's just as plausible as anything else we've come up with." James got up and sat on the arm of her chair. He put his arm around her, and she leaned against him, grateful for the comfort of the contact with his warm torso.

"I'll talk to Janie about it at your exhibit on Saturday—pick her brain about angels."

"Good thinking." He gave her shoulders a little squeeze. "It occurs to me if they are our guardian angels, then Michael is putting his stamp of approval on us dating."

She twisted her head to look up at him. "Do you think?"

"What else could it mean?" he asked as he leaned down to kiss her silky hair.

****

Mildred watched from the balcony, so angry she was amazed steam wasn't shooting from her ears. How did her plan go so awry? They'd been fighting. Mistrusting each other. And it had been music to her ears. Now, suddenly, they were canoodling and blathering about angels and having Michael's blessing to boink.

She heard the quiet rustle of wings as Michael and Zane landed on the balcony behind her. She turned to glare at them, and couldn't suppress the sting of jealousy she felt at the sight of their blindingly white wings. She flapped her own dingy, gray ones in irritation.

Zane tucked his wings away, and stepped up to the glass. He heaved a sigh of relief at seeing an unharmed Kelly and James snuggled together on a chair.

"Looks like whatever your plan was, it went down the drain," he observed with a wry grin.

Michael came up behind him and pumped his fist as he looked in the window. "Love trumps evil every time."

Mildred shrugged with feigned nonchalance. She didn't want these two do-gooders to see how disappointed she was. "We'll see. This round went to your side, but I've got a lot more dirty tricks up my sleeve."

The darkness closed in around her and she was gone, leaving behind the ominous scent of sulfur.

"She's really starting to get on my nerves," Zane stated.

"You and me both," Michael agreed in a heartfelt manner. "But she sure didn't get what she was after tonight."

Zane looked back at James and Kelly, who radiated happiness as they smiled at each other. "Nope. She sure didn't." His voice was satisfied, and he held out his knuckles to Michael, who bumped them with his own. "Looks like these two are getting along fine without us. What do you say we get out of here and give them some privacy?"

****

James faced Kelly at her front door, and couldn't

resist running his hands oh-so-slowly up and down the satiny skin of the arms her sleeveless top left exposed. She murmured a soft sound of contentment, and she sounded like a kitten happy to be petted. Okay. Bad mental image, he realized as his body reacted to the picture of her naked while he stroked every inch of her lush body.

He leaned down to rest his cheek against her shiny, brown hair. "Are you sure you'll be all right on your own? I could stay."

In their current position he couldn't see her face, but he heard the smile in her voice. "No thanks, Speed Racer. I'm not ready for a sleep-over with you."

He grinned. "Are you saying I'm moving too fast? You wound me; I just meant I'd crash on your couch."

She shook her head under his cheek, and the sensation of her hair running across his skin almost made his resolution to move at her pace break down completely. He reminded himself that in spite of the argument the lower half of his body was strongly putting forth, he was not some teenager who couldn't control his hormones. What he could build with this woman was worth the wait—and yet another cold shower when he got home.

"I actually have a guest room you could use, but kind as your offer is, it's not necessary. I'll be fine on my own."

"We still don't know what's going on, though." His lower body made a last ditch effort with that point.

She leaned back a little and looked up at him. Her hazel eyes were a little unfocused, as if maybe her body parts were in disagreement with her head, too. She gave him a slight shake of her head. "No, we don't, but if

Michael is involved in whatever is happening, then I'll be safe here by myself. He'd never hurt me."

His nether regions ran up the white flag, and he resigned himself to another lonely night in his bed. "You're right. I guess I'll head home then."

"We're still on for lunch tomorrow, right? I'm looking forward to meeting your friends."

He lowered his head and pressed his lips gently to hers. "You better believe we're still on for lunch. Why wouldn't we be?"

"We've moved into seriously freaky territory here. I thought maybe it was too much for you. I wouldn't blame you if it was."

He moved his hands up her arms to her shoulders and rested them there. "Nothing is too much for me where you're concerned. You better get used to me, because I'm not going anywhere." He paused and added with a deep sigh, "Except home. Right now. Before we do something we'll regret."

She grinned ruefully. "Thanks for being so understanding. I'll see you tomorrow."

****

Kelly leaned against the shut door for a moment after she'd locked it behind James. She held her hand up to her chest as if she could somehow control her pounding heart that way.

Gracious. The man was sex on two legs. A simple kiss from him had her body turning to liquid heat, and her mind getting ready to throw in the towel on the whole waiting-before-we-sleep-together thing. Because she was fairly certain at this point it was a matter of when they slept together and not if they would.

She looked down at the diamond rings on the hand

she still held to her breast. She stretched her arm out and twisted her hand to watch the light glint off the stones and whispered, "Was it really you, Michael?"

Her legs carried her into her room to prepare for bed, but her mind raced a mile a minute while she did so.

The telephone rang, but Kelly decided to let the machine answer. She didn't want to talk to anyone yet—not about their far-out supposition about Michael and some hot cowboy being guardian angels, out to hook up James and her. And she certainly wasn't ready to talk about the feelings James stirred up inside her.

Not just lust. She could handle lust, and explain it away as the result of the celibate state of her life the last two years, but she had deeper feelings for him. Emotions she wasn't ready to admit even to herself, let alone to one of her well-intentioned friends.

Grace's pleased voice came out of the answering machine. "You're still not home? Dare I hope you're off having wild monkey sex with James? Anyway, I just wanted to let you know how much Bill and I liked him. See you Saturday night."

Kelly had put on her pj's while Grace left the message. She twisted her hair on top of her head as she padded into the bathroom to wash up.

She spoke to her reflection in the mirror as she picked up her toothbrush. "Wild monkey sex, indeed. Where does the woman get this stuff?"

Kelly paused in the middle of putting toothpaste on her brush, her eyes dreamy as she thought about what Grace suggested. Gah! Why did Grace have to put that mental image out there for her to contemplate?

Now that she was contemplating, it was all she

could think about. She pictured James and her in his loft. Could practically feel his big, calloused hands as they ran over her body—in her fantasy, they were both naked. She cocked her head as she pondered the possibilities, and maybe body paints were involved. Yeah, that's good; she would lie on a canvas in his studio as James' expert hands painted her nude body.

Kelly snorted, shook her head, and began to energetically brush her teeth as if she could scrub the image out of her head.

Body paint. She'd been spending way too much time with Grace.

After taking out her contacts and washing off her make-up, Kelly crawled into bed. She propped the pillows up behind her and reached for the romance novel on her nightstand, but then held it in her hands unopened.

What if Michael did want her to move on with James? All of her friends certainly thought she should. Heck, she had to admit if the tables were turned and Grace or Janie were in her position, she'd think it was time for them to stop grieving and move on.

Was it really outside the realm of possibility that Michael was urging her to explore a relationship with another man? No, she corrected herself. Not with any man. With James. If they were right about the whole angel thing, then Michael had handpicked James Flynn for her.

Her heart pounded as she thought about the kind of man James was. Strong, smart, funny. He was honorable, but not in a self-righteous goody-goody kind of way. He was what Michael used to call "a real stand-up guy". James might be someone that Michael would approve of for her. And he was sexy as all get out.

She took a deep breath and threw back the covers. She walked to her dresser with purpose. When she got there, she looked at her wedding rings and said out loud, "This doesn't mean I don't love you anymore, Michael."

Kelly took off her rings and put them on a crystal ring holder. "But I think maybe you're trying to tell me it's all right to let go."

She got back into bed and turned off the light.

As she burrowed under the comforter, Michael stood invisible in the corner of the room.

He whispered, although he knew she couldn't hear him. "I understand, baby. I'll stick around until I know you're safe from Mildred and settled with James, and then it'll be time for me to move on, too, but I'll always love you. Be happy, Kelly. For me. It's what I want for you."

Chapter 9

Friday morning found Mildred in an Internet café. She read her email, feeling smug. Damn, she was good. All the pieces of her plan were falling into place. The boss would be so happy when she drove apart the two lovebirds and foiled Uriel's plan for their happy ending.

A smile twisted her mouth. She didn't need those two goody-two shoes angels to tell her James wouldn't touch his ex-wife with a ten-foot pole. She found herself momentarily distracted by thoughts of James. Did he actually have a ten-foot pole? Not the most angelic notion, but she was a fallen angel after all. And James Flynn was one fine looking male specimen.

So, yeah, as soon as she met his whiny, drunken, over-Botoxed ex, Mildred knew he wouldn't turn from Kelly back to Tracy. She grinned. But she sure got the cowboy and Michael to chase their tails about it.

She had other plans for Tracy now that she'd talked to the woman—plans that would exploit Tracy's vanity, jealousy, pettiness, and greed. Traits it had only taken one booze-soaked lunch for Mildred to see Tracy had in spades. And when Michael chose to follow Tracy in Manhattan rather than her, it gave her the chance to put her Plan B into action.

Mildred re-read the email from one of the New York based press agencies she'd contacted that day, while Michael was occupied chasing Tracy from upscale boutique to upscale boutique.

The agencies were all very interested in possible dirt on James Flynn. After all, he was young, attractive, and a world-renowned artist. However, he was known to be a recluse so they would be pleased to get an inside line on him.

And Kelly was so shy—she wouldn't even let her publisher put her picture on the back of her books. Mildred had decided two such private people would absolutely hate it if the press turned out in droves for Saturday's exhibit and spotted them together. And the gutter press would like nothing better than to find two such under-exposed public figures involved in a scandal.

So what if they were both such good scouts there was no hint of a scandal around them—with the international press and James' bitter ex-wife in her stable, Mildred didn't deserve to be called a fallen angel if she couldn't invent a drama public enough to break up the couple's fledgling relationship.

James would be left bitter and alone, and Kelly would be eaten up with the guilt of thinking she'd betrayed her husband's memory with a man who didn't deserve it. Zane would be disgraced for his failure on the mission, and Michael wouldn't be able to ascend to the next plane and would have to watch Kelly's misery, while being helpless to do anything about it.

Mildred shivered with pleasure at the thought of so many lives ruined with one simple plan. The boss would surely fast-track her path up the fallen angel ladder.

She noticed the time on her computer and logged off. Tracy's flight was due in soon, and she needed to head over to the airport to get her and let the fun begin.

****

Kelly smoothed her pink and green cotton skirt anxiously as she waited for James to pick her up for their lunch date. She'd buzzed him into the building, and was waiting for him to come upstairs.

She looked down at her hands and thought for about the millionth time how naked her ring finger looked without her wedding rings. She'd worn them around the clock for so many years there was a significant indentation around the base of her ring finger.

In her nervousness, she switched from her skirt, and began to fuss with the fitted T shirt she wore. Was it too tight? She bit her lower lip as she looked in the mirror by the door. It was too tight. She should never have let Grace talk her into buying it.

Kelly started when she heard the sharp rap at her front door. Oh well, too late to change now. Too tight or not, she had to go with it. James was here.

She took a deep breath and wiped her palms on her knee-length skirt one more time before she got a shaky smile in place and opened the door. Her smile faltered as she looked at James.

Holy mother of pearl, the man looked good! With his tanned face, blond hair—in a pink button down shirt and jeans with dock shoes, he managed to combine New England prep and California beach dude. All mixed together with a soupçon of New York artist bad boy.

Kelly licked her lips as she realized he was checking her out, too. From the tips of her shell pink painted toes as they peeped out from her sandals, to the top of her artfully tousled hair. And did he linger just a bit at her breasts in this snug T? Maybe she'd have to thank Grace for talking her into it after all. To know she could put that hungry look into the eyes of a man like this was worth a little self-consciousness.

"You look amazing," he said with deep appreciation.

"Thanks. You, too," she replied and blushed at the inanity of her words.

He smiled and took her hand. He looked at it with wonder and then raised his green eyes to meet her hazel ones. "You took your rings off."

"Yep." She nodded and could've kicked herself. Really, could she find a word of more than one syllable to say to the man? You'd think she was an awkward girl on her first date, rather than an experienced thirty-something widow who made her living with words.

"I know that's a big step for you, sweetie. Are you sure? I hope I didn't pressure you into it somehow."

He caressed the dent on her finger where the rings used to sit.

How was a woman supposed to form a coherent thought when he stroked her finger that way, and looked at her like she was a bacon-cheeseburger and he was a starving man?

She nibbled her bottom lip and saw his eyes follow the movement with interest.

Finding her voice after what felt like twenty years, but had really just been a couple of seconds, she said, "Seeing you again might have spurred me into action, but it was long overdue. You didn't pressure me."

****

Spurs? Why did she have to mention spurs? Now

139

he had to fight against the ride 'em cowgirl fantasy about her that the word put into his head. He cleared his throat. Just because she'd taken her rings off didn't mean she was ready for him to pounce on her like some kind of sex-crazed caveman.

Or did it? He mentally smacked himself. Of course it didn't. Eyes on the prize, Flynn. You're in it for the long haul with this woman. Don't let your manhood, and its rather strident demands, make you lose sight of the goal.

"Did our angel theory have anything to do with your decision?" he thought to ask as the blood began to flow back up into his brain.

"Probably. I mean if it was Michael who wanted you to get in touch with me, then maybe it's time for me to let go." She bent her neck to look him in the eye, as though she was anxious to make something clear to him. "But it doesn't mean I'll forget him. A part of me will always love Michael and what we shared. Anyone I get involved with will have to accept it as part of the package."

"Of course I don't expect you to forget. Hell, you wouldn't be the Kelly I lo—er—admire if you just threw off your rings and yelled 'bring on the next man'!"

****

Love? Had he been about to say "the Kelly I love"? Her heart pounded so hard she was afraid he'd be able to see it through the damned tight shirt. Even if it was what he was going to say, he'd stopped himself before he uttered the "L" word, so she'd just pretend she didn't notice and put it on the back burner to think about some other time.

Right now, she had to get through lunch with his best friends. She hated that shy Kelly reared her ugly head in these situation. She still got tongue-tied when she met new people—especially if they were people she really wanted to like her, and she did really want Steve and Daphne to like her. She wasn't sure if what she felt for James was love, but she did know he was important to her, and she didn't want his friends to think she was a twit. Or worse, they could think she was a snob. She'd noticed a lot of people mistook her shyness for snobbery.

Her face brightened. Maybe the other couple couldn't get a sitter for their son and would have to cancel.

James' next words dashed that flimsy hope. "C'mon, we better get a move on. Steve and Daphne are going to meet us at the restaurant, and with Friday traffic, I'm afraid we'll be late if we don't leave now."

****

Mildred searched the crowd that surged into baggage claim from the New York flight for Tracy.

She'd rented a car and moved it to a regular parking space before she came in, so Tracy wouldn't think she didn't have a car normally. It was important to keep up her human charade when she interacted with people.

But she was more used to flying wherever she needed to go, and it had been a jerky, hair-raising trip through the parking lot in the rental car. Hopefully, Tracy would just think she was a lousy driver. Maybe the souse had even enjoyed a few good belts on the flight and would be too tipsy to notice Mildred's lack of driving skills.

She saw Tracy's shock of platinum blonde hair as the woman waved cheerfully and tottered toward her on yet another pair of impossibly high heels. Today, they were red to match her skintight pencil skirt.

"Millie!" she exclaimed as she air kissed in the direction of Mildred's face. "It was sweet of you to take the afternoon off and pick me up."

"I'm happy to do it." Which was not a lie, for a change. Mildred didn't want to ruin Tracy's surprise appearance in front of the press at the exhibit tomorrow, and if James happened to see her beforehand, it would be a blow to Mildred's machinations. She intended to stick to this broad like glue until then. "Let me help you with your bags."

Tracy gestured to the rack of luggage carts, as she began to hoist what appeared to be a full set of Louis Vuitton luggage off the conveyer belt. "We're going to need one of those."

"You're not kidding," Mildred sputtered as she got a cart. "How much stuff did you bring? You're only in town for a few days."

Tracy stopped and let Mildred take over the transfer of the luggage to the cart. Her reply was petulant. "I want to make a splash while I'm here, don't I? Besides, if things work out with James, I might want to stay here a little longer."

As Mildred shoved the luggage cart to her car—had the woman packed bricks?—Tracy tripped along next to her.

"Where am I staying? Thanks again for taking care of getting a hotel for me."

Mildred popped the trunk of her rental car and hoisted the first heavy bag in, as Tracy surveyed her manicure and made no effort to help. No wonder this woman had turned James off to relationships. She brought the term "high maintenance" to a whole other level.

Her response was a little breathless from her exertion as she continued to toss luggage in the car like a stevedore. "I've been staying at the Hotel del Coronado, so I booked you a suite there, too."

Tracy's red, glossy lips formed a perfect "O" before she said with a head bob of approval, "Ritzy. Thanks, Millie. It will be a nice romantic spot, if all goes according to plan."

Mildred seriously doubted Tracy would need to worry about a romantic rendezvous with James. And more important to her secret plan than ritziness, the hotel was on the other side of the bay from James and Kelly's waterfront neighborhood. It greatly decreased the chances of James seeing Tracy before Mildred wanted him to.

The last bag finally stowed, they got into the car, and Mildred peeled out of the space in reverse, without bothering to look back before she did so. Cars squealed to a stop in both directions to prevent slamming into her car.

Tracy craned her neck to survey their near-miss accident, and said in awe. "Wow. That was a close one. You must have an angel sitting on your shoulder, Millie."

Mildred negotiated around the other cars and ignored their driver's curses and horns honking. "Something like that."

****

The hostess led them to a table next to a wall of

glass, which allowed a fabulous view of the San Diego skyline across the bay, but Kelly felt like she was walking to the gallows for her own execution.

She tried to overcome her shyness with an internal pep talk. These people were James' best friends, after all. They would be nice, and why wouldn't they like her? If Brandi with an "i" was any indication, she was a step up from the kind of girls to whom he usually introduced them.

She saw a tall, dark-haired man stand as they approached. He had a tanned face, with a huge smile that put her immediately at ease. Next to him sat a clean-scrubbed blonde woman, who looked like she'd grown up on a California beach. Her smile was friendly and understanding.

Kelly found herself returning their smiles effortlessly, as the man said in a joking manner, "We were starting to think you were going to stand us up, James. You know I thought you'd made Kelly up to put my wife off her matchmaking, but I guess I was wrong." He winked at Kelly. "Or I was right and you hired a really nice-looking woman to play the part and trick us."

His wife reached up to slap his arm playfully. "Steve! You're awful. Forgive him, Kelly, he knows not what he does." She stood up and held out her hand. "I'm Daphne Harrington, and this is the bane of my social life, my husband Steve. I hope his warped sense of humor doesn't frighten you off, as it has so many potential friends for me before."

"Nice to meet you both," she answered still feeling a bit shy, and felt James' hand rub a soothing circle on her lower back before he pulled out a chair for her.

Steve sat and grinned across the table at her. "Sorry, Kelly. I've known this one,"—he jerked his thumb at James—"for so long, we treat each other like brothers."

Daphne rolled her eyes. "They sure do. Complete with teasing, taunting, and the occasional fisticuffs."

The hostess lingered to take James and Kelly's drink orders. Daphne gestured at a wine bucket. "We ordered a bottle of Pinot Grigio. Want to share?"

"Sounds good," Kelly said.

James ordered a beer and then teased. "Drinking at lunch? What kind of school librarian are you? I'm sure mine never did anything like this."

"One who's on summer vacation, and is enjoying a rare lunch out without you egging your rambunctious godson on to fling food at the other diners," Daphne retorted without missing a beat. "And let me just say, if you were one of her students, you can bet your sweet ass your school librarian was drinking at lunch."

Kelly laughed and turned to James. "You didn't tell me you're their son's godfather."

"Yep," he said with pride, "Charlie's a great kid."

"He's all boy," his mother added, and couldn't disguise her love for her son in spite of her jokes about his behavior. "He's always into some kind of mischief."

James punched Steve's upper arm good-naturedly. "The apple didn't fall far from the tree."

"I wish I could get all outraged and deny it." Steve shrugged. "Nah. I really don't. He's just like me, and I'm proud as hell of the fact."

Kelly felt so at ease with the couple. She couldn't be more pleased as she felt her shyness melt away in the warmth of their personalities. She turned to Daphne and asked. "You're a librarian? If the writing didn't work out for me, I was going to go back to school to get my Masters in Library Science."

"I am. I love getting to work with kids and hopefully pass on my love of books and reading to them. And working in the school system will be great when Charlie's a little older. We'll have the same schedule."

Her blue eyes lit up. "I hope you don't mind, but James told us you're K.M. Lynch. He knows I just love your Tony and Tessa mysteries."

Kelly blushed, pleased but always a little uncomfortable with praise. She felt James sense her discomfort and move his arm from the back of the chair where it had been resting, to stroke the nape of neck.

At her hesitation, Daphne apologized. "I'm sorry. I must seem like some kind of annoying fangirl."

"No you don't!" Kelly was quick to disabuse that notion and then admitted with some degree of reluctance, "I'm just a little shy when I first meet someone, and I never know what to say when people praise my work. Silly, huh?"

Steve looked jovial as he poured a glass of wine to the brim and handed it to Kelly. He jerked his thumb at his wife. "So's this one. Daffy's just had the advantage of slugging back a glass of wine before you got here. It gave her a little liquid courage."

Daphne's sun-kissed complexion flamed red. "Stephen Patrick Harrington, I can't take you anywhere. I'm hoping I can become friends with this woman, and you've made her think I'm some kind of lush now!"

"What'd I do?" Steve asked in genuine surprise. "I

thought I was helping smooth the way."

James closed his eyes and shook his head. "I really should've put off this meeting until our relationship had progressed a little farther, Kel. You know, like maybe our twenty-fifth anniversary. Please, don't let this clown scare you off of Daphne or me."

"Seriously, what did I do?" Steve held out his hands, palms up and looked around the table for an answer.

His wife chuckled and rolled her eyes, before looking at him with true affection. "What you always do, Steve. You broke the ice and got the party started." She lifted her wine glass and turned to smile at James and Kelly, "To old friends and new ones."

Steve sat up a little taller and stuck out his broad chest. "See. You all bust my chops, but I did smooth the way."

James grinned. "Maybe we should send you on a diplomatic mission to the Middle East."

"Oh no," Daphne said. "The world would never survive it."

****

As Daphne took her last sip of coffee, she said with regret. "Well, the time went by so fast. I guess I was having too much fun, but we've got to pick up Charlie from my mom's. She has her book club this afternoon, and I promised her we wouldn't make her late."

Steve suggested, "Why don't you give us a few minutes to get the kid, and then you can head over to our place?" He added as incentive to James, "I know your godson would love to see you."

James looked at Kelly. "I haven't seen Charlie for a couple of weeks. What do you say, Kel? Do you have anywhere else to be?"

"Nope, I don't, and I would love to meet Charlie."

They all walked out of the restaurant together and James said. "Okay, then. We'll take a spin and meet you at your place in a little while."

He opened the car door for Kelly and waved at his friends as he skirted around the hood of his car and hopped into the driver's seat. He smiled at Kelly as he buckled up. "Anything you'd like to do on Coronado to kill some time?"

Her expression was a little sheepish as she admitted, "I know it sounds like a total tourist thing to do, but I always love to see the Hotel del Coronado when I'm here."

He put his sunglasses on and pulled smoothly out of the parking space. "Sounds good to me. Really cool architecture, and Steve and Daffy live closer to that side of the island, so it will head us in the right direction."

"Steve and Daphne are fun, and I'm looking forward to meeting Charlie. You must be the coolest godfather ever."

James blushed at the compliment. "I don't know about my coolness factor—I'm going for buying his affection. I never show up empty-handed. As a matter of fact, I've got a really cool remote control truck for him in the trunk. I've been looking forward to giving it to the little guy."

"A remote control truck? How old is Charlie? I thought he was just a baby."

"He's ten months," James mumbled as if he didn't want Kelly to hear.

She did though, and burst into laughter. "That doesn't sound like a present for someone who probably can't even walk yet. It sounds more like a present for Steve and you, than for Charlie."

He grinned without shame. "Maybe. But he'll appreciate it when he's older. And think of the enjoyment he'll get out of watching Daddy and Uncle James play with it."

She held her hand over her heart with dramatic flair. "Oh, the sacrifices you make for the child's pleasure. Throwing yourself bravely on the remote control truck—so noble."

They approached the Hotel del Coronado. "Do you want me to drive through? We've got time," James offered.

"Sure," she agreed with alacrity. "It always looks like something from a bygone era to me. We can pretend it's the 1920s, and we're a couple of flappers coming down from L.A. for the weekend."

He glanced at her and flashed a warm smile. "It always reminds me of that movie they filmed here. You know, *Some Like it Hot*. Gotta love Jack Lemmon in drag and Marilyn Monroe in…well…anything!"

She laughed and started to reply, but stopped as he slowed the car to a crawl and craned his neck to gape at the hotel entrance. All Kelly saw was a rather nondescript woman as she watched the bellman wrestle with a ridiculous amount of expensive luggage.

"James? Do you know that woman?"

He shook his head and looked at Kelly. "Not her, but I could swear I saw my ex-wife get out of that car and go into the hotel, which is impossible."

"Why? I mean if I can believe that you've had drinks with my late husband, you can certainly accept the idea your very much alive ex-wife is in San Diego."

James turned the car around to drive back out to the road. He glanced quizzically at the hotel entrance one last time as they passed by and said, "Actually, drinks with Michael is more plausible. Tracy hates to leave Manhattan, unless it's to go to Paris for a fashion show. She thinks nowhere else is 'civilized' enough for her sophisticated tastes."

He briefly took his hands off the wheel to make sarcastic air quotes when he said "civilized", and then eased out of the hotel driveway and into traffic.

Kelly rested her arm on the car window as she pondered his words and then suggested, "You said her husband owned some kind of mega-corporation, maybe he's got business in town and she came along."

"Could be. They've never come here before, but I guess there's a first time for everything."

He sincerely hoped if the Blackburns were in town that they wouldn't make any effort to get in touch with him. He was too excited by the prospect of a future with Kelly to revisit his past miseries with Tracy.

James pulled up to a cute bungalow style house and parallel parked in front. He nodded his head toward the car parked in front of them. "That's their car. Good, they got home ahead of us."

Kelly got out and stood on the sidewalk. She watched James with amused affection as he retrieved a huge, gift-wrapped box from the trunk. He seemed as excited as a little boy at Christmas about the completely age-inappropriate gift. Mr. Sophisticated Artist, indeed. She could tell he couldn't wait to get the truck out of the box, and Kelly found it all really endearing. She found she liked this child-like side to him, and was even happier that he felt comfortable enough with her to reveal it.

Steve and Daphne walked around the side of the house. Steve shoved a very grubby looking Charlie into Daphne's arms and rushed toward James and the big box.

"Charlie, look!" He glanced over his shoulder at the baby and called out with excitement, "Uncle James brought you a present, and I bet it's awesome!"

"It's not for Steve and you, huh?" Kelly asked sotto voce.

Daphne laughed. "He tried to get you to fall for that old line, did he? These two are always getting toys for themselves and pretending they're for Charlie."

James beamed as he walked to his godson, whose chubby face was wreathed in smiles at the sight of his godfather. He took the boy in his arms and kissed him soundly on the cheek, to both Charlie and Kelly's delight. This side of James could make a woman fall in love with him. Especially if she was halfway there already, which she had to admit to herself she was. Kelly exhaled sharply at the thought.

James hefted the child in the air and lowered him so their faces were level. "You love your Uncle James, don't you little man? And his super-fabulous gifts."

Charlie babbled happily in response.

James looked up in wonder. His eyes sparkled with delight. "He said Uncle James! Did you hear him?"

James turned to Kelly as he spoke, and Charlie held out his chubby arms to her.

"The boy's got good taste," James said with approval as he handed the baby to Kelly.

"Oh don't!" Daphne called out in horror.

But it was too late. Charlie had already planted one

very dirty little hand on Kelly's pale pink T-shirt during the hand-off from James.

"He's filthy!" his mother exclaimed. "I swear my mother lets him roll in mud while drinking grape juice. At least that's what he always looks like he's been doing when I pick him up from her house. He's ruined your shirt."

Kelly chuckled as she watched James chase Steve to the backyard to play with Charlie's present. She turned to Daphne. "Please don't worry about it. It's just a T-shirt. I love kids, and I understand they frequently come complete with dirt."

Daphne exhaled with relief at her understanding. "Thanks for being so nice about it. Want to come around back? I've put out some iced tea for us to have while the three little boys play." She winked as she led the way to a postage-stamp sized backyard. There was a small café-style table and chairs by the backdoor, set with a pitcher of tea and glasses.

"Coolness!" Steve shouted as he opened "Charlie's" present, "Look, Charlie. A remote control truck! Just what I...er, I mean you...wanted!"

James loped over and took Charlie from Kelly's arms, which revealed a perfect child's handprint on her chest. As she looked down at it, she thought Daphne might be right—it appeared to be composed of mud and grape juice.

"Uh oh." James said as he stared at the stain.

"Uh oh," Charlie parroted with a gleeful smile.

"Daphne was right. I shouldn't have handed him to you. Your shirt's ruined, and I really liked it," James said with regret.

Kelly dusted the spot off with her hand, although it

did nothing to clean it. The little handprint seemed to be there to stay.

"I'll get it out," she said with confidence. "It's just a cotton T, and I've got mad skills in the laundry room."

"I just bet you do. I'm looking forward to exploring them with you some day," James said with a suggestive waggle of his eyebrows. He leaned over Charlie's head to press a quick kiss to Kelly's lips. "Smart, beautiful, and a good sport, too. You're the best."

Steve used the remote control to run the toy truck into James' feet. "Break it up. No time for smoochin', we've got a truck to drive here."

James ran over with the small boy in his arms. "C'mon Charlie. Let's go play with Daddy."

Daphne rolled her eyes as she sat down and poured out two glasses of iced tea. Kelly sat in the second chair and took a sip.

"Where'd you guys go while we were picking up Charlie from his mud and juice bash?"

"We took a spin by the Hotel del Coronado."

"Great place," Daphne said with approval.

"It is, but it was weird. James thought he saw his ex-wife going into the hotel."

Daphne winced and lowered her voice. "Ouch. I sure hope he didn't; I can't stand that woman."

Kelly looked at her with interest. She knew she should ask James any questions she had about his ex, but her curiosity got the better of her and she couldn't stop herself from asking. "You knew her?"

Daphne nodded. "Steve and James went to art school together, and Steve and I have been together since dinosaurs roamed the earth, so I had the misfortune of having to hang out with her when they were married. We all lived in New York back then. We were even at their wedding at City Hall. It was the only time I cried tears of sadness at a wedding instead of tears of joy."

"She's that bad?"

Daphne shrugged. "Maybe not. She is who she is. Tracy doesn't try to pretend she's anything she's not—but they were so wrong for each other. They had nothing in common. James is smart and funny, and in spite of his love of monster remote control trucks, cares more about people than things. Tracy's kind of dumb and really materialistic."

"From what James has told me about her, that was my impression, so what I don't understand is why a woman like that wanted to marry a struggling artist in the first place. I mean the odds were astronomical against James achieving the level of success he has in the art world. If money was her primary concern in a husband she should've picked someone in another line of work."

"Back in the day, I always had the impression she thought James was a rich boy, playing at being an artist."

Kelly looked confused. "The Flynns aren't rich. I mean they're not poor, but I always thought of them as being what my grandmother used to call 'comfortable', but not rich by any means."

"Tracy just saw the house on the ocean in New Hampshire and the sailboat, and thought she'd snagged herself a trust fund baby."

"Mr. Flynn and James built that sailboat in their

yard. It wasn't a yacht or anything."

Daphne looked curious. "You seem to know a lot about James' family."

Kelly blushed. "We're from the same hometown." She held her thumb and forefinger a tiny distance apart. "And I might have had the teensiest crush on James when I was a kid."

Daphne leaned across the table; her eyes alight with interest. "If you're from Rye, you must have known the girl."

"The girl?" Kelly gulped.

"The one who threw him over the summer after college. Steve and I always thought he was on the rebound from her, and that's the reason why he let a barracuda like Tracy trap him. Have you seen the painting over his fireplace? That's her…" Daphne's voice trailed off as she stared at Kelly in recognition. "Oh, crap. You're her. The *Love Awakens* girl."

Kelly's smile was a little wobbly. She hoped this wouldn't negatively impact her new friendship with this woman. Daphne seemed distinctly disapproving of "the girl".

"Guilty as charged."

Daphne slumped back in her seat and waved her hands in the air. "I'm sorry. Forget I said anything."

Steve crashed the truck into the table, which caused both women to jump. He followed the toy over with James and Charlie in tow.

"You guys look intense. What are you talking about?"

Daphne's big, blue eyes got even bigger as she looked at Kelly. Her baby blues implored Kelly not to rat her out.

Kelly forced her lips upward and shook her head with studied casualness. "Nothing much."

Steve flopped on the ground at his wife's feet. "Doesn't look like nothing to me. What's up?"

Daphne huffed in exasperation. "Fine. I just realized Kelly is the *Love Awakens* girl. I was asking if she knew her from Rye, and then I recognized her from the painting. There. You got it out of me. Happy now?"

James laughed. "You'd never make it as a spy, Daffy. You'd crack after the first question under interrogation. Don't sweat it. Kelly knows she's the *Love Awakens* girl."

"She is?" Steve hollered. "Holy crapola! I feel like I'm meeting a movie star or something. How come you didn't tell me who she is?" he asked James with indignation.

In a clear attempt to change the subject, Daphne said to her husband. "Would you please take your son inside and clean him up so he can have his snack?"

"How come he's always my son when he's filthy?" He eyed the grubby youngster and added dubiously, "I can try to clean him up, but I'm not making any promises." He stood and gestured for James to follow him with Charlie, "C'mon men. To the soap!"

Daphne watched until the door shut behind them, and then smiled and said, "Thanks for trying to cover for me. I didn't want James to know we were talking about him and make him self-conscious. I hope I didn't make you feel bad or anything. I honestly didn't realize it was you until my foot was lodged firmly in my mouth. I don't even know all the details of the story with the *Love Awakens* girl. All I know is that after that summer James changed the type of woman he dated. He went from bimbo to bimbo, until Tracy got her claws into him. I remember thinking that the girl in the painting must have done a real number on him to have him running so scared of commitment." She blushed and paused before saying apologetically, "And I just realized how none of that is going to make you any less mad at me—I'm sorry."

"I'm not mad, but I hope it doesn't change the way you think about me. I'd really like us to be friends. Long story short, I did sort of dump him, but it was my own fear that drove me, and when we met again recently, we realized the whole thing was a big misunderstanding. I didn't think I'd hurt him." She gnawed at her bottom lip. "I'm really sorry if my immature actions contributed to his disastrous marriage, though."

Daphne reached over to pat her hand. "Everything happens for a reason, so don't kick yourself about stuff you can't change." Her smile was warm. "I want us to be friends, too. If James got over whatever happened back then, I can, too."

Kelly smiled briefly, but worry still clouded her eyes. Daphne squeezed her hand. "I meant what I said, what's past is past. We can't change it; all we can do is learn from the past and try not to make the same mistakes again."

Kelly looked thoughtful. "I don't know why those two call you 'Daffy', what you just said was really wise."

Daphne chuckled. "It's my childhood nickname. I told you, Steve and I have been together forever. They mean it affectionately."

She paused and took a sip of her iced tea.

"Whatever happened when you were kids, I like seeing James with you now. He acts so natural and at ease around you. You're good for him. He's been selling himself short in the dating department for a long time."

Kelly grinned. "Hot and cold running bimbos according to Betsy Lester."

Daphne laughed. "Good old Betsy. Leave it to her to cut to the chase. In his defense, I think he picked women like that to protect himself. They didn't expect much from him emotionally, so they didn't have the power to hurt him. He's a good man. It's nice to see him with someone like you." She paused and then blurted out, "Please don't hurt him." She slapped her hand over her mouth. "Whoops. Don't know where that came from. Sorry. I didn't mean that I thought you would hurt him, just that he's really putting himself out there with you, and he might end up hurt."

"I don't intend to hurt him. I'm not one hundred percent sure what's going on between us right now—he's the first man I've dated since my husband died, but I do know that I'll do everything in my power not to hurt James again."

"I know. You seem really sweet, and I'm relieved to find out the stuff in the past was a misunderstanding. It's just that he's like a brother to me, and I'm a little protective of him. But it's none of my business. Whatever is going on between you two is just that— between you two. I'll just shut up now."

"James is lucky to have a friend like you to watch his back. And if it puts your mind at ease, I think I'm much more in danger of being hurt by James than the other way around."

Daphne regarded her seriously. "I really don't

think so. I think he means business. He's never brought another woman to our house to meet Charlie before."

Steve burst through the door with a slightly cleaner Charlie in his arms, and spoke in a high voice as he pretended it was his son talking. "Look how spotless I am, Mommy. Can Daddy and I have our snack now?"

Daphne stood up and took her son in her arms. "Aren't you a tidy little man?"

She smiled as she looked at Kelly and James. He stood behind her chair, with his hands on her shoulders. She'd reached up and covered his hands with her own and gazed up at him, her heart clearly in her eyes. James looked back at her with adoration. Kelly might not know what was going on between them, but it was clear as glass to Daphne. Those two were head over heels in love with each other.

She spoke to Charlie. "I'd ask Uncle James and Aunt Kelly to join us for snack time, but it looks like they might want to…"

Her husband interrupted to finish her sentence, and disguised his words with a fake cough, "…Get a room."

Chapter 10

Zane cocked his head as he sat on the roof of a cabana and watched Tracy by the hotel pool in a tiny white bikini, studded with silver.

Michael sat next to him and scoffed. "You can't even call that thing a bathing suit. She could never go swimming in it. A little contact with water and it would be completely see-through."

Zane chuckled. "I think that's the point, Mike. You know, she reminds me of the saloon girls from my time. They looked good at night. In dim light. But by the harsh light of day…" He shuddered.

Michael grinned. "I imagine a few weeks on a cattle drive, or whatever the heck you used to do, only helped make them look prettier."

"You got that right," Zane conceded and added after a moment's consideration, "And a good bit of whiskey didn't hurt, either."

There was a disruption in the air next to them, and Uriel appeared. "None of which will apply to James tomorrow night. Well, maybe the whisky, but not the dim light or the female-less cattle drive. Meaning, he won't be vulnerable to this woman's dubious charms. So what is that fallen angel really plotting? Any leads on that front, Michael?"

"No," the angel admitted with slumped shoulders. "Whatever Mildred has planned, she's been careful not to plot it in front of us."

"How about you?" Zane asked his boss. "You're the all-knowing one. How come you don't know what she's up to?"

"First of all, I am not the all-knowing one, and He wouldn't appreciate you calling me that."

"Sorry," Zane mumbled.

Uriel inclined his head. "It's all right, I understand you're frustrated, but my guardian angels work with billions of souls, and I normally only get personally involved with the big stuff—war, famines—I'm only involved with Kelly and James for Michael, so he may ascend to the next level."

"And your interest is what drew the fallen one here?" Zane asked.

Uriel had the grace to look somewhat abashed. "I'm afraid so. Her boss really doesn't like me, and she hopes by upsetting me on this case she'll please him."

"Why is he so hot to annoy you?" Michael asked.

Uriel's eyes took on a faraway cast as he remembered. "We were friends a long time ago. Before the fall. I chose to stay on the side of good, and he's never forgiven me for what he considers my betrayal. He's forbidden to take me on directly, so periodically he tries to get to me through the humans in whom I've expressed an interest."

Zane drew one knee up and rested his forearm on it. "And right now you're interested in James and Kelly."

"Indirectly. As I said, my interest lies more with Michael. It's past time for him to move on. He has good things waiting for him and good work to do for my Corps, and all of that is on hold until he decides to leave this earthly plane."

Michael couldn't help the flash of interest he felt in his future, but then set his jaw and said stubbornly. "We've been over this before. I'm not leaving until Kelly is settled."

Uriel looked around the hotel pool as if he was searching for someone he knew he wouldn't find. "Where are Kelly and James? And why are neither of you with them?"

"I was with them all day, up until a little while ago," Zane answered with a careless shrug. "I didn't have to interfere once. It seems like they're doing just fine on their own, so I thought I'd scope out the enemy camp and see what there is to see."

Uriel clasped his hands together and beamed. The golden aura around him impossibly became even brighter. His glow dimmed the sun the poolside humans were soaking up, and it was a good thing they couldn't see him at the moment or they would be struck blind. Even his two angelic companions had to blink in his glare.

"Wonderful," he intoned. "If they're beyond needing assistance, it's time for me to escort you to the next level, Michael."

Michael squared his shoulders and squinted as he looked through the brilliance surrounding his boss and straight into Uriel's eyes. "I am not leaving until I know Kelly is safe from Mildred."

The light around Uriel dimmed.

"I'm sorry, sir, but Mildred's up to something, and I want to stick around long enough to see her plot through and make sure no harm comes to Kelly. Surely my destiny can wait a little longer?"

Zane narrowed his eyes. "Look, Michael, I want you out of this mess and onto the next plane. If anyone deserves to be there, it's you, but I'm starting to think this situation with Mildred will never be resolved to your satisfaction."

He turned to Uriel. "Mildred implied that even if we get rid of her, more fallen angels will come. What if Kelly is never actually safe from the attention of the fallen ones while Michael is here trying to protect her?"

"Traitor," Michael muttered under his breath.

Uriel laid a fatherly hand on his shoulder. "He's not a traitor, Michael. Zane is looking out for your best interests."

Zane locked his eyes on Michael and said with sincerity. "I really am, Mike."

"I know. I'm sorry, man. I just really don't want to leave until Mildred's plan unfolds, and I know she's been stopped. Please, Uriel."

Uriel pursed his perfectly molded lips as he considered Michael's request. As Michael waited for his response, he studied his boss's appearance. He looked like a Renaissance sculpture of an archangel come to life, with his chiseled features, full lips, and wavy hair that looked like spun gold.

At long last, Uriel answered. "Fine. You can stay to see this business with Mildred through, but then you must ascend."

"Even if more fallen angels come after Kelly and James?"

"Even then. I'm sorry, but as I've said again and again, you're already long past the time you should have left this realm."

Michael turned his head to hide his disappointment

from his companions.

"If it's any consolation, I don't believe what Mildred told you. If she fails, it is highly doubtful her boss will expend any more precious resources on these two humans."

"You think Millie was just blowing smoke out of her ass?" Zane asked and after a strong look of disapproval from Uriel, amended, "I mean out of her behind."

Uriel sighed in a long-suffering manner. "That word isn't much better, Zane, but yes, I do believe Mildred was trying to scare Michael with empty threats."

"But you're not one-hundred percent sure?" Michael asked.

"No. But staying long enough to stop Mildred is the best deal you're going to get from me. It's time, Michael."

Michael considered and sighed with resignation. "Fine. I'll take it." He quirked his lips into a half-smile. "I'm ready to get to the next stage of my afterlife. It's just that Kelly…"

"Is no longer your responsibility," Uriel interrupted with an air of finality.

"And from what I've seen of her, she's a pretty strong lady," Zane added to console his friend. "She'll be okay."

Uriel beamed. "Fine. It's settled. Now, I've got places to be, tragedies to avert." With a flash of light visible only to Zane and Michael, he was gone.

Zane looked at Michael out of the corner of his eye and then focused his attention back on Tracy. "After you ascend to the next plane, I'll keep an eye on things here for you, Mike. If Uriel's wrong and more fallen angels come after Millie fails, I'll protect Kelly."

"Thanks, man. I appreciate it."

****

James turned his car in to the parking garage and said with studied casualness, "So…what were you and Daffy talking about?"

Kelly shrugged. "Nothing much. About how long you've been friends and how I better not hurt you. Yada, yada, yada."

James laughed as he slid into his space and cut the engine. "Funny. Bill had that same talk with me last night."

Kelly turned to gape at him, her jaw dropped. "No kidding! And Grace and I thought you were debating the merits of gas versus charcoal."

"Oh, we did that, too—it's in the guy rule book, you know." He cleared his throat and pretended to quote. "'When by a grill, beer must be consumed and debate on barbecue methods must ensue.'"

Kelly slapped his arm in mock annoyance, and he rubbed it as if she'd really hurt him.

"Ouch, slugger. Easy there." He looked at her and his expression went from playful to heated. "I know we're home, but I'm not ready to say good-bye yet. Do you want to come up to my place? Maybe we could hang out and order a pizza for dinner in a little while."

Kelly pretended to think. It had been a while since she'd taken a dip in the dating pool, but she knew it was never wise to look too eager. She tried, but couldn't completely disguise her happiness at his invitation. "Sure. That sounds good."

"Great." He got out of the car and had her door

opened before Kelly could get her seat belt unbuckled.

"No anchovies, though," he cautioned. "There are limits to what a man will do for a woman, no matter how amazing she is. And that's mine. No anchovy pizza."

He put his hand on the small of her back as they strolled to the elevator.

"People always say that—'no anchovies'—but I've never actually seen anyone order anchovies on a pizza. Does it really need to be said?"

They got into the elevator, and James pushed the button for the top floor.

"Good point," he conceded. "Then my limit will be, no green peppers."

Kelly fiddled with the hem of her shirt. "Do you really think I'm amazing? Although, not amazing enough to eat an anchovy or a green pepper pizza for, apparently."

James took her by the shoulders and turned her to face him. His gaze drifted down to his godson's little handprint on her top and he smiled. "You are the most amazing woman I've ever met, Kelly Morrison Lynch."

Her eyes flickered up to meet his intent stare. He dipped his head to kiss her, and the elevator binged as it jolted to a stop and the doors opened.

The man in the hallway asked, "This one going down?"

James and Kelly moved apart. Kelly stared at the floor and James cleared his throat before he answered, "No. We're going up."

The man stepped back. "Oh, okay, I'll wait."

James pushed the button to close the doors and groused. "I suppose his timing could've been worse, but

I don't know how."

Kelly gulped and blurted out, "I think you're amazing, too."

James turned to her, his green eyes wide as she gathered her courage, stood on her tiptoes and pressed her lips to his.

The elevator jerked and stopped again.

"Now what?" James asked in irritation at the interruption. "Oh. It's my floor."

He pulled away from Kelly and put his hand on the elevator door to hold it open for her. Kelly stepped off and felt amazed at her own boldness in laying that kiss on him. Grace would be so proud.

James opened the door to his condo and gestured for her to go in. "Have a seat. Would you like a glass of wine?"

He put his phone on a docking station, and fiddled with it until soft music filled the air.

She settled on the sofa. "Sure. I'm not driving anywhere tonight. All I've got to do is walk across the street to get home."

He walked to the kitchen area, which in keeping with the industrial style of the loft looked a little like a laboratory with its gleaming stainless steel appliances and counters. He pulled two wineglasses out and asked, "Is red okay?"

"Of course. What else does one drink with anchovy and green pepper pizza?"

****

Mildred landed next to Zane and Michael on the cabana roof with a loud thump, and tucked her dingy wings away. "What are you two idiots up to? Still trying to figure out my diabolical plan?"

She looked down at Tracy as the woman adjusted one of the three miniscule triangles, which made up the front of her bathing suit. "Or are you here to admire my girl's attributes? She is a looker. Still think she can't lure James into the sack?"

They watched as a man by the pool walked into a lounge chair he hadn't noticed, as his attention was focused entirely on Tracy's bikini adjustment. He grimaced and rubbed his shin as he tried to surreptitiously continue to check out Tracy's surgically-enhanced body.

"Sure she's flashy…" Michael began.

"But James has been there, done that, and had the STD testing," Zane finished.

Mildred turned a level gaze to the cowboy. "You're not at all the usual good guy material. Sure you don't want to switch sides? We could use someone like you on our team."

"No thanks. I'm happy where I am." A slow smile tugged at one side of his mouth. "I like being on the winning team, and you're going down, Millie."

Mildred whipped her head around to glare at the two angels. "Just like your beloved wifey. She's probably going down right about now, too. On James."

With a malevolent grin, she stretched her gray wings and flapped away.

"Don't let her get to you, Mike," Zane advised with sympathy.

Michael waved his hand in dismissal. "She didn't. Look, I'm not a dummy. I know Kelly and James are going to get physical. It's a natural path for their relationship to go on, and I've come to terms with it. It's part of what Kelly has to do to move on, and I'm okay with that." He grimaced. "I just don't want to have to see it."

He thought for a moment and narrowed his eyes as he cautioned his friend. "And I don't want you to see it, either."

"I know, Mike. That's why we're sitting on this cabana and watching that skank strut her stuff. I may have my faults, but I'm no voyeur."

Michael looked impressed. "I didn't know nineteenth century cowboys even knew a word like 'voyeur', let alone be able to use it in conversation."

One side of Zane's mouth quirked up. "It wasn't a word we tossed around on the range, but I've seen a lot of crazy shit since then. Like Millie said, I'm not your average good guy."

****

As dusk fell, James went to a switch on the wall by the fireplace and turned on the recessed lighting. He used the dimmer to lower the bright lights to a more romantic level and retrieved the wine bottle from the kitchen island. He topped off their glasses. "Pizza should be here soon."

Kelly stretched like a cat and settled back on the sofa with her feet tucked under her; she might have actually purred. "I'm in no hurry to move. I've gotta say, for your typical single guy sectional sofa, it is wicked comfortable."

James put his glass on the coffee table and pulled Kelly into his arms as he sat back down. He rubbed his cheek against her hair and murmured, "Is it just me, or has this been one of the best days ever?"

She shifted so her back was against his chest and her long legs were stretched out on the sofa. She wrapped an arm around his neck, "It's definitely been one of my favorites."

James snaked a hand around her waist and slipped it under the bottom of her shirt. He smiled a little as he heard the catch in her breath as he began to stroke her silken skin. He slid his hand to rest just under her breast and kissed the top of her head.

"I know how I can make it even better," he said in a low voice as his hand moved up and teased the peak of her breast through her satiny bra.

When Kelly spoke, her words were tough, but he was pleased to note that her voice was husky with desire. "Big talk, Art-Boy. Think you can back it up?"

As his hand continued to work its magic and he felt her arch into his caress, he replied with confidence. "Oh, I know I can, Writer-Girl."

She gave a breathless laugh before his lips claimed hers. He pulled her onto his lap, and Kelly twined her arms around his neck and ran her fingers up into his hair.

James moved one hand under her T-shirt to the tantalizing dip at the base of her spine. He ran his other hand up the hot, smooth skin of her thigh. He didn't want to push Kelly too far, too fast, but she sure seemed as ready as he was to move their relationship to the next level. His grip on the hem of her shirt was tentative. He wanted to see her, to touch, to taste her. But if she gave any resistance when he lifted her shirt, James swore to himself that he'd stop. It might very well kill him, but he'd stop.

Instead, when Kelly realized what he was doing, she tore her mouth away from his and raised her arms to help him. James felt relief, lust—and God save him—love, at her maneuver. He lifted her shirt off and tossed it aside with a chuckle of pure masculine satisfaction.

Kelly's hands reached for the buttons on his shirt, as she turned on his lap to straddle him for easier access. When this position caused their most intimate, and already highly aroused, places to come in direct—and oh-so-delicious—contact with each other they both moaned. James shrugged out of his shirt with impatience and reclaimed Kelly's mouth.

He placed his hands at her waist and slowly slipped them up her back to release the clasp of her bra, which she slipped out of and threw over her shoulder with a seductive smile.

"My God, woman. You're killing me," James rasped before he took a full breast in his mouth. Kelly moaned deep in her throat and twisted his hair that she had clutched in her fingers. Her head rolled back and her eyes drifted shut with pleasure as his tongue worked its magic on her body.

She jumped and her eyes popped open at a loud knock on the door. James pulled away from her and blinked a couple of times. He took a deep breath to clear his head and lifted Kelly gently off his lap. He placed her next to him on the sofa, and ran his fingers through his already messy hair.

****

"Must be the pizza guy," he observed with a casualness he was far from feeling.

Kelly looked around frantically. James had reached the door, pulled his wallet out of the back pocket of his jeans, and waited for Kelly to cover her partial nudity. She put her arms across her breasts in a vain attempt to cover herself and whispered, "I don't see where my shirt went."

"You can wear mine. It's next to you on the sofa."

She snatched it up and stuck her arms into the sleeves. She didn't bother with the buttons—she just pulled it across her chest and scurried for the bedroom.

Once she was safely out of sight, James opened the door.

****

Kelly leaned her backside against his dresser and gripped the edge with one hand. She used the other to hold James' button-down shirt closed.

She tried to get her breathing under control and listened to James make small talk with the deliveryman as he settled the bill. How could he sound so calm? Maybe he wasn't as affected as she was by what they'd been doing. After all, he'd been with a woman much more recently than Kelly had been with a man. This might not be as much of an event for him as it was for her. It had been two years since Michael's death, and he'd been so ill for months before that, so it had been a mighty long time since Kelly had been intimately touched.

She closed her eyes and admitted to herself that her long dry spell wasn't the only reason she was so aroused. She realized that somewhere along the line she'd fallen in love with James, and that emotion amped up her physical reaction to him.

Kelly heard his deep voice as James bade farewell to the pizza man and then heard the front door click as it closed.

She leaned against the dark wood dresser and looked around. Good golly, she was in James Flynn's bedroom—and she was half-naked! She gulped and looked at the king sized bed with its charcoal gray spread and red sheets, and shivered with anticipation. She really wanted the night to end with James and her tangled in those sheets, but maybe she'd presumed too much. When all was said and done, he was the talented, handsome object of her youthful dreams, and a part of her was still the dorky girl who'd admired him from afar. Of course, his heart wasn't racing the way hers was. She sighed and tried to brace herself for what she feared was his inevitable rejection of her.

Kelly knew she should try to act unfazed and walk out of this room to join him, but her body was not in sync with her mind's plan. It still burned for his touch, and she stood rooted in place in the bedroom.

Through the opening next to the glass blocks, which divided the bedroom from the rest of the loft, she saw James stroll by with the pizza box. He tossed it on the counter and turned to the bedroom.

Here goes, Kelly told herself, try to act sophisticated and not like some crazy, hormonal groupie.

He paused at the door and leaned one shoulder against the glass bricks. Kelly felt her heart stutter at the sight of him clad only in his jeans. His streaky blond hair tousled from where she'd clutched him when he'd kissed her breasts.

His grin was devilish, as he looked at her, and while his gaze was heated, she worried about how she must look—barefoot in her skirt and swallowed up by his pink Oxford shirt.

"How do you feel about cold pizza?"

"Cold pizza?" Kelly squeaked as he stalked toward

her like a big, sexy cat.

"Mm hm," he murmured as he reached her. He put his hands on her shoulders and stroked down the length of her arms to capture her hands in his, which caused her to release her grip and the unbuttoned shirt to fall open. "Because I really, really want to get back to what we were doing before the pizza got here and interrupted us."

"You do?" Kelly's jaw dropped, as all her attempts at sophisticated nonchalance flew out the window.

His crooked smile was puzzled. "Of course I do. Why do you sound so surprised?"

He pulled her against him and she could feel his body's evidence that he was still as turned on as she was. He ran his fingers through her hair, from the roots to the ends, and cocked his head as he looked at her.

"You have to know how much I want to make love to you. I was hoping we could have the pizza later. Like maybe for breakfast."

Kelly was so relieved at his words she wasn't able to answer right away. He still wanted her, too. This was really going to happen. She was going to make love to James.

He seemed to misinterpret her silence and said with real reluctance. "But if you've changed your mind, we can just eat dinner, and then I'll walk you home."

"No! I haven't changed my mind. I'd love cold pizza for breakfast."

James' head lolled back on his neck and his sigh was heartfelt. "That's a relief. You know I'm not the kind of man to force his attentions on a woman, and if you had changed your mind I would've handled it, but man, Kelly, it wouldn't have been easy."

He steered her to his bed, and slipped his shirt off her shoulders and stroked the bared flesh it revealed to him. He leaned toward her face and breathed against her cheek. "I want you so much. Now. In my bed."

****

James couldn't believe he was making love to Kelly. When he had come into the bedroom, he suspected she was having second thoughts, and he felt disappointment like he'd never experienced before in his life, but here she was, in his bed. So warm and wet and responsive. She was everything he'd ever wanted and more. She was smart, funny, kind, and successful in her own right. And hotter than hell. A point that couldn't be overstated at this point in time.

He looked down at her as they made love. Her lips were swollen from their kisses, and her eyes were heavy-lidded and cloudy with passion. Her dark hair was fanned out on the pillowcase, and her skin looked impossibly fair against the crimson sheets.

"You're the most beautiful thing I've ever seen." He breathed the words with awe.

At his words of praise there was a sharp intake of breath as she arched her spine, and he felt her release. Her climax caused her body to grip his inside her, and it made his control break and his own release soon followed.

As his body exploded, he called out what was in his heart. "Kelly—God—Kelly, I love you."

He held himself frozen in place above her and was afraid to look into her eyes for fear of seeing a rejection of his declaration of love. Why had he said it? Way to scare the woman away, asshole.

And then he heard her voice—soft, stunned, and a

little hesitant, and what she said was like the most beautiful music to his ears.

"I love you, too."

Chapter 11

When Kelly first awoke she had a brief moment when she didn't know where she was. It didn't feel like her bed, and she was most definitely not alone. She felt someone snuggled against her back who was all hot, hard, and most definitely male. Then all the delicious events of the previous night rushed back to her, making love with James and then having a two in the morning naked pizza picnic in the middle of his king-sized bed. Then making love again.

She sighed in contentment at the memories and nestled into James. His thigh was intimately wedged between her legs, and his arm was thrown across her, with one breast cupped in his hand.

Kelly really would be happy to stay here in bed with him all day, but David was coming into town this morning. She forced her eyes open with great reluctance and was shocked to see the condo bathed in sunlight, which poured through the exterior glass walls of the living area and through the glass blocks into the bedroom.

She gasped and sat up. James cracked one eye open, and then a knowing grin spread across his face as he opened both eyes to look at her. Suddenly very aware of her nudity, Kelly pulled the sheet up to cover herself.

"What's wrong, darlin'? You can't possibly be

feeling bashful with me after last night."

"Oh, yes I can," she scoffed. "But that's not what's bothering me. What time is it? It looks like the middle of the day."

He rolled over, unashamed of his own nudity, which was revealed to Kelly's appreciative eyes when she'd yanked the sheet away from him. He picked up his cell phone from the nightstand to look at the time.

"It's ten forty-five." He rolled over and propped himself up on his elbows. "And much as I hate to say it, I've got to be at the gallery soon for that special tour for Lydia's art class. Want to join me for a quick shower before I go?"

Kelly jumped out of bed, and found her skirt and panties on the floor. She pulled them on and grabbed her eyeglasses from the nightstand and shoved them on her face.

He yawned as he sat up and stretched. "Good thing you had all your contact lens stuff with you last night, so you could take them out to sleep." He narrowed his eyes and asked with playful suspicion, "Why, Mrs. Lynch, that seems awfully prepared on your part, now that I think about it. Did you plan to seduce me last night?"

She rolled her eyes. "Nice fantasy, Art-Boy. I always carry my glasses and a lens case in my purse. I've got allergies and sometimes my eyes get irritated with my contacts in, and for the record—you seduced me."

He chuckled. "Not the way I remember it, Writer-Girl."

"Where the hell are my bra and shirt?" she asked as she looked around in agitation.

James stood and strolled out to the living room, seemingly oblivious to the fact he was gloriously naked. Kelly craned her neck to enjoy the rear view as he walked out and bent over to pick something up off the floor. As he rose and turned, she wiped the smile off her face and straightened up with a lurch, so as not to get caught ogling his very fine behind.

"They're right where we threw them last night. On the living room floor."

Kelly flushed and snatched them from him. She turned her back to wriggle into her bra.

As she pulled her T-shirt over her head, he asked, "Seriously, Kelly. What's your hurry? I was hoping you'd hang out here while I give Lydia's class their tour, and then when I got home we could pick up where we left off."

He nuzzled the side of her neck and she sighed.

"That sounds wonderful, but I can't. David's coming into town this morning, and I've got to get back to my place before he gets there."

She pulled a brush and a clip from her purse in order to wrestle her unruly bed hair into a messy ponytail.

"Just give him a call and see if he's there yet. If he's not, then you have time for a shower before you go. And you can borrow one of my shirts, if you don't want to wear that one. It's still got Charlie's grubby little handprint on it."

"No, no, no." Kelly shook her head so hard the ponytail swung back and forth. "If I do that stuff, then David will know I spent the night here."

"And that would be bad, why? Is David that puritanical?" James pulled on his jeans, without worrying about underwear or a shirt. He fastened the jeans, and slowly raised his head to look at her with narrowed eyes. "Are you ashamed of last night? Of what we did? Because I'm not. It was the greatest night of my life. Bar none."

Kelly's expression softened. "No, I'm not ashamed. What we shared was unbelievably beautiful. And private. I'd just like to keep it between us for a little while."

James thinned his lips and cocked his head. "See— that sounds a lot like shame to me."

"It's not. Really! I love my friends, but they can be the most incredible buttinskys. If David found out we made love, he'd probably be so frantic to spread the news he'd send smoke signals from the roof for Grace and Janie to see. Then they'd both race over to my condo, and they would all want to quiz me about it, and I want to savor it by myself for a little while yet."

She flashed him a seductive half-smile and put a little extra swing in her hips as she walked to him and wrapped her arms around his neck. "Right now, it's like you and I are in our own little bubble world, with this delicious secret. I want to keep it that way for as long as we can."

He grinned down at her and rested his hands on her hips. "Funny. My instincts are the complete opposite, because I feel like running out to my balcony and shouting to the greater San Diego metropolitan area that I just spent the night making love to Kelly Lynch. But, I'm completely incapable of saying 'no' to you, so our little secret it is. For now."

****

Kelly tapped her foot as the elevator made its way

to her floor. Could it go any slower? She knew David was planning to get an early start this morning to beat the weekend traffic, and she really hoped she'd get to her condo before him. She hadn't meant to sleep so late, but rest hadn't really been on James' and her agenda the night before, and it was almost dawn by the time they fell asleep.

The elevator dinged and the doors opened to reveal David, where he sat on the floor with his back against her door. His motorcycle helmet and bag were on either side of him, and he had one knee drawn up. He looked up from his cell phone, and flashed his sparkling white smile at her as he stood up and waved the phone at her. "Hey, Kel. That nice old lady from the 3rd floor let me in the front door—you know the one who's always at the pool? She's such a doll, and good thing I ran into her and she remembered me, or else I would still be waiting on the street. I was just getting ready to call you. Where've you been?"

She gave him a quick kiss on the cheek and lowered her eyes as she squeezed by to open her door.

"I had to run out for something. I thought I'd be back before you got here."

"For what?"

"What do you mean, for what?" She tossed her keys in the bowl and kicked her sandals off, careful to avoid eye contact with him.

"You don't have a bag, and quite honestly, babe, you look like crap. So I was just wondering where you went."

She pulled self-consciously on her ponytail. "Thank you very much for the fashion critique."

David laughed and went to the kitchen to pull a

181

soda from the fridge. He popped the top and took a sip, while his eyes watched her over the can. He leaned back against the counter. "You just don't normally go out in your glasses, and your outfit looks like you pulled it off the floor to put it on."

He gestured with his soda can to her top. "And it looks like you got groped by a little person while you were out on your mysterious errand."

Kelly glanced down at Charlie's tiny handprint over her breast. "No lascivious little people. I met James' godson yesterday. What a cutie he is—ten months old and full of mischief—anyway, he reached for me while James was holding him and left his dirty little handprint."

David took another swig of his soda as he thought it through. "Let me get this straight—you're in your glasses and the dirty, wrinkled clothes you wore yesterday. Your hair's a mess, and it looks like you just rolled out of bed..." He gasped. "Oh my God! You weren't out running an errand. This is the walk of shame."

She frowned at him and shook her head vehemently. "No. No shame."

He laughed. "I should hope not. You slept with James Flynn, didn't you? Nothing to be ashamed of there. Yummy James, my God! Tell Uncle Davey all about it."

Kelly scowled at him as she went through the bedroom and into the master bathroom. "I must have missed the part where this is any of your business."

David rolled his eyes, pulled his motorcycle jacket off, and threw it on the sofa, as he turned to face the bedroom and replied facetiously, "Oh, I don't know what makes it my business. Maybe the lifetime of friendship? Or the fact I was with you the first time you laid eyes on Yummy James on the playground in elementary school?"

Kelly came out in a fluffy, white terrycloth robe. She poured herself a glass of water from the dispenser on the door of the fridge, and sat on one of the barstools on the opposite side of the kitchen island from David.

"You're my very best friend, David, but you know I'm private about my love life."

"Who said anything about love? I'm asking about your sex life. This is the first person you've been with since Michael—of course I'm interested. It's huge!" He grinned and leaned across the granite countertop to waggle his eyebrows at her. "Speaking of which, was it huge?"

Kelly choked on a sip of water. "Private means no talk of measurement. David, please leave this alone. At least until it's not so new, and I've had time to get used to it."

"Okay. I won't press for details," David conceded with a dramatic show of reluctance. "But you have to admit, this is a major development for you. Last time I was here, you were still wearing your wedding ring and resisting all our attempts to fix you up. What happened to change your mind?"

She thought for a bit before she answered. "James and I aren't exactly strangers. We've got a history together. It's not like I ran out, grabbed the first man I saw off the street and slept with him."

"But still, it's a big change for you in a pretty short amount of time. I feel like something must have made you jump off the cliff that we've been trying to push you off for such a long time."

She sighed. "You know me so well. Yeah, something did happen that made me think it was time, but you'd never believe me if I told you what it was."

"Try me."

"You know Janie's theory about guardian angels?"

David wrinkled his brow and said slowly. "Yes. Where are you going with this, kid?"

"It seems that a man James met in a bar convinced him to go online and get in touch with me."

She paused and David gestured for her to continue. She took a deep breath and blurted out, "And we think that man was Michael."

David's blue eyes widened and his jaw dropped. "Michael? Like his ghost or something?"

She shook her head. "I told you that you'd never believe it—no, not a ghost. A corporeal being. Possibly an angel."

David raised his eyebrows at her words. "An angel? What makes you think it was Michael?"

She pointed to the photo in the living room. "The first time James came here he saw that picture and told me he's the guy who encouraged him to look me up."

David frowned. "Maybe this man just looked like Michael."

"He drank the same whiskey, he had a Boston accent. Hell, he even smelled like Michael! I know it sounds nuts, but I think Michael wants me to be with James."

"Wow." David blinked. "That's a wild story, all right, but I trust you. Actually, there's no one on this earth I trust more than you, so, if you believe it was Michael, then I believe in you."

She smiled and reached across the island to squeeze his hand in gratitude. "Thanks."

David furrowed his brow. "But that's not the only reason you slept with James, though—it's more than just because you think Michael wants you to, right? You're attracted to James without Michael's stamp of approval?"

"Attracted like a magnet to metal. I was really falling for him, but I felt guilty about it—like it would be cheating on Michael. Then it seemed as though Michael was telling me it's okay to love someone else. That it doesn't take anything away from what we had together."

"Of course it doesn't," he said with staunch loyalty and then his look grew speculative. "Wait. Did you just say you love James?"

She looked down at her glass then peeked up at David through her lashes and spoke in a rush. "Sort of. But it's too soon, right? I mean I can't love James already. Except I kinda do."

David frowned and shook his head. "I've got to admit I googled him the other night. He's got kind of a reputation as a playboy. Well, as a recluse and a playboy, which don't exactly seem like they'd mesh, but he seems to pull it off. Anyway, just be careful. I don't want him to hurt you."

"He hasn't been serious about anyone since his divorce, so it might look like he's a Casanova, but I think he was so hurt by his ex-wife's betrayal that he put walls up to protect himself. Now those walls are starting to come down with me, and I really don't think he'll hurt me, David."

"He'll answer to me if he does," David threatened

in his best big brother manner. His voice was casual—too casual to fool Kelly—as he asked, "Does he feel the same way about you?"

"I think so; I mean, he said he loves me. Once. But it was in the heat of the moment so I'm not sure it counts. And my God, he's James Flynn and I'm…" She laughed self-consciously and waved her hands up and down her body. "I'm just me. It's hard for me to believe he loves me, but he said he does, and he's sure acting like it."

"He better not be leading my best girl on." David glowered. "I'm looking forward to checking him out with my own two eyes at this charity exhibit tonight. Hopefully, I'll get a chance to talk to him alone, and to make it clear to him that his life will be worth nothing if he hurts you."

Kelly laughed. "My big, brave defender. Thanks for the protection, David, but I really don't think it's necessary. What we have is different for James than what he's had with other women. I don't know if it's really love for him, but I do know it's not a game to him any more than it is to me. Sometimes I just let my insecurities get the best of me. I really need to work on that."

At David's "we'll see" shrug, she added, "But you'll definitely get your chance to be menacing tonight. James gets nervous about being at public showings of his work, so he asked if I'd go with him tonight to lend moral support. I said sure, but you were staying with me, so we were kind of a package deal tonight."

David raised his eyebrows. "And he was okay with me tagging along?"

At Kelly's nod, he pursed his lips and bobbed his head. "Points to him on that, then. If he's willing to have your best friend along on a date, then his intentions can't be too dishonorable."

****

James rushed out of the locker room of his gym, where he'd changed into his standard weight training clothes, a ratty old concert T, shorts, and sneakers.

Steve waited for him in a similar outfit and flung his arms out in exasperation. "Where the hell have you been?"

"Sorry I'm late, thanks for waiting for me. I did a special tour of the exhibit for one of Kelly's friend's kids and her art class this morning. Man, did they ask a lot of questions. It took way longer than I thought it would. Look, since I held you up, you can do the first circuit, and I'll spot for you."

They walked to the first piece of equipment. Steve squinted at James. "Hanging out with a kids' art class as a favor to Kelly, huh? You are seriously trying to score points with this woman."

James shrugged and tried to look nonchalant. "Maybe."

"Okay. Here's the deal—I'm on a mission for Daphne, and she wants to know all about what's going on between you two. She thinks it's serious. We can do it the hard way or the easy way, but I'm not going home with nothing to tell her. So spill, dude."

"Kelly's a great woman, what can I say?" James was very aware of Kelly's desire for privacy, and to be honest, he wasn't completely comfortable talking about their relationship with Steve either. It was new, and based on Kelly's reaction this morning, he was afraid she'd get freaked out and pull away now that they'd made love.

His other fear was that he hadn't compared to her late husband. He still saw the light in her eyes when she talked about Michael. Bill and Grace had talked at length about what a great guy he'd been. How could James measure up to his memory? Would he ever put the same expression on Kelly's face that she'd had when she sniffed her late husband's cologne the other night? She'd been quick to school her expression, but James remembered all too clearly the flash of bliss in her hazel eyes before they'd drifted shut, and the beatific look on her face as the aroma clearly brought back good memories of her late husband.

He'd spent a good chunk of his adult life avoiding commitment with women. How could he ever love this woman the way she deserved to be loved? Feeling inadequate with a woman was a new emotion for James, and it wasn't a comfortable one. Sure, he could bring pleasure to Kelly in bed, but he wanted to do more. To be more. And he was afraid he wouldn't know how and would hurt Kelly in the end. His stomach clenched at the thought. No. He'd never hurt her. He couldn't. If it looked like he might, he'd get out of her life before he could bring her a moment's pain.

His thoughts were interrupted when Steve grunted as he worked out. "Earth to Flynn—what are you doing gazing at nothing like some character in a soap opera? You've totally fallen down on your spotter duties here, and I need you to tell me more than that Kelly's a great woman. I could tell she was great yesterday, and she got serious good sport cred for not minding when Charlie ruined her shirt. Daffy wants to hear more than 'she's great', so give me a freakin' break and tell me something else."

"Like what?"

"I don't know. Have you done her yet?"

"Done her? Thank you, Mr. Romance. For your information, Kelly isn't the kind of woman you 'do'."

Steve stood up and wiped down the equipment with his towel before he moved on to the next machine. "You've got it bad, my brother. I've never seen you like this about a woman before." He grinned devilishly. "Since you didn't like my choice of words before, let me rephrase the question—have you made sweet love to her yet?"

James rolled his eyes. "Man you can be a dick sometimes. Remind me again why we've been friends for so long?"

"Because you know I've always got your back, and this is odd behavior for you. I just don't want her to hurt you." He shook his head in disgust and resumed his workout. "And I could feel the testosterone draining from my body even as those words were coming out of my mouth."

"Kelly won't hurt me," James said with conviction, and then paused before adding, "I don't think."

"You don't think? That's underwhelming. What makes you think she might hurt you?"

James wrinkled his nose as he thought. "I don't know. We had a great day together yesterday. An unbelievable night last night. But this morning…"

Steve interrupted with a triumphal shout that had the other gym patrons looking their way with curiosity. "I knew it! I knew you had sex with her!"

"Amazing deduction, Sherlock," James said with

sarcasm. "And I'd been meaning to tell every other freakin' person in the gym about my sex life, so thanks for saving me the trouble, but now can I get back to the point of my story?"

Steve gestured regally for James to continue as he wiped up and moved on to the next machine in the circuit.

"This morning she couldn't get out of my place fast enough, and she doesn't want her friends to know we spent the night together. I'm just worried that she regrets what happened last night, or..."

"Or what?"

"Or I scared her off. I'm the first guy she's dated since her husband died, and I was trying to take it slow, but I kinda told her that I loved her."

Steve dropped the weights back into place with a clang. "Dude, what the hell?"

James went on the defensive. "It just came out. I didn't mean to say it. Shit, I hadn't even really admitted it to myself yet."

Steve tore his shocked eyes off James' face and began to lift weights again. "So, she freaked out after you dropped the 'L' bomb on her?"

"No. She said it back."

Steve draped his towel around his neck and bobbed his head as he considered the situation. "That's okay then. I mean, for the record, I think you're both nuts. It's way too soon to be tossing around the 'L' word, but at least you're both nuts together."

"I know it hasn't been long, but I've never felt like this before. Not even with Tracy."

"Yeah, well, I never understood why the frig you married *her* in the first place, but that's another story.

Just do me a favor and don't rush into another marriage."

"Kelly's nothing like Tracy." James bristled.

"That's clear to anyone with functioning eyes, buddy. I didn't mean that—Kelly is no gold-digger, and it's obvious she means a lot to you. You've never brought another woman around Charlie before. Daphne really liked her, and she was great with Charlie."

He sat up and wiped the sweat off his brow, as he looked at James with his jaw somewhere in the vicinity of his knees. "Well, shit. You're getting all dreamy-eyed about this woman holding my kid. You're really serious about her. You want the whole package with her, don't you?"

James nodded. "I do. Marriage, kids, house in the 'burbs."

"I better put my affairs in order, then, because James Flynn thinking about settling down and moving to deepest, darkest suburbia is one of the signs of the Apocalypse."

"Very funny. Just don't say anything about this in front of her tonight. I think I made her nervous enough already with the love talk. There's no need to send her screaming into the night with talk about mortgages and carpools."

Steve pressed two fingers together and held them up. "Scout's honor, man. I won't say a word."

"You were never a scout."

Steve lowered his chin and glared up at James. "Whatever. It's just a saying. I mean you have my word. My lips will be sealed."

James punched Steve's bicep lightly in a friendly gesture. "Thanks. I appreciate it."

Steve grinned at him. "And I'll try to keep Daffy under control, but no promises on that score. She's going to freak out when I report back to her that you're ready to tie the knot with this woman already."

****

Zane materialized on the beach at the Hotel del Coronado. The late afternoon sunshine reflected off Michael's mirrored sunglasses as he sat stretched out on a lounge chair and sipped a tropical drink.

Zane ambled over and flopped onto the neighboring lounger. "Don't wear yourself out with this frenzied pace, Mike."

Michael gave an abrupt laugh. "This was the most boring day ever. I've earned this little break. Tracy spent the whole day getting salon and spa treatments."

"And Mildred?"

"She was on the phone or at the computer for hours, but she created some kind of white noise around her, and I couldn't hear a blessed thing. How'd she do that?"

Zane leaned back in the chair and closed his eyes. "The fallen ones have ways. I thought she was too low-level to have those abilities, though."

"Well, she's not. And I've got nothing. How about you? How are things going with James and Kelly?"

"Right on track. If it wasn't for the fallen angels out to sabotage their relationship, I think we could almost leave them to it and both get on with our own afterlives."

"Good." Michael gave a brief nod. "What time is the charity thing tonight?"

"It starts at seven, but I was thinking it's too risky for you to go. There are going to be too many people who know you there tonight."

Zane opened his eyes and squinted into the golden sunlight and continued, "I'll go in corporeal form, and you can stick to Mildred."

"But what if she goes to the exhibit with Tracy?"

"Follow her. But be sure to stay invisible."

"Okay." Michael looked thoughtful as he sipped his drink through a straw. "Do you think it's all going to be over tonight?"

Zane shook his head once. "I don't rightly know, buddy. It depends on what ole Millie has planned, and we're in the dark there. We've just gotta be patient and let the hand play itself out." He snorted. "And hope like hell she's bluffing about having an ace up her sleeve."

Chapter 12

"Hustle woman, I buzzed James in the front—he'll be up any second now!" David called through the closed bedroom door.

He gave a low whistle as Kelly emerged from her bedroom. "Look at you, all glamorous."

She blushed and looked down at her white, raw silk dress. It was sleeveless and dipped into a V in the front that gave her just the right amount of cleavage—not so much that she'd look like a girl gone wild on spring break, and not so little that she'd look like a nun on a pilgrimage. She'd accented it with turquoise jewelry. The dress ended a little above her knees, and she'd left her lightly tanned legs bare. Strappy silver sandals adorned her feet. "What? Is it too dressy? I thought it struck the right balance between looking desperate to impress, and so casual it looked like I didn't care."

"You look perfect." David soothed her. "And you did your hair all va-va-vavoom."

She touched her hair self-consciously. "Somewhere between desperate and not caring lies 'come and get me'."

A firm knock sounded at the door.

"I'll get it!" David offered with alacrity.

"Be nice," she warned.

David turned and flashed her a smile before he opened the door. "Aren't I always?"

He threw open the door to reveal James on the other side.

"James Flynn, as I live and breathe. Good to see you, man."

****

James shook the hand David extended. "You, too, David." He looked the handsome man over and felt glad he was gay—otherwise he'd be jealous of the man's close relationship with Kelly. He grinned. "You look exactly the same. Have you got a portrait aging for you in the attic or something?"

"Oh, Kelly, I like him. Keep him around for a while, okay?"

James turned to look at Kelly for the first time when David spoke to her, and he felt like the wind had been knocked out of him. She looked gorgeous. Her dress was fitted to accentuate all her curves, but not too tight. And she'd styled her hair in a tousled way that vividly brought back every teenaged Brigitte Bardot fantasy he'd ever had.

When he could get his voice working he said, "Wow. Kelly. You look amazing."

She blushed and peeked at him from under her lashes. "Thanks. You don't look half bad yourself."

He looked down at his dark wash jeans, a crisp white shirt, and wheat-colored linen sports coat. "Thanks, but I bet Ellen is going to tell me I should've dressed up more."

David perched on a stool by the island that divided the kitchen on the right from the rest of the living room on the left. "I'm just glad I won't be the only one in jeans tonight. I rode my bike down, so I couldn't bring anything that would get too wrinkled in my bag."

"Cool. What do you ride?" James asked with interest.

Before David could answer, Kelly interrupted, "On that note, I'm going to go put on my lipstick and get my bag, and then I'll be ready to go."

James moved toward her with purpose and put his hands on her bare shoulders. "I better get this in before you do the lipstick thing."

He lowered his head to capture her lips in a brief, but meaningful kiss. He pulled back and Kelly swayed a little on her feet, with her lips still parted and her eyes closed.

David broke the moment by saying, "Since I just have my bike here I'm assuming we're taking your ride tonight, James? Or do we all have to pile into Kelly's silly little clown car?"

Kelly opened her eyes and her mouth formed an "O". "I hadn't thought about that. We won't fit in your car, James. I guess we'll have to take mine." She swung her head around to glare at David. "Notice how I'm ignoring the rude clown car comment for the sake of keeping the peace."

David grinned at her and spoke to James, "What do you drive that we won't fit in?"

"A 1960 Corvette."

David looked impressed. "A classic. I'd love to take a spin in that baby sometime, but I guess it's the clown car tonight." He looked hopeful, "Unless you want to take me in the 'Vette and let Kelly go in her own ride."

James laughed at both David's suggestion and Kelly's outraged expression at it. "Actually, we're set. My agent wanted me to show up in style, so she arranged a limo for us. It'll be downstairs in a few minutes."

Kelly sighed with relief. "Good. I won't have to listen to David bust on my car all night." She went into her room and called over her shoulder. "I'll be back in a minute."

David's smile faded as he rose to put himself on equal footing with the standing James. He spoke in a quiet voice, so Kelly wouldn't overhear, "We don't have much time, so I'm going to cut right to the chase. It seems like you turned out to be a good guy. Cool car, too, which I sincerely hope I'm not about to blow my chance to drive someday."

He took a deep, fortifying breath and continued, "I love Kelly more than anyone on the planet. She's been the best friend I could ever ask for. She's stood by me through thick and thin, so believe me when I say, I'd kill for her." He glared at James. "Literally. You've got kind of a reputation as a ladies' man, so I'm a little leery of you with my girl. Just know if you hurt Kelly in the least little way—even if you just cause her to get a hangnail—I'll hunt you down to the ends of the earth and make you pay in the most painful way possible. We clear on that?"

"You've grown up to be one scary s.o.b., Taylor," James said, allowing awe and amusement to mingle in his tone. "But Bill beat you to the 'hurt Kelly and get your ass kicked' speech."

David grimaced and snapped his fingers. "Damn. I was more menacing than Bill, though, right?"

"Totally. He only threatened me with an ass-kicking, not death as hangnail revenge." James grinned. "Seriously, David, I'm glad Kelly's got a friend like you, and I don't intend to ever hurt her. She means a lot to me. I want to take care of her—cherish her, not hurt her. My past history with women is less than stellar, I admit, but Kelly is special. I want to give her everything she deserves."

To be everything she deserves.

"Good. See that you mean it," David said, and then gave James a winning smile. "So, now that's out of the way, I've got to ask—can I drive your Corvette sometime?"

"Sure. Next time you're down this way. What do you do for a living in L.A.?"

"I'm a cameraman. Right now I'm working on a new HBO series."

James nodded appreciatively. "What a great job."

"Being an AV Club geek in high school paid off for me," David joked as Kelly came back into the room, her lips freshly glossed, and with a small, silver evening bag in her hand.

She rolled her eyes. "Oh, please, not the high school geek reminiscences."

James looked at his watch. "We'll have to save this trip down nerdy memory lane for another time. The car should be waiting for us."

Kelly looped an arm through each of theirs. "Lucky me. I've got the two best-looking dates all to myself tonight."

David laughed. "The gossip rags would have a field day with our little *ménage à* geek."

Kelly's smile faltered. "Bite your tongue, David. James and I have both worked really hard to be successful in our chosen fields, but maintain some degree of privacy."

"No worries, Kel," James said as he opened the front door and stepped back to let Kelly through first. "This is for a local charity. The San Diego media will probably give it a little coverage, but nothing major. Ellen isn't expecting any national news outlets there."

****

When they pulled up in front of the gallery a short time later, James and David hopped out before Kelly, and both turned to help her out. She swung her long legs out as she let the two men each take one of her hands, as she tried to emerge as gracefully as possible from the limo. If she couldn't manage graceful, she issued a fervent prayer against flashing the photographers waiting on the sidewalk to record the moment for all posterity. Merriment danced in both their eyes as they acted the part of her faithful swains, and Kelly tossed back her head and laughed with pure joy.

James tucked her hand in the crook of his left arm, and David loped along on her other side. James patted her hand and said, "See. Just a couple of photographers. Probably from the San Diego Union Tribune. No big deal."

She smiled up at him. "You were right."

Ellen rushed up to them as they entered the gallery. She looked glamorous in her chic black dress. Diamonds at her neck sparkled in the gallery's lighting. She had a glass of champagne in her hand and a pleasant-looking sixty-ish man at her side.

"I'm glad you're here early. It will give us a chance to get situated before the hordes arrive. Kelly, this is my husband, Saul Markowitz. He just got in from New York today."

Kelly shook his hand. "Nice to meet you."

She gestured to David. "Ellen, Saul, this is my friend David Taylor."

David greeted them politely, but his eyes drifted back to the dark, handsome man behind the couple from New York, who was looking back at him just as intently.

Ellen followed his gaze. "Oh, Enrique, this is James' date Kelly Lynch and her friend David Taylor. This is Enrique Martinez. He owns the gallery."

He took Kelly's hand, but his chocolate brown eyes were only for David. When the two men shook hands, he flashed a grin, his teeth white against his olive skin. "May I show you around before everyone else gets here?"

"Sounds great," David said almost before Enrique finished speaking.

As they moved away, Kelly said with mock regret, "So much for my two hot dates. It looks like one of them might have his eye on someone else."

James took two champagne flutes off a waiter's tray and handed one to Kelly. "You'll just have to make do with me." He winked at her. "And I only have eyes for you."

A slight commotion at the door heralded the arrival of Steve and Daphne. Hot on their heels were Grace and Bill. While Kelly and James introduced their friends, the gallery began to fill up with the other guests.

By the time Janie and her husband Greg arrived, a crush of people filled the big, airy gallery. The sound of so many voices speaking at once bounced off the gleaming wood floors and white walls.

When Janie made her way to Kelly's side, she had to raise her voice to be heard above the din. "I'm sorry we didn't get here sooner. I know you wanted to talk to me about something. There was an accident on the 5 and the traffic was dreadful."

"It's okay," Kelly shouted back. "We can talk about it at brunch tomorrow. You're coming over, right?"

"Wouldn't miss it." Janie beamed at her friend. "Your James is really talented. Greg and I are going to walk around and look at all his work. It's realistic, but there's a magical quality to it, too."

James appeared at her elbow, as Janie walked away. "I can't get over how many people are here."

"It seems like all of San Diego jumped at the chance to see our famous reclusive artist," Kelly teased.

He flushed and frowned. "As long as they're ponying up for the youth art program, I can put on a happy face for one night."

Kelly patted his cheek. "My brave hermit, facing his adoring public for the greater good."

Her words had their desired effect as he shook off his embarrassment and laughed at her joke. She looked around and asked, "Do you know where the restroom is?"

He pointed behind her. "Down that hallway. I learned this all-important fact when I was here with Lydia's art class this morning."

She laughed and kissed his cheek. "You are a keeper. Try not to miss me. I'll be right back."

****

He watched with what he feared was a goofy smile on his face as she wended her way through the crowd.

He didn't know what he'd done to deserve a second chance with this amazing woman, but he was going to do his damnedest not to blow it. She might have been joking, but damned if he wasn't going to miss her in the next few minutes. Having her at his side was making this event a lot more tolerable.

At the sound of shrill female voices, and the clatter of what sounded like a battalion of high heels on the polished wood floor of the gallery, he turned to find himself surrounded by women. And not just any women, he realized with dawning horror, all women he'd dated in the past. He looked around frantically for Kelly and caught a glimpse of her white dress and sexy, tousled hair as she disappeared down the hall to the restroom. Damn it all to hell, it looked like he was on his own.

He pasted a false smile on his face and turned to the pack of his former girlfriends. "Ladies. I hope you all came prepared to make a generous donation to a good cause."

****

A few minutes later, Kelly came out of the ladies' room. She was so proud of James tonight. The charity exhibit was a huge success, and their friends were all getting along as if they'd known each other forever. She'd been nervous about the whole evening, but it appeared her nerves were for naught—everything was going really well.

Kelly scanned the room, looking for James, and her heart sank when she spotted him surrounded by what had to be a dozen of the most gorgeous girls she'd ever seen. She was at least a decade older than the oldest one.

She'd felt beautiful tonight, especially after she'd seen James' jaw drop when he'd looked at her for the first time, but looking at these girls, with their miles of leg and pert breasts barely covered by their glittery, little cocktail dresses, she felt positively frumpy in her chic, but definitely more modest, white dress.

James smiled, but was she just kidding herself by thinking it was a little too bright to be sincere? It was probably just wishful thinking on her part. What man wouldn't be thrilled to be the center of attention for so many beautiful women? She chuckled to herself. Actually, she could think of two men here tonight who wouldn't be. David and Enrique seemed to have eyes only for each other since they met.

She sensed someone step up next to her and turned to see Saul Markowitz. She smiled gamely and jerked her head toward James and his harem. "Wow. Were they lying in wait for me to leave before they pounced? I just ran to the ladies' room for a minute and he's been swarmed by supermodels."

Saul's eyes crinkled and he said with a New York accent that managed to be even thicker than his wife's, "They're showy, I'll give you that. Like orchids, but you remind me of those little wild violets we have at our place in the country."

Kelly furrowed her brow. "Wild violets? I'm sorry, but I don't understand."

"Ellen and I have a weekend place in Connecticut. There are all sorts of beautiful flowers in the garden that require around-the-clock maintenance from our landscaper—roses, lilies, peonies, but my favorites are these little wild violets that grow in the yard. I suppose technically they're weeds, and the other flowers might demand your attention, but if you look closely, these little violets are the most exquisite things there."

He patted her back in a fatherly manner. "The smart man looks for the violets. And James is nobody's fool."

She could tell the exact moment when James spotted her—relief was clear on his face as he extracted himself from the women and headed for Kelly and Saul with determination in his stride.

Saul looked from James to Kelly. "And it looks like he's just found his wild violet."

Kelly felt the tension in her shoulders ease as he weaved his way through the crowd to her. He kept his eyes trained on her as he moved to her as if she had a homing beacon aimed directly at him.

She really needed to lock her inner dork in the closet the next time she felt insecure about her appearance. She might not be as glamorous as these girls, but she was attractive, funny, and smart, and she was the one James had chosen to be by his side tonight. Not any of them.

"There you are, Kelly!" James exclaimed. "Hi, Saul. I don't know what the hell that was all about. Every one of those women claimed my assistant called them today to invite them here."

Kelly gave the awkward geek within a slap on the wrist for the pang of jealousy she felt over James having his assistant invite other women here when he'd said he wanted to be with her. Wait—assistant? What assistant? He'd never mentioned one before.

She drew her brows together and said, "I didn't know you had an assistant."

"I don't. Which begs the question, who the hell

invited a pack of my ex-girlfriends to come here tonight? And more to the point—why?"

****

Zane popped up in an alley around the corner from the gallery. He shook his legs to ease his starched and pressed dress jeans down over his cowboy boots. He'd had no idea what to wear to a shindig like this one, so he opted for dressy jeans, a western style shirt, and bolo tie. On his head he wore a snowy cowboy hat, as a way to thumb his nose at Mildred who always referred to him as a "white hat". He hoped his clothing choices wouldn't make him stick out too much, but if Uriel wanted someone more polished, someone who'd be at ease in this setting, then he should've picked another guardian angel for the job.

He turned the corner, handed his invitation to the man at the door of the art gallery, and stepped inside, where the crowd and the noise instantly overwhelmed him. The din of so many conversations taking place at once buzzed like a swarm of cicadas.

Mildred was not in sight, but that didn't mean she wasn't here. There were so many people he couldn't even find James and Kelly, and he knew they were around somewhere.

Kelly's friend David was talking to a good-looking Hispanic man over by the bar. Zane noticed David wore jeans with a shirt and tie also, and was satisfied his own clothes wouldn't draw too much attention. Guardian angels were supposed to keep a low profile.

A gaggle of women shrieked and Zane turned to see what was happening. The women surrounded James and all talked at once. He shook his head in disgust. This little situation had "Mildred" written all over it.

She probably hoped to cause trouble between Kelly and James by bringing in this troupe of trollops.

He elbowed his way through the crowd to get closer. When he was near enough to hear the women, he was even more positive the fallen angel had arranged this scenario. They all claimed a woman who said she worked for James had called to invite them to the exhibit as James' date. At least now he knew who Mildred had been on the phone with all day.

Before he could intervene to help James out of his predicament, the artist had broken free of the group and fought his way to Kelly's side. Zane followed him, but unfortunately so did his pack of "dates". There had to be ten women here, and Zane wasn't sure if he had a strong enough angelic mojo to influence so many people at once. He wished Michael could be here with him, because he'd have a chance at getting things under control with a second angel to help.

One of the women attached herself to James' arm and cast a dismissive glance in Kelly's direction. "Is this woman your assistant, James? She can straighten all this out."

The woman then addressed Kelly as if she was an inconsequential minion. "Tell them that you called me today for James, and invited me to come tonight as his date."

The rest of the women exploded in an outraged babble as they pressed closer to Kelly and demanded she admit that she called them.

James wrenched his right arm away from the woman on his right and wrapped his arms around Kelly in a protective manner. Drawn by the hubbub, David, Enrique, Steve, and Daphne all came over and helped to form a defensive cordon around James and Kelly as the women's behavior became more mob-like.

James raised his voice to be heard above the cacophony. "Kelly is not my assistant. Leave her alone."

"Who is she then?" one of the women demanded with her hands on her slim hips.

James and Kelly responded in unison.

"I'm his date."

"She's my girlfriend."

They turned their heads sharply to look at each other. Each one looked a little surprised by the other's response. They blurted out, again simultaneously.

"I'm his girlfriend."

"She's my date."

Steve rolled his eyes in exasperation. "Oh, for Pete's sake. She's his girlfriend, ladies. His very serious girlfriend. So back the hell off."

One petulant woman refused to be put off. "If they're so serious, why did his assistant tell me he couldn't wait to see me tonight?"

Her question got the group of women, who'd been somewhat subdued by Steve's statement, all riled up again. The babble of their angry voices grew louder and more shrill.

James shouted to be heard, "I don't have an assistant!"

David emitted a loud, high-pitched whistle between his teeth, which silenced the irate mob of women. "That's enough! Someone has obviously played a cruel prank on you ladies. Clearly, James didn't invite you here as his date, so show a little pride and take a hike."

Enrique feigned a cough to cover his laughter at

David's blunt suggestion and grabbed a tray of champagne from a passing waiter. He smiled. "Ladies, please have a glass of champagne. Enjoy the exhibit and support youth art programs here in San Diego County."

Appeased by the free drinks, and Enrique's charming manner and rakish good looks, they each stepped up to grab a champagne flute from the tray.

Kelly and James took advantage of their distraction to ease away from the crowd.

Zane heaved a sigh of relief. Crisis averted and he didn't even have to get involved. If this was the best Mildred had to offer, Michael would be moving on to the next plane very soon.

He allowed himself to relax and took a glass of champagne. Things were under control, so he figured he might as well take a look around at James' paintings and enjoy the night.

****

James pulled Kelly into an alcove, shielded from the room by a potted palm. He gathered her into a protective embrace and rested his chin on top of her head.

"Are you okay?"

She felt the comforting thud of his heart where her cheek was pressed against his muscular, warm chest. She closed her eyes and nuzzled against him.

"I'm fine. Although, I did think I was going to be the victim of an angry all-bimbo lynch mob for a minute there."

She felt, more than heard, his answering rumble of laughter.

"Quick thinking on Enrique's part to lure them

away with free booze," James said.

"And with his Latin-lover good looks. Good thing they haven't figured out yet that he's playing for the other team, and they don't stand a chance with him." Kelly chuckled. She twisted in his arms to smile up at him.

James cocked his head, "I couldn't help but notice you looked a little freaked out when I called you my girlfriend. What's that all about?"

She lowered her eyes. "I didn't want to seem presumptuous."

He took her gently by the shoulders and hunched his lanky frame down a little to look her straight in the eyes. "After last night, how could you have any doubts about how I feel or what you mean to me?"

"For a lot of men, sex doesn't necessarily mean anything. Plus, you do have a bit of a reputation as a man-about-town, and then we got hit with the bimbo brigade." She raised her chin. "I don't think it's unreasonable for me to have questions."

He heaved a deep sigh. "No, I guess it's not. I'm sorry that my past has made you feel this way. My timing could have been better last night, and you might think I just blurted it out in the throes of passion, but I meant what I said. Kelly, I lo—"

Sounds of further commotion from the gallery floor interrupted him, and it was with real annoyance that he asked, "What in the hell is going on now?"

Kelly peeked around a palm frond. "I'm not sure. It looks like the press just got here en masse."

They stepped out from the alcove and saw a platinum blonde in a red sequined dress, which could generously be described as being the size of a handkerchief. A non-descript middle-aged woman and a wall of reporters and photographers flanked her. Her eyes, heavily rimmed with eyeliner, lit up when she saw James.

She exclaimed with obvious glee, "James, there you are! You naughty boy, what are doing hiding behind that plant?" She threw open her arms. "Come, give me a kiss!"

James grew pale and gulped. "Tracy? What are you doing here?"

Kelly whipped her head in his direction. She went from feeling mildly amused at what she thought was another old girlfriend lured here under false pretenses, to dismayed when she realized who the newcomer was. "Your ex-wife, Tracy?"

He tried to smile at her, but it came across more like rictus. He injected a light tone into his voice, but it still sounded strained. "Just when you thought the night couldn't get any weirder, huh?"

Tracy launched herself into James' arms, and the press closed in around them. Kelly blinked in the sudden, blinding glare of flashbulbs as the photographers clicked away at Tracy as she latched on to her ex-husband's very unwilling lips.

Kelly muttered under her breath, "What was it you said about the night not getting any weirder?"

Chapter 13

"Damn it all to hell," Zane exclaimed at the fresh commotion around Kelly and James. He looked around for somewhere to put down his glass and saw Michael.

"What are you doing here?" He hissed the words. A couple of people gave him perplexed looks and edged away from the crazy cowboy who appeared to be talking to himself.

"Chill. I'm non-corporeal. Only you can see or hear me. Well, you and Millie over there."

Zane moved closer to Michael and his voice was little more than a breath. "I should've known she had more planned than all the old girlfriends. What's happening now?"

"She brought James' ex-wife here, just like we expected. But all this press arrived at the exact same time, so I'm thinking she tipped them off."

"Look at that swarm around them. They're like locusts," Zane said with disgust. "How do we get rid of them?"

Michael looked thoughtful. "Too bad there's no one more famous in town right now—like that Natalie Seattle girl."

"Who's she? And why would that help us?"

"James and Kelly aren't mainstream celebrities. You've got to know about art or books to have heard of them. If there were someone more famous around, the press would leave to chase after them. And right now that teenaged pop star, Natalie Seattle, is as hot as you can get."

Zane's eyes narrowed and the right side of his mouth quirked up. "I've got it covered."

He surveyed the mob of photographers and reporters until he spotted a likely prospect. He snaked his way through the crowd until he was at the man's side and addressed him in a stage whisper. "Hey, man, I'm surprised y'all are here for these two-bit celebrities. Especially when Natalie Seattle's out on the town tonight."

The photographer's eyes gleamed with interest and he turned to block his potential tip source from his competitors. "I didn't know about Natalie, my friend. Where did you hear she's in San Diego?"

Zane shrugged. "I was at a club over in the Gaslamp District before I came here, and she was there."

The photographer leaned in; his eyes alight with interest. "Are you sure it was her?"

"Positive. Although I didn't know she was old enough to drink, and she was tossing back margaritas like they were water. Just before I left, she grabbed some guy who looked to be at least thirty—way older than her anyway—and pulled him up on the bar to dance—or at least what kids call dancing nowadays. It looked more like sex with clothes on to me. All that bumping and grinding."

"Thanks, dude! I owe you," the photographer exclaimed after he secured the name of the club from Zane and bolted for the door.

News spread like wildfire among their ranks, just

as Zane intended, and soon all the press had deserted the gallery.

The guardian angel now had a clear view of Mildred across the room, and he tipped his hat to her in an old-world manner. Mildred narrowed her eyes and her scowl was fierce as she strode toward him.

Michael flitted over and said in awe. "That was great! How'd you do it?"

"I'll tell you how he did it," Mildred hissed with barely-contained fury. "He lied."

Michael's mouth fell open and his eyes widened. He asked with disappointment in his voice. "You lied, Zane?"

"Like a rug," Mildred spat out. "Not very white-hat behavior, in spite of his current head gear."

Zane shrugged with apparent indifference, but when he spoke to Michael his eyes begged his friend's forgiveness. "I wanted them out of here. Fast. So I might've told them Natalie Seattle was causing a scene at a bar nearby." He dropped his eyes and continued, "That she was drinking and carrying on with a man."

Mildred regarded the cowboy angel with grudging admiration. She pursed her thin lips and inclined her head. "This round goes to you, I admit it, but don't think it's over. I'm going after the press to try and lure them back here."

Her small eyes darted around, and when she saw no one was watching, she made herself invisible to the humans and rushed out to the street, where she unfurled her dingy wings and took flight.

Michael watched her with disgust. "I better go after her." He gestured between Zane and him. "But this, between us, isn't over."

His friend lowered his eyes and looked at his boots, which he scuffed on the floor. Michael shook his head and patted Zane on the back.

"I know you were trying to help me, and it did work like a charm. But lying? And about a girl who's just a kid. I can't approve of your methods."

"I'm sorry. I felt like the ends justified the means," Zane explained.

"We'll talk about it later. I've got to catch up with Millie before she can do any more damage tonight." Michael frowned and raced after the fallen angel.

****

Tracy looked around with a moue of disappointment, and Kelly was relieved to see the woman had lowered her leg from where she'd hitched it up on James during her fervent embrace.

"Where'd all the photographers go?" Her bee-stung lips pouted, and if the Botox had left her capable of movement, her face would have fallen.

Kelly shrugged. "I heard one of them say something about Natalie Seattle and dirty dancing. I guess we're small potatoes compared to her."

James extricated himself from Tracy's grasp, through a complicated series of moves that would make a pretzel proud. He smoothed out his sports coat where she'd been clutching it, and stretched his hand out to Kelly with a loving smile.

"Kelly, this is my ex-wife Tracy Blackburn. Trace, this is my girlfriend, Kelly Lynch."

Tracy whipped her head around so fast, Kelly was afraid it might pop right off her neck. She looked Kelly up and down with disdain. "Girlfriend? I didn't know you had a girlfriend."

James pulled Kelly into his side and ran his hand over her hair. "Why would you know? We've barely spoken to each other since our divorce was finalized years ago."

Steve and Daphne walked up, and as Steve issued a chilly greeting to Tracy, Daphne went to Kelly and pressed a glass of champagne in her hand. "Here you go, sweetie. I thought you could use a little fizz right about now."

Tracy ignored Steve and watched the women's exchange with narrowed eyes. "Sweetie? You never called me 'sweetie' back in the day. As a matter of fact, it was pretty clear you couldn't stand to be around me. Now, you and James' *girlfriend*," she spat out the last word with obvious distaste, "are BFFs?"

Daphne shrugged. "She's a writer, I'm a librarian. We have more in common than you and I ever did. But there's something else, too. What is it?" She paused as if trying to remember something and then hit her forehead with the heel of her hand. "Oh, yeah. I knew there was another reason Kelly and I are friends, and you and I never were—Kelly's not a gold-digging whore out to ruin my best friend's life."

Steve chuckled. "Good one, babe." He held out his fist to his wife, which she promptly bumped with her own.

Tracy clenched her hands so tightly her knuckles were white. As she took a breath to shoot back an angry retort, James spoke up to diffuse the situation. "Where's your husband, Trace? Is he here with you?"

She took a breath to calm herself and flashed a blinding smile at James. "Nope. Arnold's back in New York." She tiptoed her fingers up James' chest and said flirtatiously, "It's just little old me, here all by myself, rattling around in that big hotel suite all by my lonesome."

Kelly tossed back a hearty swig of champagne. She knew there was no reason for her to be jealous of Tracy, but she couldn't help but let the green-eyed monster rear its head. She saw James look at her with the hint of a smile, and returned it with a wave of her champagne glass.

Tracy followed his gaze to Kelly, and she could tell the other woman was trying her damnedest to hide her irritation at this unexpected girlfriend development. Tracy brushed some imaginary lint from James' shoulders and forced a smile on her face. "I'd heard you hadn't been serious about anyone since we split up. I sort of hoped that meant you were..." Her voice trailed off as James' jaw dropped to the floor.

"You thought I was pining away for you, Tracy?" He shook his head and snuck a glance Kelly's way. "I'm sorry, I'm not trying to be hurtful, but if you came all this distance because you felt that way, then you deserve the truth—you were never the woman I pined for."

Tracy's blue eyes were bright with angry tears, but she seemed determined not to let them fall. She pressed her glossy, red lips together in an obvious attempt to keep her emotions in check, and the impossible happened at her transparent show of dismay—Kelly actually felt sorry for the woman. Tracy had clearly come here to try and win back James, and she was just realizing there was no way that was going to happen.

While she did feel some sympathy for Tracy, Kelly also felt relief wash over her as she realized that

Tracy's dismay meant James had chosen her. She thought about how she would've felt if the tables were turned and she was in Tracy's expensive shoes. It would be awful to be rejected by James. and especially to have it happen so publicly. Given the circumstances, Kelly could afford to be magnanimous. At least she could make the situation a little less of a public display for Tracy.

Kelly touched Daphne's arm. "With all the hubbub tonight, I haven't had a chance to walk around and look at the artwork. Will you two show me around?"

Steve and Daphne exchanged a look that made it clear they were both reluctant to leave the scene that was about to unfold, but Kelly linked arms with Daphne and led them away.

"Why'd you do that?" Daphne whispered. "I wanted to hear."

"Me, too," Steve chimed in.

"I know, guys. I'm sorry, but she looked so crestfallen that I felt bad for her, and I thought it might be easier if they could have this conversation without me there. It looks like she's going to be hurt enough without the added embarrassment of having it happen in front of James' girlfriend and two people who are clearly not her biggest fans."

"You're a way nicer person than I am," Steve said with a disbelieving shake of his head.

Kelly tucked her hand in his elbow. "I seriously doubt it. Now, tell me all about Charlie's latest antics."

As she intended, Charlie's doting parents couldn't resist her interest in their beloved child. and launched into a story about him.

****

"But I was your wife. How can you say something like that to me?"

James looked sympathetic to her pain, but didn't want to give her false hope. "I didn't mean to hurt you, but I haven't been pining for you. Hell, we both know our marriage was a mistake, there's no sense trying to rewrite history and turn it into some great love story."

"Maybe the mistake was splitting up," she suggested in a small voice.

James' eyebrows shot up so high he was afraid he might have to peel them off the ceiling. "What? No. Splitting up was the only thing we got right."

She pouted in what he remembered was her best seductive manner, designed to get him to do whatever she wanted him to do. "That's not true. Think about all the good times we shared. We loved each other."

"We were too young when we got married, and I think we got love and lust mixed up," he disagreed.

Wounded pride infiltrated and sharpened her voice. "What are you trying to say? You never loved me?"

"We *never* loved each other, Tracy. Let's be honest."

She gasped. "How can you say that?"

He shrugged. "You cheated on me and left me for another man. At the time you were pretty honest about your motivations, and they had nothing to do with love and everything to do with money."

Her mouth opened and closed like a fish on a dock.

James didn't understand why his words would trigger this reaction. Tracy had always been a practical woman, and he didn't think she had any romantic illusions about their marriage. As far as he knew she was perfectly content in her loveless marriage to the rich old coot, but if that were the case, why would she be here in San Diego putting on this big show with the press in tow? And why would she be so angry at his having a girlfriend?

A reason for her behavior occurred to him, but it was so outside the realm of his own nature his first instinct was to dismiss it out of hand. But knowing Tracy as he did, James had to admit it wasn't all that crazy an idea. His eyes narrowed as he looked at her face. "What's this all about? Are you having trouble with Arnold and thought you'd hedge your bets with me, since I'm not a starving artist anymore?"

His supposition must have been a little too close to the truth for her comfort. Her eyes widened and with a sharp intake of breath she hauled off and slapped his face. "How dare you say something so insulting to me? You do realize you just implied I'm a whore, don't you? How dare you!"

She reached back to slap him again, but Kelly appeared and pushed between them to press a cool hand to his inflamed cheek. He suspected he had a red mark in the shape of Tracy's talons on his face.

David and Enrique hurried over, and David grasped Tracy's wrist to prevent her from getting another shot in on James. It seemed, in spite of their efforts to act like they were doing otherwise, all of his friends had been keeping a careful eye on the scene with his ex.

Enrique frowned. "James, I'm appalled something like this happened in my gallery. Would you like me to get the police here so you can press charges against this woman?"

"Press charges? What the hell are you talking

about, Chico?" Tracy shrieked.

David's grip tightened on her arm and she winced. He growled in a low voice, "Now you're going to start with racist bullshit on top of everything else? His name is Mr. Martinez, as in the Martinez Gallery, where you are currently a guest, and I would assume the charges he meant involve assault."

James laid his hand over Kelly's on his face. "I don't want to press charges, Enrique. This is a personal matter, and things just got a little out of control."

Enrique looked at him for a long moment and then turned to Tracy. "In that case, Madam, I'm going to have to ask you to leave my gallery. I'll allow you to go on your own if you can behave. If not, I'll have security escort you out."

Tracy wrenched her arm out of David's grasp, and snapped her response at Enrique although her eyes never left Kelly and James. "I'll leave your pathetic little gallery."

At her harsh words, James and Kelly turned to face Tracy. He was expecting to see her winding up to keep the tirade going, but was surprised to see Tracy speechless, with a sort of shocked recognition on her face as she looked at Kelly. And hatred. Lots of hatred. He felt Kelly shiver and knew she saw the same emotions on his ex-wife's face. He didn't understand her expression at all—she had never met Kelly, as far as he knew, and he didn't believe for one moment that she still loved him—if she ever had—and he couldn't imagine anyone hating the kind, intelligent woman by his side.

Enrique gestured discreetly for security, and Tracy's glare followed his movement. "No need for security. I said I'm leaving and I am."

She tossed her head, raised her chin in the air, and left with whatever dignity she could salvage.

Enrique smiled apologetically at James. "I was on my way over here to let you know it's time to give your spiel about the youth art program and get our guests in a donating frame of mind. Would you like a few moments before we do it?"

James shook his head. "No. I'm fine. A little embarrassed, but fine. Let's go raise lots of money. The least all these people can do is cough up some cash after the floor show I just gave them."

****

As the limo pulled up in front of Kelly's building, David grinned. "I've got to say James, you really know how to throw an event for charity. Usually those kinds of parties are one big snore-fest, but this was certainly a night I'll never forget."

"That was my goal," James joked as he folded himself out of the vehicle and turned to help Kelly out.

David pounded him on the back. "I'm going to head up now and give you crazy kids a chance to say good night. Kelly, can I have your key?"

She pulled it out of her silver evening bag and handed it to her old friend. Then she took out the key card to the entrance and slid it in the slot to buzz him into the building. "I'll be up in a minute."

"No hurry. See you at brunch tomorrow, James. Hey, do you think any of your women will be there?"

James hugged Kelly and smiled. "Only one of them, God willing."

He watched David enter the building and then pressed his lips to Kelly's forehead. "I'm so sorry about everything that happened tonight. It was nuts."

"It was all pretty out there, but none of it was your fault, so no apology needed."

"I don't suppose there's any chance I can convince you to spend the night with me tonight?" James asked as he swiveled his hips against Kelly's where their embrace joined them.

"Don't tempt me. David's my guest, and I can't abandon him. Besides, I have a houseful of people coming for brunch tomorrow. I'm going to have to get up at the crack of dawn to start cooking."

"You can't blame a guy for trying. Can I bring anything tomorrow?"

"Just yourself. I've got it under control."

"It was really nice of you to invite my friends to come, too."

She grinned deviously. "Or very tricky of me. This way I get all the inside dirt on you from the people who know you best."

"Then I'm in serious trouble." He winked. "Although, one good thing about tonight is that I don't have very many skeletons left in my closet."

Kelly laughed and stood on tiptoe to kiss him. "Good night, James. I'll see you in the morning."

He returned her kiss and stepped up the passion. He teased her lips open with his own, and she parted them for him and moaned as his tongue tangled with hers. He pulled back and said, "Just a little something for you to think about tonight when you're in your cold, lonely bed."

"Tease," she quipped as she put the keycard into the lock. The front door opened with its grating sound and she strolled through.

James called after her. "I'm only a tease if I don't intend to follow through. And I fully intend to follow through at the first possible opportunity."

She turned around and walked backwards, blowing him a kiss as the doors shut behind her.

As he watched her stroll to the elevator, James let out a whoosh of air, and muttered, "After last night, I thought my cold shower days were over. Guess not."

****

Zane left the gallery after Kelly and James departed. Uriel stepped out of the shadows and frowned at him.

"You lied tonight, Zane. Deliberately and maliciously. You know my rules about lying, and you did it anyway."

Zane took off his hat and ran his hand through his coal black hair. "I did. I'm real sorry, Uriel. I thought it was the fastest way to get the press away from Kelly and James."

"You took the easy way out, Zane, and I'm disappointed in you."

Zane hung his head. "I'm sorry, sir. I'll take my punishment."

"I'm going to have to add time onto your service to me, and as it is, you won't be moving on to the next plane anytime soon. Don't you want to?"

"I don't know; I like it here on Earth. And I feel like I'm doing good. I did a lot in my lifetime to atone for, and I don't rightly think I'm done yet."

"That's not for you to decide. The big guy thinks you could move on, but you keep shooting yourself in the foot."

When Zane didn't reply, Uriel waved his hand in

frustration. "Fine. When this assignment is over, I'll have another one for you."

"Thank you, sir."

Michael flew up the street to them. He landed and tucked his downy wings away. "Hi, Uriel. Mildred didn't have the juice to control all those photographers. They're all still looking for Natalie Seattle."

"And where is Mildred now?" Uriel asked.

"Last I saw of her she was heading back to the hotel. Tracy called to tell her she'd left the gallery and was grabbing a cab to the Hotel del Coronado."

Uriel pursed his lips. "I can't help but think this wasn't Mildred's whole plan. There's got to be more coming. So, I want you two to stay on this case for a little longer."

"Fine by me," Zane said.

"Me, too," Michael agreed. "I hate to sound like a broken record, but I want to be good and sure Kelly is safe from the fallen angels before I move on."

Chapter 14

James was just leaving his condo to go to Kelly's for brunch when his cell phone rang. He recognized his sister's ringtone and answered. He held the phone to his ear with his left hand and locked his front door with his right.

"Hey, Becky."

"Please, God, tell me you're not getting back together with that evil bitch."

"Nice greeting, Becks; do you kiss your children with that mouth?" He chuckled into the phone.

"I'm sorry, James, but when I saw the picture of that slut hanging all over you I flipped out, and Dad's not happy either."

James stepped into the empty elevator with a perplexed look on his face. "Whoa. Slow down. What are you talking about? You don't mean Kelly, do you? Because, trust me, she's not a slut."

"Kelly? Who's Kelly? I mean that piranha of an ex-wife of yours! Imagine my horror when I walked by a newsstand this morning and saw your picture on the front page of all the rags, with Tracy all over you like a cheap suit. Dad saw it online and called me in a panic to see if I knew what was going on, since it was too early for him to call you with the time difference, so I promised him I'd call you as soon as I could."

James got out of the elevator in the lobby. He

forced a grim smile at the security guard as he passed by the desk and walked out to the sidewalk. He stopped and leaned his back against the building with one leg bent at the knee and his foot flat against the wall.

"I am so not getting back with Tracy. She ambushed me at my charity exhibit last night and brought the press along for the ride. Trust me—I had no idea she would be there, and she was an extremely unwanted guest."

Becky heaved an audible sigh of relief. "That's good. You better call Dad and put his mind at ease. He was all for both of us flying out to California to knock some sense into you. That's why I wanted to talk to you first; I didn't trust him to just not start off with guns blazing."

"I don't know how you two thought I would even consider picking up where I left off with Tracy, but don't worry, I'll call Dad," he reassured her and then frowned. "What are the papers saying about me? Why would Tracy's scene last night be considered news?"

"Tracy's husband is one of the richest men in New York, and they've been having marital problems. They're big news here in Manhattan. The papers are calling them the Battling Blackburns. Today's article said Tracy was getting ready to dump Arnold and reunite with her ex-husband."

"Oh brother. No wonder you were scared. Believe me; it's not happening. I think that's why she came to San Diego, but pigs will be flying over the frozen tundra of Hell before I get back with Tracy."

"Glad to hear it. I don't think I could've stomached seeing her face across the family Thanksgiving table again."

She paused and continued, her voice all innocence. "Who's Kelly?"

The tension left James' shoulders and a smile spread across his face. "She's my actual girlfriend—Kelly Lynch. She was in your high school class, but she was Kelly Morrison back then."

"Kelly Morrison." Becky sounded thoughtful. "I think I remember her. Brown hair? Kind of shy? Smart?"

"That's her. She lives in San Diego now, too."

"Cool. So with the name change, I assume she was married. Is she divorced now, also?"

"Widowed, actually."

"How sad. She's young to have lost her husband."

"Cancer," James said shortly, by way of explanation.

"That's really awful," Becky sympathized, and then her voice brightened. "But at least now she's got a good guy in her life again."

"Thanks, Becky. I never really know what to do when you compliment me." He laughed.

"Oh c'mon. It's not that rare an event. You know I think the world of you. That's why the thought of Bitchzilla reeling you back in had my blood running cold."

"Get back to 98.6, little sister. Tracy's well and truly history."

He pushed off the wall and strolled toward Kelly's building. "I'm on my way to brunch at Kelly's. Can I call you back later?"

"Sure, but be prepared to tell me all about Kelly. And tell her I said 'hi'. If you're busy, I can give Dad a quick call to let him know we're safe. And you might want to look online at some of the trash they're writing. Best to be prepared in case you get ambushed by the press about it."

****

Mellow jazz music played in the background as David mixed a pitcher of Bloody Marys and Kelly bounced to the door to open it. She'd buzzed the building door open for James a couple of minutes ago, so it had to be him now. As she suspect, James stood on the other side of the door and dragged his gaze up from his phone to stare at Kelly. Normally, his face had a light, golden tan, but it was pale, his mouth tight and his green eyes were somber.

Her smile faded. "What's the matter? Bad news?"

He held the phone out to her in silence. She took it and waved him in, as she shut the door behind him and looked at the small screen.

"'*Ménage à trois*: Artists are different from you and me'," she read in bemusement. "Why are you showing me this article?"

The speaker box by her front door squawked. Without raising her gaze from the phone, she said absently, "David, would you please get that?"

As David pressed the button to buzz in her other guests, her eyes widened when she touched the screen to scroll down and saw the photograph that accompanied the story. "Oh. My. God. That's David, you, and me getting out of the limo last night."

The box emitted its harsh buzz again, and David pressed the button to open the door again, before walking to the kitchen counter to pour a drink from the pitcher there. He pressed the glass into James' hand and then peeked over Kelly's shoulder.

"They're saying the three of us are doing the wild thing?" David asked, his blue eyes wide and a huge grin on his face.

James took a swig of his drink and spoke for the first time since he'd arrived. "Yep."

Kelly bustled to her desk and booted up her computer. "I can't believe this garbage! How can they print these lies?"

As the computer started, she walked to the kitchen area to retrieve her Mimosa. She took a fortifying gulp and went back to sit at her desk. With a few keystrokes, she called up the news headlines.

She gasped. "Look at all the stories about us."

The two men stood on either side of her and stared at the computer, each one with a Bloody Mary clutched in his hand.

Kelly's eyes were locked on the screen, "How did you find out about all these articles?"

James rested his hand on her shoulder. "My sister just called—she says 'hi' by the way—in a complete panic that I was getting back with Tracy "

David gestured to the screen with his glass. "Well, 'Love Triangle: The Industrialist and the Artist Duke It Out for One Woman's Love' certainly seems to think you two are back on."

Kelly scrolled down the screen and read one of the headlines aloud. "'Love Quadrangle'? What does that even mean?"

David leaned over her shoulder and read. "'Which famous artist, author, businessman, and socialite are locked in a Love Quadrangle?'"

Someone knocked at the door and Kelly stood to answer, still staring at the computer in horror.

James hung his head. "I'm sorry, sweetheart. I know how much you value your privacy."

Kelly smiled weakly and squeezed his hand before walking to the door. "About as much as you value yours, I imagine. I know this mess isn't your fault, there's no need to apologize."

She opened the door to Ellen and Saul. Ellen's sharp eyes spotted the article up on the computer screen right away. "You've seen what they're writing."

James shook Saul's hand and gave Ellen a peck on the cheek. "My sister called from New York this morning. She said we're all over the newsstands there."

"Speaking as your business manager, remember that any publicity is good publicity." She patted his face fondly. "But speaking as your friend, I'm sorry. That woman is toxic. I'll be back in New York tonight, and I'll start damage control immediately."

The elevator dinged and the doors slid open to reveal a group of their friends, who poured in through the open front door. Kelly heard her telephone ring above the babble of voices and she rushed to answer it.

"Hello." She raised her voice to be heard and then shut her eyes in a long-suffering manner. She held the phone away from her ear, due to the angry yelling on the other end. When the voice on the phone quieted, she put the phone back to her ear.

"No, Daddy, 'that damned bohemian artist' did not talk me into participating in an orgy. I'm having people over for brunch, that's what all the commotion is."

Steve laughed at her words and pounded James on the back. "Way to get in good with the father, dude. He thinks you're luring his only daughter into a life of sleaze."

****

Michael and Zane, in their non-corporeal forms, watched the scene from Kelly's balcony. Steve's joke drifted through the open door.

"Her father doesn't seem happy about Kelly dating James. Could that be Mildred's game? To drive a wedge between Kelly and her folks?" Zane asked the other angel.

Michael shook his head. "I don't think so. Her dad is old school. I don't think he really has anything against James; it's just that for him, no one is good enough for his baby girl. Heck, we were married for years, and I think he still has himself convinced she's a virgin. The thought of any man touching his daughter makes him apoplectic."

Zane gave a rare chuckle and Michael continued. "But her mom's the voice of reason in their marriage. She'll see how happy James makes Kelly, and she'll bring Mr. M. around."

Zane hoisted himself up to sit on the railing of the balcony as he pondered the situation. "What's Millie's deal, then? Sure, Kelly and James are mortified by this kind of attention from the press, but it seems to be bringing them closer together. Not driving them apart."

"Maybe Mildred miscalculated," Michael suggested hopefully.

"Maybe," Zane replied. "Or maybe there's even more to come."

Michael eyes grew wide. "I better hunt Millie down and see what she's up to."

"Good idea." Zane jerked his head toward Kelly, who was still trying to reason with her father, and James, who stood beside her and rubbed soothing circles on her back. "I'll stay here and make sure these two don't go off the rails."

****

The amorphous gray shape floated in front of Mildred. The stench of sulfur filled her hotel room, until even an evil being like Millie wanted to hold her breath. She couldn't believe the big boss's right hand man was here to see her.

"I'm honored to have you here, Master," she said with what she hoped was proper subservience. "I've made this room safe. You're free to take your true form."

A deep, evil laugh emitted from the dark cloud like smelly steam belched from a smokestack. Mildred fought to keep from gagging.

"My true form is too horrible, even for one of my agents of discord to behold."

His voice was so deep that Mildred could actually feel it when he spoke. It felt like the vibration of the bass on a too-loud stereo system.

"Thank you for your consideration then," she said with unaccustomed meekness. "How may I serve you?"

"I'll tell you how you may serve me," the blob roared in obvious displeasure. "By not making a total hash of this Kelly Lynch-James Flynn case, that's how! I am not impressed with your work thus far."

If Mildred were still alive, her heart would be pounding out of her chest. The being before her was the first Lieutenant to the most evil entity in the universe, and she had caught his attention. And not in a good way. Her voice shook when she answered and she hated that show of weakness. "I'm sorry, Master. B-b-but I'm not finished yet. I've got more planned for them."

"I know all. You think I don't know what you're plotting?"

She twisted the hem of her shirt with shaky hands. "Of course you do. I'm sorry. I'll do whatever you like. Please give me guidance."

"You have delayed Zane's ascending to the next plane, so you haven't been a total failure." Her master's voice sounded somewhat appeased at her show of obeisance.

"Th-th-thank you," she stuttered.

"But you need to do more. I want to hit Uriel where it hurts, and he wants these insignificant humans together. Therefore, I want them apart."

Mildred blinked her eyes, which had teared up due to her fear and the foul odor, which surrounded the charcoal-colored form. "With all due respect, Master, I think the second phase of my plan will break up Kelly and James."

"You're wrong," he bellowed. "You've miscalculated. You're working from the assumption these two will react the way you would—the way any reasonably behaved evil being would react. But they won't. These two are full of goodness." He spat the out the last word as if it were something vile.

"How do you suggest I proceed?"

"Go ahead with Phase Two of your plan, but then you need to take a more active role, and use their goodness and consideration of others against them. Manipulate their actions; so that our goal is achieved by the two of them doing what they're convinced is right." There was an audible sneer in his voice.

Mildred's small eyes narrowed and a tight smile played at the corner of her mouth, as she thought of a way to use the couple's weaknesses against them. "Thank you, Master. I believe I now know how to proceed."

"You'd better hope so, little one," her master threatened. "Because if you don't succeed in this mission I will be most displeased. If Michael Lynch moves up the ladder of goodness, you will go down a rung on the ladder of evil."

She swallowed hard. "I'll do my best, Master."

His laughter echoed in the room, even as his smelly, gray mist dissipated. "If we were the praying sort, I'd tell you to pray your best is good enough. You don't want to even think about the repercussions for you if it's not."

****

The party was breaking up, and Kelly gave herself a mental pat on the back. It had all gone well, aside from the talk about the bad press James and she had received. Her food had been a hit, and their two groups of friends had rubbed along together well.

"This has been lovely, doll, thank you, but I need to call for a cab," Ellen said. "We've got to get to the airport."

"We can take you," Grace volunteered. "Bill's got a flight this afternoon, so I was going to drop him at the airport on the way home anyway."

David tossed back the last of his coffee, and moved toward the guest room. "I better get a move on, too. I've got to ride back to L.A."

Lydia looked at James and Kelly. "Don't forget about Tuesday."

Kelly hugged the girl. "We won't, sweetie. I'm looking forward to it."

"Me, too," James put his arm around Kelly and added with a kind smile.

"Me, three," Lydia chirped. "Imagine having a real, live artist take you to the museums at Balboa Park."

Daphne began to gather all of Charlie's baby paraphernalia together in an oversized diaper bag. She said with regret, "We've got to go, too. We have an appointment with our realtor to look at a couple of houses this afternoon."

"I love the house you live in now," Kelly said.

"Me, too," Daphne agreed. "But it's like a little dollhouse, and it's too small for us now that we've got Bonnie Prince Charlie."

As Grace began to tell Daphne about a house for sale on her street, Janie touched Kelly's arm and said quietly, "We haven't had a chance to talk yet. Do you want Greg and me to stay for a bit longer?"

Kelly nodded eagerly and whispered back. "Yes, please. There's something James and I want your opinion on."

****

Once everyone else had left, Kelly poured another cup of coffee for Greg and a Mimosa for Janie. Her friend accepted the champagne cocktail and settled on a stool expectantly. Kelly stood opposite her on the other side of the granite island next to Greg, and James took his coffee cup and sat next to Janie. Greg leaned back against the kitchen counter and smiled at his wife's barely contained excitement.

"Tell me. What's up? I can't imagine what you want my advice about."

"It's a little out there," James warned.

"Probably not too out there for my Janie," her

husband joked.

Kelly bumped Greg's shoulder with affection, and warmth shone in her eyes and explained to James. "These two are the classic case of opposites attract."

James looked from Janie to Greg with interest. He took in Janie's colorful, flowing dress, dangly earrings, and the assortment of bracelets she wore on her wrist, and then he compared them to her husband's light blue dress shirt and tightly creased trousers. Greg's gray eyes were intelligent behind their tortoise shell glasses. They looked like a gypsy and banker had wandered into the same party by mistake, but there was no mistaking the love and respect the pair shared for each other, in spite of their outward differences.

"You're not into the whole New Age thing, too?"

"Nope," Greg took a sip of his coffee. "But that doesn't stop me from supporting Janie in her beliefs."

Janie flapped her hands impatiently, which caused the bangles on her arm to clank together. "Enough about us. What's going on with you two?"

Kelly took a deep breath. "We want to pick your brain about angels."

Greg raised his eyebrows at James, who shrugged at the other man.

Janie bounced in her seat. "Angels? I've done a lot of research on them. What do you want to know?"

"We're interested in guardian angels. Do you think our loved ones who've passed on can linger here to guide us?" James asked.

"Absolutely," Janie stated with a confident nod. "Why do you ask?"

James cleared his throat and spoke sheepishly to Greg. "I think I met Michael in a bar, and he convinced me to find Kelly and re-connect with her."

"Michael?" Greg said with a healthy dose of skepticism. "Kelly's late husband, Michael?"

"This is *so* exciting!" Janie enthused. "Ignore Greg's negativity. Tell me everything."

Kelly and James recounted the whole story, tossing the parts of the tale between them like a beach ball.

"You two are so unbelievably cute together." Janie beamed when they finished talking.

"Angels, Janie." Kelly blushed and tried to get her friend back on topic. "Do you think it's possible Michael could be playing Cupid for us?"

"Sure. Everything you've told me is in line with all the instances of guardian angel intervention I've read about."

"And it's true to Michael's character," Greg interjected. He chuckled at their shocked expressions at his agreement. "I know I'm usually pretty dubious about this woo-woo stuff, but if Michael were going to hang around for anything, it would be to see Kelly happy and settled with a good man. He was always thinking about other people—what would make them happy—especially Kelly."

****

Kelly suddenly seemed absorbed in her Mimosa. She stared into her glass and a delicate flush bloomed on her cheeks. "Slow down, Greg. It's a little fast to have James and me settled down together."

Although it was clear Kelly was clearly trying to avoid eye contact with anyone else, James stared at her, and knew his heart was in his eyes, but couldn't do anything to control it. Was this just a fling for Kelly? A rebound to get over her late husband? For him it was so much more, and he'd thought it was for her, too.

"Every relationship has got to start somewhere," James said with quiet dignity.

Kelly slowly raised her gaze at his words to look at him. He saw confusion, apology, and sadness in her eyes, and feared what he'd been hoping was going to be his future, was about to become his past. God, he hoped Kelly was as ready to move on as he thought she was, because he didn't want to imagine his life without her again.

Intuitive Janie, with her gypsy soul, picked up on the change in atmosphere and put her glass down on the island. "We've got to leave now, but I'll email you information on guardian angels when we get home. Let me know if you have any questions after you read it."

Greg extended his hand to James, who tore his eyes from Kelly's face with reluctance to attempt a smile at the man. "Nice to meet you."

Kelly walked her friends to the door and kissed them both. "Thanks for your help, Janie."

James kept the forced smile on his face. "Thanks, Janie. I'm looking forward to reading what you send, and thanks also for believing what I said and not trying to send me to the loony bin."

As the door closed behind the couple, his smile faded. "Your reaction to what Greg said leads me to believe we need to have a talk about our relationship."

Chapter 15

Kelly's smile was a little too bright and didn't reach her eyes as she brushed past James to bustle into the kitchen. "I hope you can dry as you talk, because there are a ton of dishes to do. I don't like to put the crystal in the dishwasher, so I've got to do all these glasses by hand."

He followed her and took the striped dishtowel she handed to him as she babbled on and filled the sink with hot, soapy water. James tossed the towel on the counter, and he interrupted her steady flow of chatter. "I risked my membership in the Dude Club by using the phrase 'let's talk about our relationship'. I wasn't expecting to get the brush-off from you about it."

Kelly stopped talking, but didn't turn around to face him. Instead, she took a glass and plunged it into the sink and began to wash, as if it took all her attention. "You belong to a Dude Club?" she finally asked, her voice full of false cheer.

He shrugged and winked. "Not really, but don't let Steve know. He thinks I'm the treasurer. He's the president, of course. It means a lot to him."

She laughed, but it was devoid of humor. She reached for the dishtowel he had cast aside and spread it on the counter next to the sink. She rinsed the glass and put it upside down on the towel to dry. As she reached for a second glass, James took her by the shoulders and gently turned her to face him.

He left his hands on her shoulders, and she held her soapy hands up in the small space between their bodies. "Do you want to tell me why you got so flipped when Greg talked about us like we're a couple?" he asked softly.

She lowered her gaze. "I'm sorry I reacted that way. I could tell it hurt your feelings."

"Hell, yeah, it hurt. I told you I love you. Not counting my sister and my mother, I've said that to a grand total of one woman besides you."

She looked up slowly, disbelief clear on her face. "That's hard for me to believe."

"It's true. My ex-wife is the only other woman I've said it to in a romantic sense, and now I realize what I felt for Tracy wasn't love. It doesn't compare to what I feel for you. I know you loved Michael, and I don't want that to change, but it wasn't the same in my marriage." He paused, and his voice was low and gentle when he continued, "Is your love for him why you reacted that way to Greg?"

She sighed. "My feelings for Michael are part of why I reacted that way. Everything is happening so fast, and sometimes it still feels like I'm cheating on him."

"I get that, really I do, but even if he isn't my guardian angel, from everything your friends have said about him, I think Michael would be happy for you. For us."

He didn't want to think too much about Michael as it filled him with unaccustomed feelings of inadequacy. If the tables were turned, he wasn't sure he'd be nice enough to share Kelly with another man. There'd been a moment earlier today when he was standing by the window talking to Steve and Bill. He'd looked across the room and saw Kelly laughing with Janie and Grace, and he was filled with a fierce possessiveness he'd never felt before for any woman. *Mine,* his inner alpha male had growled.

He didn't doubt the depth of Michael's feelings— he clearly loved Kelly—but he thought the other man had to be on the fast track to sainthood to try and fix Kelly up with him.

She nodded and wiped her hands on her cotton shorts. "I know he would. Those feelings are only part of it. There's a huge part of me that's just waiting for you to get bored with me and move on. I can't believe you love me, because you're…well…you."

He looked confused. "What do you mean?"

She blushed to the roots of her hair. "Okay. Confession time. You're James Flynn. I can still remember the first time I met you."

"Me, too. We were at Becky's graduation party."

"Nope." She shook her head. "It was during recess in elementary school. I was a little, nerdy first grader. I already wore glasses, and you were a big, cool fifth grader. Some older boys were picking on me—calling me names like 'four-eyes'—and you made them stop. I think I fell a little in love with you then and there."

"I'm sorry. I don't remember it."

"No reason for you to remember. You were just being yourself, and helping a little kid who was being bullied, but for me, it was a huge event. I had a crush on you for years. That's one of the reasons I got so scared and ran when we went out when I was eighteen."

James looked deep into her eyes and thought about her words. Finally he said, "And I fell a little in love

241

with you when I was twenty-two, but please don't let all that history stand in the way of us again now. Don't get scared and run." His mouth quirked up. "This time, I'll know what you're doing and chase you. I'm not letting you get away again."

She grinned at him sheepishly. "I'm trying to be a grown-up, I really am, but that little four-eyed first grader is still inside me, and she keeps saying there is no way James Flynn could love her."

"But I do. Love you. Look, I'm enough of a Dude Club member that it's hard for me to talk about this kind of stuff. Guys aren't very good with being verbal about their feelings."

"I've always thought that was a cop-out. Some men are excellent communicators."

"There are a couple of notable exceptions, I'll give you that. Like Shakespeare and Browning. But most of us regular twenty-first century guys have trouble with the words. We do better at showing those feelings physically. That's why I blurted it out the way I did when we were in bed—it was all I was feeling and all I was thinking. Before I knew it, the words just flew out of my mouth. I've been afraid that you thought it was just a heat of the moment thing, and that I didn't mean it. Because I really, really do."

"That thought did cross my mind," she conceded. "Especially since you didn't say it again until now."

He caressed her arms, and then took her face carefully in his large hands, as if she was made of precious china, and he was afraid of breaking her.

"Let me love you," he whispered and lowered his head to brush his lips ever so softly against hers. "Let me show you how I feel about you. Let me love you."

Kelly's breath was uneven when she whispered in response, "'Kay."

He looked over her shoulder to her bedroom. "Do you feel comfortable doing this here or do you want to go to my place?"

Her brow furrowed. "Here is fine. I'm not sure I'd make it across the street before I spontaneously combusted. Why wouldn't I be comfortable here?"

"You lived here with Michael. This is the bed you shared. I just thought…"

"But it's not," she interrupted. "Toward the end, he needed a hospital bed, so we got rid of ours and got one for him and a twin bed for me. I bought this bed for myself after he passed. Here is fine, but thank you for thinking about that. You're almost too good to be true."

He shook his head ruefully, reminded of his earlier thoughts about Michael. He really feared he wasn't nearly good enough for the amazing woman who stood before him with her soapy hands and trusting eyes so full of love. "I'm no saint, Kel. I just want this to be about you and me. I want you to be as much in the moment as I am."

James rubbed his cheek against her silky hair before he picked her up in his strong arms and carried her to the bedroom.

****

Zane watched from the balcony and rasped out a laugh at Kelly's surprised squeal when James lifted her up and strode away with her. For an anxious minute there, he was afraid she was going backwards and was about to shut James out, but the man didn't let her. He managed to make things right, even without Zane's angelic interference.

Not wanting to intrude on the couple's private interlude, he decided to hunt down Michael to see what he'd learned about Mildred's plot.

He flashed to the Hotel del Coronado, where he found Michael in the hall outside Millie's room. A foul aroma of sulfur lingered in the air, where it mixed with the familiar scent of the carpet cleaner that all hotels seemed to use. He wrinkled his nose against the stench.

"Smells like Millie had herself a pretty powerful visitor," he observed.

Michael grimaced. "I thought this stink was way more potent than Mildred's usual odor."

"The bigger the evil, the fouler the stench."

Michael held his nose. "Then this has to have been one of their top guys, because, man, I've never smelled anything this rotten before."

Zane jerked his head to the door. "Is she in there?"

"No. I was just trying to see if I could sense who had been here with her. She's with Tracy in her suite, but she's put up an even stronger block. I can't get in or even hear a thing they're saying."

"She isn't a high enough level fallen angel to keep you out. I wonder if her aromatic visitor gave her a little extra juice. Let's go to Tracy's suite and see if I've got any better luck at breaking down her wall of silence."

****

Once in Kelly's bedroom, James lowered the shades against the afternoon sun. It dimmed the light in the room, but left enough of a soft glow through the ivory shades that he could still see Kelly. He wanted to be able to watch her while he showed her with his body how much she meant to him. He moved toward her with quiet purpose, and when he reached her, he slowly unbuttoned her blouse and pressed a light kiss to each piece of skin the button had previously covered.

Kelly sighed in contentment and reached for the hem of his polo shirt to try and lift it over his head.

James playfully twisted out of reach and said, "Uh, uh, uh. This is about me loving you. Not the other way around."

"But…" Kelly began to object.

He grinned. "Later I won't give you any argument if you want to love me, but right now I'm going to show you just how much I love you, in the best way I know how."

He'd reached the last button on her shirt and ducked his head down to press a kiss to the soft flesh of her stomach. He teased her navel with his tongue, and then straightened up to his full height. He pushed the shirt from her shoulders and nuzzled her neck, where her pulse pounded in her vein. Without missing a beat, he reached down to unfasten her shorts.

Once he had her completely undressed, he threw back the covers of the bed and eased her onto it. He nudged his shoes off, but remained in his jeans and polo shirt as he stretched out beside her. His hungry eyes took in the sight of her displayed on the sunny yellow sheets.

He smiled in satisfaction as he ran one large hand from the swell of her breast to the curve of her hip. "Beautiful. You're so unbelievably beautiful, Kelly."

She blushed at his praise, and he was interested to see the color wasn't only heightened on her face. Very interesting parts of her body turned a rosy pink as well.

"I can see you're going to need a little convincing." He kissed her nose. "I think I'll start here, with your adorable nose, and work my way down to your cute little toes."

****

Zane stood a few feet back from the door to Tracy's suite. Michael watched with interest as the angel closed his eyes in deep concentration and slowly extended his hand in the air between him and the door. There was an audible noise, as if an invisible bug zapper had been triggered. Zane's eyes shot open, and he jerked his hand back.

"I feel like less of a lightweight now since you can't get past her barricade either," Michael said in a pleased tone of voice to the more experienced angel.

Zane glanced at him out of the corner of his eye. "That's good, because I exist to make you happy."

"No need for sarcasm. I know it would be better if we could get into the suite, but I felt like a loser before. I can't help but feel better that you can't do it either."

The door jerked open without warning, and Mildred stood framed in the entryway with an amused tilt to her narrow lips.

"Don't feel too good, rookie. The cowboy came a lot closer to breaking down my barrier than you did."

Zane inclined his head. "This is a new low for me. Having a fallen angel defend my abilities."

"Millie, is that room service?" Tracy's voice trilled from another room in the suite.

"Not yet. It's just a couple of guys from the company I'm auditing. They'll be gone soon," Mildred called over her shoulder.

"Tracy sounds awfully cheerful," Michael observed.

Mildred shrugged noncommittally in response.

"What's she got to be so happy about?" Zane pondered. "Her second husband is getting ready to dump her, and her first husband rejected her advances last night. What could possibly have her so chipper?"

"Something that will warm every fallen angel or shallow woman's heart. Revenge," Mildred replied with a cocky grin.

"Revenge against Kelly and James?" Michael asked, unable to hide his concern.

"Yep," Mildred said with satisfaction. "Who else would it be against, Einstein?"

Zane narrowed his eyes. "Just what are you up to, Millie, old girl?"

"That's for me to know and you to find out." Mildred stuck out her bottom lip and said with false contrition, "That wasn't a very mature response, was it? I'll make it up to you and give you a little hint. Be sure James and Kelly watch *The Intrepid Inquiring Reporter* tomorrow night on television."

Zane looked puzzled, as he didn't keep up with television shows.

Michael asked, "That entertainment news program?"

Mildred nodded happily. "That's the one. It should be a really informative episode." She waggled her fingers at them. "'Night boys. Give my love to Uriel."

The door slammed in their faces.

"What do we do now?" Michael asked.

Zane shrugged. "I don't know about you, but my clothes reek of fallen angel stink. I'm going to zap myself some fresh duds and go get a beer. Not much else we can do tonight."

****

All of her bones felt like they'd melted into liquid. Kelly had never felt so relaxed and sated in her life. James was a man of his word. He'd used his talented mouth and clever fingers to love every inch of her body.

She opened her eyes to see him lying next to her on the bed. He was still fully dressed and propped up on an elbow facing her. The grin on his face held a hint of smugness and was full of pure masculine satisfaction.

"You look awfully pleased with yourself," Kelly teased.

"Oh, I am. There's nothing a man likes more than making his woman scream in pleasure."

Kelly felt her cheeks heat up and said defensively, "I did not scream."

"Yeah. You did," he disagreed with a cocky grin. He looked so pleased with himself Kelly couldn't help but feel a burble of joy in her chest. He might be James Flynn, her idealized childhood crush, but right now he was just her man, and he was filled with satisfaction at her pleasure, but it wouldn't do for him to get too full of himself.

"So, have I convinced you yet that I love you?"

She tilted her head and tapped a finger on her chin before she answered, her eyes wide with feigned innocence. "I don't know. I think I might need a little more convincing. I'm not absolutely positive yet."

James reached for her and heaved a playful sigh of weariness. "A man's work is never done."

Kelly rolled just out of reach. "Sorry. It's my turn."

Heat flared in his eyes. "Your turn for what?"

She pressed against him and they both shivered a little at the sensation of her bare body on his fully clothed one. Her hand slipped between them and slid the button of his jeans open, with her other hand, she tugged the hem of his polo shirt up. "It's my turn to love you. You said you wouldn't give me any argument if I wanted to love you after you had your chance to love me."

She rubbed her soft lips on his hard abdomen, as she continued to lift his shirt.

He grinned and raised his arms above his head to facilitate the removal of his polo shirt. "No argument here. Do you hear me arguing?"

Kelly tossed his shirt aside and ran her fingers down his torso. She followed the tempting trail of dark blond hair back down to his jeans. She drew the zipper down and he raised his hips to help her pull off his pants and briefs.

She looked up the length of his body at him, the corners of her mouth tilted up "So very helpful. I like that in a man."

His laugh ended with a sharp intake of breath as she took him in her mouth. His voice sounded a little strained as he quipped, "I'll do whatever I can to help you do that, whenever you're so inclined—never say I'm not helpful."

****

Kelly gasped as she squinted at her alarm clock. "I can't believe it's six o'clock at night already!"

James kissed her shoulder, "You know what they say, time flies when you're having fun, and boy, did we ever have fun."

Kelly's smile was a little shy as she remembered their afternoon. First, James had convinced her of his love. Then, she'd convinced him of hers. Finally, they'd convinced each other.

She glanced over her shoulder at James and noticed he looked like a cat with a half-gallon of cream in front of him. She nestled her back against his front and felt a stir of responding interest in his body.

"Tempting as you are, and believe me darlin', you are tempting, I've got to call my dad before it gets too late in New Hampshire."

Kelly looked at him in disbelief. "Do you always call your father after spending the afternoon in bed with your lover? Because, if so, that's just creepy."

James snaked his arm around her waist and reached up to cup her breast. He breathed into her ear. "My lover. I like the sound of that."

He flicked his tongue in her ear and nipped gently at her lobe, before he pulled away from her with obvious reluctance. "But I promised my sister I'd call Dad today. According to Becky, he was scared shitless I was about to bring Tracy back into the Flynn family fold."

"Oh, that poor man," Kelly said with sympathy. "From what I've seen of Tracy, that would be a terrible scare for him."

James sat up and retrieved his shirt, which hung rakishly from the bedpost. "Damn! My cell phone is dead."

"Do you want to use my phone?"

He thought and then shook his head. "That's okay. I think I'll run home to call him. That way, I can grab some of my stuff and come back here to spend the night. If that's all right with you?" he concluded anxiously, as if he was worried that he might be overstepping a boundary by asking to spend the night.

Kelly murmured and stretched in satisfaction. "You spending the night here is more than all right with me. We might need to convince each other some more."

"Are you hungry? I can grab some Chinese carryout from the place on the corner on my way back."

Kelly sat up too and pulled the sheet up to cover herself modestly. "An afternoon like we just spent, and you'll bring me a spring roll? You are close to being the perfect man."

He grinned as he pulled the shirt over his head and leaned out of bed for his jeans. "Close to being the perfect man? If I promise to bring back dumplings, too, will that push me over the edge to perfection?"

She pursed her lips as she considered the matter. "You're going to Ming's?" She mentioned the restaurant on the corner of her block in a tone of great gravitas.

He replied with a smile, "Where else?"

She nodded as if she'd come to a great conclusion. "Throw in their Pork Lo Mein, and you are officially Mr. Perfect."

Chapter 16

"I can't believe you were going to have Floyd and Betsy stage an intervention." James stood next to his bed. He had the cordless phone propped between his ear and shoulder as he tossed clothes into a duffle bag and listened to his father's response. "Dad, I swear to you, I'm not getting back together with Tracy. You can't believe everything you read."

He stopped packing and switched to using his hand to hold the phone as he listened to his father's anxious ranting. When his dad paused to take a breath, he cut in, "The Lesters are right. I'm dating someone who's not Tracy and she's great. She's from Rye even."

James threw back his head and laughed. "Betsy didn't lie to you. Kelly is not, in fact, a trollop, but she is waiting for me to bring dinner to her place, so she's probably a hungry non-trollop right about now. I'll talk to you soon, Dad. And please, stop worrying. The Flynn family is officially a Tracy-free zone. She's Arnold Blackburn's headache now."

He paused as his father spoke and replied with warmth in his voice, "I love you, too, Dad."

****

Kelly finished washing up the brunch dishes and placed the last glass upside down on the towel on the counter to dry. She smiled as she thought they looked like little crystal soldiers all in even rows. She shook her head and wondered where that odd image came from—jeez—one afternoon of good lovin' and she was getting soft in the head.

She padded into the living room on her bare feet. After James left, she'd thrown on the pajamas he liked so much when he saw her on the balcony last week. She'd changed from her contacts to eyeglasses, too. Might as well give him the whole fantasy naughty librarian look. If he was getting dinner for them from Ming's it was the least she could do, since it really seemed to float his boat.

****

Unseen by Kelly, Michael had popped into the living room in his non-corporeal form. He'd been deliberately keeping his distance from her, in case she could sense his proximity and it would keep her from moving on with her life, but he just needed to see for himself that she was doing all right.

He watched as she picked up the framed photograph of the two of them on the sailboat.

"Hey, Michael."

He jumped at her words, afraid that she could see him. Then he realized Kelly was talking to the picture.

"Everyone keeps telling me you'd be happy I'm seeing James now, but I'm not so sure. I wish you could tell me it's okay with you, because a part of me still feels guilty."

"For Pete's sake, Kel! You and the guilt. You'd think you were the one raised Catholic and not me. I'm fine with you dating James—I even set it up for you to meet him again."

The photo fell from Kelly's fingers, and clattered to the hardwood floor. All the color drained from her face. She whispered, "Michael? Is that really you?"

"Crap!" he cried out when he realized he hadn't properly shielded his presence and that his voice had been audible to her

Kelly whipped her head around to where he stood next to her desk, and he knew that she'd just heard him again—double crap! But her eyes darted right over him, so at least he could take a little comfort in the fact that while she could hear him, she definitely couldn't see him. One fewer of Uriel's rules broken, anyway. Jeez, at this rate, he was going to be on this plane as long as Zane, with his repeated flouting of the rules.

"Okay. That was definitely you, Michael. Although 'crap' is not the most angelic word I've ever heard. You're here, aren't you? And you're an angel now."

Michael screwed his eyes shut and pounded his forehead with his fist. What the heck, he'd already broken two cardinal rules of Uriel's Guardian Angel Corps—he'd allowed himself to unintentionally be heard by a human, and he'd cussed. Although crap was barely a swear word, in his opinion, but he knew Uriel would feel differently about it. If he was going to get into hot water for those two things, he might as well go for broke and let Kelly hear him one more time.

"I've got to go now, Kelly. Someone's waiting for me." She didn't have to know it was a dead cowboy, and he was waiting for Michael in a bar. "I just want to ask you to, please, let yourself be happy. It's what I want for you. Ease up on the guilt, baby, you're not doing anything wrong by being with James. Okay?"

She blinked back tears, and Michael was unsure if she was crying because she was sad or happy. Maybe it was a little bit of both.

"I'll try to be happy, Michael; I've been so lonely without you that I have to admit I'd like to have someone in my life again, but I've been feeling guilty about you. Thank you for letting me know how you feel. I love you. So much."

"Me, too, baby. That's why I want what's best for you. Live your life and fill it with joy. For me."

With those words he left the room and went to meet Zane at the bar where the cowboy had told him he'd be drowning his Mildred-induced sorrows. Thinking about the possible repercussions of what he'd just done, he needed a beer, too.

****

Kelly almost jumped out of her skin at the knock on the door. She exhaled shakily and went to open it. James stood on the other side with an overnight bag and a sack of yumminess from Ming's.

"That nice Mrs. Schwartz we saw from the party this afternoon let me in the front. Sorry if my knocking startled you." He rustled the bag and grinned. "I come bearing Lo Mei! Am I Mr. Perfect yet?"

Kelly stood on her tiptoes to kiss his cheek. "You sure are."

He smiled at her, but she could tell his happiness gave way to concern when he looked down into her face.

"Have you been crying? What's the matter?"

She pulled the door shut behind him and locked it. "I am crying a little, but they're mostly happy tears. The weirdest thing happened while you were gone, but I'll tell you all about it over dinner."

****

"Uriel is going to be so pissed." Zane whistled

softly through his teeth and took a swig from his longneck bottle of beer. The neon signs over the bar cast a reddish glow to his dark good looks. It made him look more like a fallen angel than the non-descript Mildred ever would, but Michael knew the goodness Zane kept hidden in his heart and wasn't fooled by appearances.

Michael sat next to him, hunched over the bar. "I know, man, and just in case that's not bad enough, I let her hear me, and then I said 'crap'."

Zane squinted at him. "So? What's the big deal about crap?"

"It's a swear word. And you know how Uriel feels about swearing."

Zane's eyes opened wide. "It is?"

Michael lifted his head to give his friend a well-duh expression. "Yeah. It is."

The cowboy shrugged. "Well, shit. It's not much of a cuss word."

"Zane! Why do you do that when you know it'll get you in trouble with the boss?"

"Just now, I did it to see you make that face. You got all red and your eyes looked fit to pop out of your head. It's funny."

Michael chuckled reluctantly. He looked around as he spoke to make sure no one could overhear their conversation, but the blues music booming from the jukebox made his worries unnecessary.

"Okay, I can see where it might be a little amusing, but it's not worth it for you. You keep getting time added on before you can move on to the next plane."

"It was worth it for me, because I got a laugh out of you when you were feeling like crap just now. Don't worry about me, buddy, I don't do anything I don't want to do."

"You really are a good friend. I'm glad I picked you to help me get Kelly and James together." He paused and took a drink from his beer bottle. "But now you said 'crap', too. And worse."

Zane shrugged. "I took a calculated risk, just like you did. And, who knows, maybe Uriel won't know what you did tonight."

Michael looked dubious. "I'm not going to count on that happening. He doesn't miss a trick." He signaled the bartender for two more beers before he continued. "What do you think we should do about the *I.I.R.* thing Millie's got cooking?"

"*I.I.R.*, what's that?"

"You know. *The Intrepid Inquiring Reporter*."

At Zane's blank look, Michael continued with a hint of impatience. "That television show Mildred wants James and Kelly to watch tomorrow. I've been thinking, if Mildred wants them to see it, maybe we should try to prevent them from watching it."

Zane leaned his elbows on the sticky bar and slowly shook his head. "I see your point, but if it's more of the same kind of garbage that was printed about them in this morning's newspapers, it might be better to have them see it. It would keep them from being blindsided like they were today."

"I guess so," Michael said with uncertainty.

"I admit it does go against the grain to give Mildred what she wants, but I think it will protect Kelly and James in the long run."

"A 'knowledge is power' kind of thing?" Michael asked.

"Yeah, pretty much. If Tracy is going to be talking smack about them on national television, they need to know about it. Then they're in a better position to fight back."

****

James popped the last of his egg roll into his mouth and chewed it thoughtfully. He swallowed and said, "Wow. That's just...wow."

Kelly sat on a stool by his side at the kitchen island, where they were enjoying their takeout from Ming's as she recounted her odd experience. James had pulled his stool close enough to hers that she could feel the warmth of his thigh pressed against her leg.

She put a dumpling on each of their plates and said, "I know. Trust me, I wouldn't tell just anyone that I had a conversation with my late husband—not unless I wanted to get carted off in a straightjacket, but I knew you'd understand, with all the guardian angel stuff we've been talking about."

He took a sip of his soda and bumped his shoulder against hers companionably. "I've talked to your dead husband, too. If they're taking you away over this, I'll be in the padded cell next to yours."

She laughed and clinked her glass of diet cola against his in a toast. "Good point. So, you believe it was Michael I heard tonight?"

His face grew serious. "I do. And not just because I've heard him, too."

Kelly interrupted, while she dunked her dumpling in its sauce. "Technically, you did more than just hear him. You saw him. Had a cocktail with him. Cocktails with an angel might get you into an extra special padded cell."

James rolled his eyes in mock annoyance, but his grin gave him away. "My point was, that I would believe you anyway, because I trust you. You can tell me anything, and I won't have you carted away." He dunked his dumpling in the ginger-soy sauce. "Although, that courtesy is not a two-way street, I guess, with your talk of my special padded cell."

****

The next evening, Kelly tapped away on her computer and chuckled at the sound of James singing in the shower with more spirit than talent. She hadn't realized how lonely she'd become until she had another person around.

It had been nice to share the day with someone. Of course, it was almost noon by the time they were able to drag themselves away from each other and out of her bed. And she realized she'd missed the physical connection with a man more than she thought, too.

Beyond the sex, it was fun to eat leftover Chinese food for breakfast with James. And while she always enjoyed spending time by the rooftop pool in the summer, it was even lovelier today with someone by her side. No. Not just someone. It was having James by her side that made it special.

Suddenly aware the shower had turned off and James had stopped singing, she turned around to see the object of her reflections watching her from the bedroom door. James rested his shoulder against the doorframe and all he wore was a white towel tied around his lean waist. His blond hair looked darker when it was damp; it matched the tempting trail leading to the terry cloth.

He grinned at her and said, "I really wish you had joined me in the shower. I missed you in there. I was lonely without you."

"I'm not sure I believe you. The singing sounded downright cheerful."

He laughed and then said with joking suspicion, "That looks an awful lot like work you're doing on that computer, Mrs. Lynch."

Kelly sighed. "The real world calls. I just thought I'd check my email, and my editor had gotten back to me about some revisions to my manuscript, so I need to get started."

"Tonight?"

She grinned. "No, not tonight. And we can still go to Balboa Park with Lydia tomorrow, but after that I'm afraid my vacation is over."

James went into the bedroom and pulled on a pair of shorts and a T-shirt. "I suppose it was inevitable. Our little bubble world together couldn't last forever."

Kelly nodded, as she watched with regret as he covered all that tight, tan, yummy flesh. She shook her head once to clear it and said, "Oh, and I heard from my agent, too. Believe it or not, she's thrilled with all the publicity we're getting. She thinks she can use it as leverage in negotiations with my publisher when my contract is up."

He came back in the living room and flopped on the sofa with a grimace. "Ellen implied the same sort of thing to me. But she sent me a text a little while ago—the gossip about Tracy, Arnold, and us…"

Kelly held up a finger to interrupt him. "And David. Don't forget David. What's that—a love pentagram?"

James chuckled. "At what point does it just become the orgy your father thought we were having yesterday when he called?"

"I'm not sure what the rule is to qualify as an orgy. I've led such a sheltered life." Kelly shook her head sadly, but then winked at him.

James smiled back. "Regardless of the official orgy rules and regulations, Ellen said there's some politician involved in a sex scandal in New York, and she thinks that will take the heat off us in the press."

Kelly sighed. "I'm sorry someone else is having problems, but heaven forgive me, if it pushes us off the front page of the tabloids, I can't feel too bad about it."

"Me either," James confessed and then changed the subject to something more cheerful. "Did you get anything fun in your email or was it all just work and spam?"

Kelly nodded. "I heard from David, and he's coming back down this weekend. It seems Enrique asked him out to dinner on Saturday night."

James raised his eyebrows. "Enrique Martinez? From the gallery? He's a good guy."

"He better be, because David only deserves the best."

****

Zane appeared in the kitchen, although Kelly and James couldn't see him. According to Michael, that *I.I.R.* show came on at seven and it was almost time. He knew his fellow angel still had reservations about Kelly and James watching it, but Zane felt strongly that the two humans needed to know what they were up against.

The cowboy focused his attention on James and caused him to have a sudden desire to watch television.

James picked up the remote and asked Kelly, who was in the process of logging off her computer. "Mind if I put on the TV? I haven't seen the news in a couple of days."

"Except for the trash about us we saw online," Kelly corrected with a chuckle. She moved to the sofa, and curled up next to James as he clicked on the television.

The local news was just ending and the anchorman said, "Stay tuned for *The Intrepid Inquiring Reporter*. There's a San Diego connection on their program tonight, as the ex-wife of a reclusive, local artist talks about what really broke up their marriage. You won't want to miss it."

Chapter 17

Kelly and James slowly turned to each other, their eyes wide as saucers and their jaws dropped.

"Please tell me you know of another local artist with an insane publicity-hound of an ex-wife?" Kelly asked hopefully.

James shook his head with regret and dragged his eyes back to the television set as the interview began. He reached out and took Kelly's hand as they watched Tracy talk to the chipper reporter.

Tracy was dressed in a somber-looking suit, which James suspected she had to buy for the interview, as most of her clothes were more suited to an off-duty stripper than the society matron she looked like right now. She appeared pale and wan, which had to be due to clever makeup application, as she'd been glowing with health and spray tan at the exhibit.

She dabbed delicately at her eyes with a tissue as the reporter brought up the subject of her first marriage.

"I realize now that my marriage to James didn't stand a chance from the start," she said in a fragile voice. "He was in love with another woman the whole time."

"You left me for a rich old man, you liar!" James roared.

On the television set, Tracy responded to the interviewer's prompt about the other woman's identity.

"Yes. It was the mystery author, K.M. Lynch."

Kelly groaned and buried her head in her hands as Tracy continued.

"She was with James at his charity exhibit on Saturday night. At first, I didn't recognize her, but then I saw her in profile and I knew," Tracy made her voice break in a pitiable way.

The reporter leaned forward eagerly and asked, "Knew what?"

"That she was the woman in James' painting *Love Awakens*."

"I'm not familiar with that piece." The reporter furrowed her brow.

Tracy shook her head as if she was afraid her fragile-looking neck would break if she moved too fast. "You wouldn't be. James would never sell it. Even when we were young and broke and couldn't pay our rent, he couldn't bear to let it go." She ended on a strangled sob and went on with wounded outrage. "It hung in our home—his portrait of his mistress."

"Mistress?" Kelly and James both shouted in disbelief at the blatant lie.

"But wasn't K.M. Lynch married, too?" The reporter tried to keep the grin from her face, but the gleam in her eyes said all too plainly that she was thrilled to be getting this scoop.

"Yes, her poor husband died a couple of years ago. I don't know if he ever knew about James and Kelly. It's so painful for me, that for his sake, I hope not."

Kelly's voice was low and dangerous. "There was nothing to know. I never cheated on my husband. That bitch! I can sue her for this, can't I? Libel, right? Or is it slander if it's spoken? Never mind, my lawyer will know."

The reporter smirked at the camera. "So, I guess James Flynn and K.M. Lynch aren't the hermits they always pretended to be. It seems they stepped out plenty with each other, as they had a long-running love affair, which spanned both their marriages."

She tossed it back to the host of *I.I.R.*, who managed to look like a basset hound at a funeral as he intoned, "That poor, poor woman. Imagine having to look, every day, at a painting of the woman who's stealing your husband's love."

He shifted gears for the next segment and brightened visibly. "And now, over to Tiffany, who's got the latest on Natalie Seattle's summer tour."

James lifted the remote and clicked off the television, just as their cell phones rang in unison.

They both ignored the ringing, and clutched each other's hands.

James looked deeply into Kelly's shell-shocked eyes and vowed, "I won't let her get away with this, Kel. I don't know how, but I'll set the record straight."

Tears filled and overflowed her intelligent, hazel eyes. "But you can't, James. Once something like that is out there, there's no taking it back—there are always people who are going to believe it."

He squeezed her hands and gently wiped a tear from her cheek. "Not the people who matter. They would never believe it about either one of us."

Their cell phones both began to ring again, and this time they were joined by Kelly's landline telephone.

"I can't talk to anyone right now."

"You don't have to, Kelly. Let the voicemail pick up." He paused and suggested nervously, "Do you want me to go home?"

Her jaw fell down and her eyes popped open. "No, of course not! Unless you want to go?"

"I don't, but I thought you might want me gone."

She crinkled her nose. "Why? None of this is your fault. The woman is clearly deranged."

"Yeah, but she's my ex-wife. You wouldn't have gotten dragged into any of this drama if it wasn't for me."

Kelly winked. "True, but you're worth a little hassle, and maybe this will blow over. People have very short attention spans nowadays." She continued sheepishly, "Plus, I don't want to give Tracy the satisfaction of having gotten between us. Petty, I know, but it's how I feel. I want you to stay here, and for us to spend the day at the museums with Lydia, just like we planned to do. How many people watch that trashy show anyway?"

Their phones all rang again and James replied with grim resolve, "It seems that most of our friends do, based on the steady stream of incoming calls, but you're right. Let's not let her win—we go on with our lives, and see what we can do to set the record straight about your marriage to Michael and why my marriage ended. Even if some people choose to believe the lie, we'll have done what we can to get the truth out there."

****

Zane watched James and Kelly come to this conclusion with satisfaction. Millie thought she was so smart, but it seemed like their love would beat out all of her hate-driven plans.

Michael popped in next to him. His face was red and his hair looked as if he'd been in a wind tunnel.

The reason for the hairdo became apparent when he ran his hands through it in an agitated manner. "Can you believe they can get away with running a program like that? I mean it's all lies!"

Zane smiled placidly and gestured to the couple snuggled on the sofa. "But they're not letting it get to them. Kelly mostly feels bad that your memory is being besmirched. Man, I wish I could've met a woman like her when I was alive."

Michael beamed. "She's one in a million, all right. I'm dead, why is she worried about me? I hate that people are thinking she's the sort of woman who'd cheat. She's so honest, it's not who she is at all."

"James pointed out to her the people who know her will know the truth."

Michael's eyes softened as he looked at Kelly and James. "He really loves her, doesn't he?"

"Yep. You picked a good man for her."

"Want to go find Mildred and gloat about her plan failing?"

Zane pursed his lips and nodded. "Sounds good, Mike. In fact, I'm surprised I didn't think of doing it already."

****

James brought in burgers from the grill on the balcony, as Kelly wrapped up a telephone call with Grace. "Seriously, we're looking forward to spending the day with Lydia. If we let this interview get us down, then Tracy's won, and it may be small of me, but I don't want to let her win."

He put the burgers on the granite island by their plates and pointed to them and mouthed, "Dinner's ready."

"James just brought dinner in from the grill, so I've got to run. But we'll come and get Lydia at around noon tomorrow. Will that give you enough time to get to your meeting?"

She listened and nodded. "Stop already. We'll be there. If you don't mind your daughter spending the day with two such notorious cheaters."

Kelly held the phone away from her ear, as Grace's loud voice seemed to indicate she'd taken exception to that statement.

"Kidding. I was kidding, Gracie. Seriously, I did not take any of this to heart. It hurt a little at first, but it's not true. And anyone who'd believe such horrible lies about us isn't really our friend in the first place."

She said her goodbyes and hung up the phone. "Yum. The burgers look great! Thanks for cooking them."

"Boys and briquettes, baby. You know none of us can resist the siren song of the grill."

Kelly laughed and pulled a couple of beers from the fridge and popped the caps off the tops. "I think these are in order tonight."

James took his and clinked her bottle. "Amen to that. You're a saint among women."

He took a long draw and said, "Ellen called while I was outside. She thinks we should do an interview together to get the real version of our marriages out there. What do you think?"

Kelly put ketchup and mustard on her cheeseburger and cocked her head as she thought before she said, "I don't know. I hate those kinds of interviews. I do book signings and some speaking engagements, and I like the online chat interviews my agent sets up with my fans, but those all involve talking about my work. I really don't like to sit down with a reporter and have her ask about my personal life."

She took a bite and said after she swallowed, "On the other hand, I don't want people believing bad stuff about Michael and you—neither of you deserve it."

He gulped down his mouthful to answer heatedly, "And you do deserve it? I don't think so. You're one of the most honorable people I've ever met. It bugs the crap out of me that some people are going to believe Tracy's lies about you. That's the only reason I'd even consider doing this interview; I don't care what people say about me."

Kelly took a swig of her beer. "We don't have to decide right now. Let's wait and see how this plays out, maybe the public won't care about a reclusive painter and a two-bit mystery writer, and this hubbub will all die a natural death."

****

Tracy clicked off the television in the living room of her suite and sashayed to the ice bucket, which stood on a room service cart. She poured a glass of champagne and raised it to Mildred in a triumphant toast. "I think that went rather well, don't you?"

Mildred took a sip from her glass. Man, this broad was a piece of work. She had no remorse about lying on a syndicated television program about two innocent people. When Tracy's time on earth was up, there was no doubt in Mildred's mind which direction the woman would be going. Down. Straight down. Do not pass go. Do not collect $200.

"You certainly said what you set out to say."

"I wish I could have worn something a little

flashier, but you were right, I had to look like the injured little woman. And, I must say I pulled it off nicely."

Mildred agreed. Tracy had lied like a pro. She'd given no indication that everything she was saying was a load of horse hooey. She'd chosen well, when she picked Tracy to help her achieve her goal of splitting up James and Kelly. Speaking of whom, she remembered her boss' suggestion that her plan wouldn't be enough to come between them; that she needed to play on their goodness. She swallowed the rest of her champagne in one gulp.

"I've got a little work I need to do tonight. Can we have our celebration tomorrow?"

Tracy frowned. "If you have to. I was hoping we could have a little fun tonight. I'm in the mood to party."

"It's probably not a good idea for you to be whooping it up in public, after you went to all that trouble to appear like a wounded bird on *I.I.R.* tonight."

Tracy took a sip of champagne and pointed at Mildred. "You are so right. I don't know what I would do without you, Millie. You've been great through this whole thing."

Mildred rose and patted Tracy on the shoulder. "You too, kiddo. I'll see you in the morning."

****

The fallen angel transported herself to Kelly's condo. She sat on the counter and swung her short legs as she watched Kelly and James canoodle on the sofa. She scowled. It appeared the boss was right. These two were not going to let the interview alone get them down. Good thing she had some follow-up planned for the next day. After that, she'd get going on playing these two goody-goodies for her own evil ends.

James stood and held out his hand to Kelly. "Ready for bed?"

She grasped his hand and he pulled her to her feet. "Am I ever."

"Me, too." James grinned devilishly and swept her into his arms to carry her into the bedroom.

Mildred rolled her eyes. These two were so full of love and goodness, it made her nauseous. They certainly weren't making her job easy. If they had just a little more selfishness and evil in their souls, she'd be done with this whole shebang by now.

Her ears perked up as she heard them stop kissing and begin to talk.

"You'd really do this interview just to clear my name?" Kelly asked in disbelief.

"Of course. I told you—I don't care what the hell people say about me. I've got a hide like a rhinoceros."

"Well, I don't want them thinking you'd cheat on your wife. I mean Tracy was the cheater in your marriage, and now she's coming across like she was 'Wife of the Year'. It's not fair."

Interesting, Mildred thought. I can work with this self-sacrificing malarkey. As the talking stopped and it became apparent the kissing was beginning again, she popped herself out of the condo and back to her hotel room. She had a lot of calls to make if she wanted the next stage of her plan to be in place for tomorrow.

Chapter 18

The next morning, Kelly and James emerged from the elevator in the marble lobby of her building. James had on worn jeans and a dark T-shirt, with a pair of sunglasses covering his eyes. He had his arm slung around her shoulders.

Kelly suspected that she looked as happy as she felt as she strolled along next to James in her white Capri pants, short-sleeved navy top and flat sandals. Her sunglasses were pushed up on her head like a hair band.

She looked at her watch and felt her smile fade a little. "We probably should've gotten an earlier start. We'll just have time to grab a cup of coffee and check out the newspapers in the coffee shop to see how bad the fallout is from Tracy's interview before we need to pick up Lydia."

"My bad." James grinned without a hint of regret in his voice or demeanor. "I couldn't drag myself away from you in bed. Or in the shower..."

She blushed and looked away. He frowned as she looked through the glass doors to the sidewalk. "I wonder what's going on out there. It's quite a mob scene."

James cocked his head and drew his brows together as he held the door open for her. "Yeah. It's unusual, even for this busy neighborhood."

Kelly stepped through the door he politely held

open for her and was blinded by flashbulbs as she was greeted by a wall of photographers and reporters. She squinted in the glare and held one hand up to shield her eyes. James stepped out of the building behind her and put his hands protectively on her shoulders; he felt big and solid against her back, like a safe haven determined to protect her as best he could.

The cameras flashed and clicked incessantly, and the reporters all shouted questions at them.

"Kelly, is it true you've been lovers since you were only eighteen years old?"

"Why did you marry other people if you were still going to sleep together?"

"Do you regret cheating on your husband now that he's dead?"

"And do you think his grief at your infidelity with Mr. Flynn contributed to his death?"

James' grip on her shoulders tightened at the last question, and she blinked away tears as he roared, "No comment!" and used his grip on her shoulders to steer her back into the building. He shut the self-locking door firmly behind them, and she felt the tightness in her chest ease a little with its click, knowing it meant the reporters couldn't follow them back into the building.

No one could follow, but the cameras continued to flash through the glass door and wall to the outside, and the now muffled voices of the tabloid reporters continued to shout their insulting questions.

James rushed them into the elevator. He reached for the button to her floor, but Kelly shook her head and leaned forward to press the one for the underground garage.

She straightened up and crossed her arms tight

across her chest and struggled to keep her voice steady as she explained. "Grace has a business meeting this afternoon, and Bill's out of town on a flight. She needs us to watch Lydia. If we can get to my car fast enough, maybe we'll get out of here before the vultures even realize we're gone."

James wrapped his arms around hers and pulled her back tight against him as the elevator went down one floor to the garage. "Are you sure? If we call Grace, she'd understand, and I'm sure she can reschedule her meeting."

"I'm positive," Kelly said with a terse nod, resolved. "She's counting on us and she's just starting up her business. I don't want her to be seen as unreliable by a potential client. She can't afford to lose any at this stage in her career, but we might have to go to Balboa another day. I'm afraid we'd be mobbed there today, too, and it might scare Lydia."

"But not you. I think it's incredible—the way you can face the most unimaginable things and just keep going," James said against her hair. She felt his breath as he spoke against her ear, and in spite of all the turmoil couldn't hold back a little shiver at the sensation.

The elevator dinged and the doors slid open. Kelly grabbed James' hand and spoke as she tugged him along, "I don't think I'm that incredible—things might suck, but you keep moving. What else can you do? It's what everyone does."

He loped along beside her. "No—it's most definitely not what everyone does. When the road gets rocky, lots of people take to their beds and pull the covers over their heads. You are one hell of a woman,

Kelly Morrison Lynch."

She peered toward the garage exit. "Thanks. Unfortunately those reporters don't seem to share your good opinion of me. I don't see them at the exit, do you?"

He followed her gaze and squinted in the square of bright sun at the top of the ramp that led up to the street.

"Nope. Looks clear. We might just make it."

They hopped into the car, and James was still buckling up when Kelly threw it into reverse. "Hold onto your hat, Flynn. With a little luck we'll be on the 5 before they realize we're not in the building."

She paused only long enough to wait for the motion-activated gate to lift and her tires squealed as she hung a hard right turn out of the garage.

James gripped the door handle so hard his knuckles were white. "Good thing your garage leads to a side street and not the front of your building where all the press is camped out."

He swallowed hard as Kelly wove in and out of the downtown Tuesday morning traffic. "Did you go to one those race car driving schools or something? Because all of a sudden I feel like I'm in the lead car at Daytona."

Kelly cast an anxious glance in the rearview mirror. "I guess I can slow down now. It doesn't look like anyone followed us."

She eased up on the gas and settled into one lane. James pried his hand off the armrest and flexed his long fingers to get the blood flowing again

"Seriously, Kel. Where did you learn to drive like that? You were totally badass."

She surprised herself by actually laughing. After

the ugly accusations the press had hurled at them, she'd doubted she would ever laugh again.

"I went through the same driver's ed program you did in high school. I guess fear and adrenalin just kicked in and brought out my inner badass stock car racer. It's just that I'd never forgive myself if I led those vultures to Grace's house."

****

Mildred sat unseen in the backseat and snorted. Badass, indeed. These two were about as badass as cotton candy.

The ambush by the reporters went just the way she'd planned, and she couldn't believe her luck was holding. She'd managed to catch James and Kelly alone and unprotected by their guardian angels.

She barely needed to concentrate to hear James' thoughts. He was screaming in his head with fury over the way Kelly had been treated. He knew she didn't deserve the ugly accusations, which had been hurled at her, and he blamed himself for this pain and upheaval in Kelly's life. Her late husband would never have dragged her down into this kind of mess. Michael put Kelly's happiness above everything else, and it was crystal clear in the way he was spending his afterlife making sure Kelly found love again.

Okay, Mildred could work with that kind of self-flagellation.

She focused her foul energy, and James looked out the window and frowned as the thoughts she'd planted hit his mind.

Kelly would be better off without him. She was such a private, bashful person, and she was being thrust into the harsh spotlight of the gutter press. And it was all his fault it was happening to her. If they weren't dating, Tracy never would have dragged Kelly into her twisted scheme.

God knew he loved Kelly, and it would break his heart to end things with her, but it would be better for her if he did. She was the best woman in the world, and she deserved to have a better man in her life—one who didn't have a grasping ex-wife out for blood. One who was more like Michael and less like him.

Kelly glanced at his stormy and pained expression then looked back at the road as she drove. "It's okay, James. I'm okay. It was startling, and…well…just lousy to be confronted that way outside my own home, but the things they said were all lies."

His heart twisted in his chest as he listened to her brave words. He felt like pond scum, dragging a good woman like Kelly into such a cesspool. And she was trying to make him feel better. He felt unworthy of her loyalty. While he didn't understand where all these insecure thoughts were coming from, he couldn't deny the truth he felt in them. He couldn't bring himself to speak and merely grunted in response.

Kelly's wounded expression caused Mildred's heart to sing, and the fallen angel decided it was time to listen in on Kelly's thoughts to figure out how to use them against her.

They were pretty similar in nature to James' self-recriminating ideas. Interesting. She'd be able to use the same tactics she had with James. She dropped her noxious thoughts into Kelly's head.

Kelly exhaled a whoosh of air as a terrible thought crossed her mind. Maybe James was regretting their relationship. After all, her image in that damned painting was the ammunition Tracy had used against him. It was all her fault.

He'd been pretty happy with his parade of bimbos before her, and if he'd been with one of them at the charity exhibit on Saturday night, none of this would have happened. They were all young, beautiful, and uncomplicated. They didn't come with the baggage she did. And Tracy had left James alone for years when he was dating all those girls. It wasn't until Kelly had come back into his life that Tracy had unsheathed her talons and tore into James. A realization came to her with a shocking clarity—nothing had ever been so obvious to her before, and her certainty at it felt preternatural. This whole mess with Tracy was Kelly's fault.

Her eyes were bright with unshed tears and her throat burned with the effort it took to keep them from falling.

James would be better off without her. If she truly wanted what was best for him, she had no choice—she needed to pull away from him. Their time together had been like a lovely dream for her, but she had to face facts. She caused trouble and unhappiness in his life, and she loved him too much to harm him any longer.

They'd spend the afternoon together babysitting Lydia, but when they got back to the city she'd go home alone. She felt as though someone had punched her in the gut at the thought, but she'd survive. She'd made it through the loss of Michael and she'd get through this, too.

Mildred patted herself on the back. These two pinheads were just too easy. With all their ludicrous notions about love and self-sacrifice, they'd played right into her hands. She decided to take a moment to bask in their misery, which filled the car like poisonous smog. She inhaled deeply with satisfaction in her evil deeds.

Suddenly, the tiny backseat of Kelly's car became very crowded as Michael and Zane appeared next to her.

Zane looked every inch an avenging angel as he glared at her across Michael, who had the misfortune to be stuck in the middle seat.

"Just what the hell do you think you're doing, woman?" he asked with quiet menace.

Mildred twisted her mouth. She really shouldn't have stuck around to gloat. Much as she hated to admit it, the cowboy scared her, and if she hadn't stayed to watch the results of her handiwork, she could have been gone before he got there.

During this time Michael, concentrated on the people in the front seat and punched his thigh in irritation at what he saw. "I'll tell you what she's done, Zane. I just listened in on their thoughts, and Millie has each of them thinking the other would be better off without the other."

He turned to his friend and asked with a hopeful nod, "We can fix it, right? We can replace those awful thoughts with something else?"

Zane squinted at Mildred, his hat low over his narrowed eyes. "It doesn't work that way, buddy. Once the thoughts are there we can't get rid of them. We can try to steer Kelly and James in the right direction, but we can't make them forget. The damage has been done."

Mildred forced a bright smile to her face as a show

of bravado. In reality, the cowboy's anger made her anxious to tuck her tail firmly between her legs and run.

"He's right. The damage is done," She licked her index finger and gestured as if she were scoring a billiards game in a tavern. "Score one for my side."

And with that taunt, she flashed out of the car.

Michael scooted to the right into the seat the fallen angel had vacated.

"What a mess. I guess Millie was cleverer than we gave her credit for, she did have more planned than Tracy's lying television interview. How do we fix this, Zane?"

His friend shook his head once. "I don't rightly know. I've got to cipher on it for a while. Mildred was good, I'll give her that much. She exploited feelings and insecurities they both already had. They're both essentially noble people and she turned that against them. It's going to make it hard to repair the damage."

Michael huffed in frustration. "If Mildred wasn't already dead I think I could kill her."

He looked at the couple sitting in strained silence in the front seat. "At least they're together now, and they still plan on spending the afternoon together."

"That's true," Zane acknowledged. "What do you say we leave them alone for a bit, while we figure out what to do next."

****

James and Lydia sat side-by-side on the sofa in Grace and Bill's formal living room, a large sketchbook balanced between them as James gave the child an impromptu art lesson instead of the museum tour they'd promised her.

Kelly sat in a wingback chair opposite them and

flicked absently through a magazine she'd picked up off the coffee table. It was clear her mind was on other matters as she flipped through the pages so fast the turning almost created a breeze. She was so lost in her thoughts she jumped and tossed the magazine when the door to the garage slammed shut.

"We're home! Sorry we're a little late. Bill's flight was behind schedule, and I had to wait at the airport for him."

Grace tossed her portfolio on the floor, and slipped out of the high-heeled shoes she wore with her sophisticated linen suit. Bill followed, and looked sharp in his airline pilot's uniform.

"Daddy!" Lydia called out with glee and pushed the sketchbook to James as she hurried to her father's waiting arms.

"The only good thing about these long-haul flights is the greeting I get when I come home." Bill beamed at James over his daughter's head.

James felt a sharp pang of envy. He'd dared to hope he could have this kind of loving family with Kelly. Instead, he'd brought ugliness and pain to her world. What a prince he was.

"You're a lucky man," he said with a voice rough with unspoken emotion.

"Gracie filled me in on what's been happening to you two. I'm really sorry."

Grace sprawled gracefully in the matching chair to Kelly's, and she reached across the piecrust table, which separated them, to squeeze her friend's hand in support.

"Were you able to reach your publisher or your lawyers?"

Kelly bit her bottom lip as she nodded. "The P.R. person at my publishing house said he could set up an interview with a reputable journalist for me to set the record straight. But he did warn me that a lot of people will still prefer the more salacious lies to the less titillating truth."

James rolled his neck in a vain attempt to release some of the tension that had taken up residence there. "And my lawyer said we could sue Tracy for slander. The documents from our divorce will show she was the one who…" He hesitated and glanced at Lydia as he tried to formulate a child-friendly way to describe the end of his marriage. "Um…strayed. Further proof is that Arnold and she were engaged before our divorce was final."

"I sense a 'but'," Bill observed sagely.

James inclined his head. "But I did date Kelly before I married Tracy. And I do have a painting of Kelly, which has hung in my home since I was twenty-two years old—including the brief, disastrous time of my marriage to Tracy. He said a jury might feel misguided sympathy for Tracy because of it."

Kelly cleared her throat and her voice was thick with the unshed tears James could tell she'd been fighting all afternoon. "And my lawyer agreed. I was never unfaithful to Michael, but it's almost impossible to prove something didn't happen, rather than something did happen. We could put the burden of proof on Tracy and in theory she wouldn't be able to produce anyone to testify I'd had an affair with James during my marriage, since I never did. But her TV appearance proves she can lie like a rug and she has no scruples about doing it, so she could find a disreputable lawyer and someone willing to perjure himself for a price to lie and testify that I did cheat on Michael. And again, the jury's sympathy would be with her. They would see me as nothing but a homewrecker."

"What are you going to do?" Grace asked with a sympathetic frown.

Kelly shrugged and managed a tight, anxious smile as she replied, "Go home and try not to cry in my beer."

****

She looked around at the somber expressions of James and her friends and decided to drop her attempt at a cheerful mask, as she clearly wasn't fooling anyone in the room.

"Honestly, Grace, I don't know what to do. I need time to think."

James nodded tersely. "Ditto. My instinct is to go after Tracy with both barrels, but I don't want to drag Kelly through any more mud in the process, and I don't see how I can do one without the other "

Bill bobbed his head in sympathy, and then turned to Kelly. "I was looking at your car on the way in the house tonight."

She wrinkled her brow at his serious tone. "What's wrong with my car?"

Bill smiled. "Nothing. It's very you. But it does kind of stand out. I was thinking if those vermin were still staked out at your condo, my car might be less conspicuous."

Kelly thought of his very nice, but non-descript, dark sedan in comparison to her cute, sunny yellow convertible, with its vase of Gerbera daisies on the dashboard and agreed with a brief nod.

"You can take it home tonight and leave your car

here. We can switch back later this week when things have calmed down a bit."

"Or you could just stay here for a few days," Grace suggested.

"I'm not hiding." Kelly's response was fast and firm. "I won't give Tracy or those horrible reporters that kind of power over me. I refuse to be run out of my own home."

She smiled at her friends' concerned faces. "Although I'm grateful for the offer of a hideout. It's very tempting, but I couldn't look at myself in the mirror if I let them control my actions to that extent. But I will swap cars with you for a couple of days, if you're sure?"

****

James took the keys from Bill as they stood in the driveway and prepared to leave after dinner. He flashed a brief grin at Kelly and teased, "I'll drive home, Maria Andretti."

She forgot her sadness and her plans to break things off with him for a moment. Her face lightened and she joked back, "Hey, I got us out of town without a single reporter following us. It's not my fault if you're too chicken to handle my fabulous driving technique."

"Yeah. It's all on me. Whatever helps you sleep at night. But, I'm driving home." James took possession of the driver's seat.

Kelly felt herself go all soft inside at their light, teasing banter, and she smiled at him. When she saw the hopeful expressions on Grace, Bill, and Lydia's faces her own grin faded.

She couldn't let herself fall back into the easy relationship James and she shared, albeit briefly. She was bad for him and needed to end things for his sake.

Kelly shrugged as she waved at the little family and got in the passenger side. "Whatever. You can drive home."

****

For miles James and Kelly sat in the luxury sedan in a most uncomfortable silence. Kelly stared out the passenger side window as if she didn't want to look at James. With both hands gripping the steering wheel, James doggedly kept his eyes on the road straight ahead.

James couldn't stand the deadly quiet any longer and blurted out, "It was nice of Bill to loan us his car. Clever of him to think of it."

"He's a smart guy," Kelly said, but kept her gaze fixed on the dark night outside her window.

"Have to be smart to be a pilot, I guess," James added casually, but inside he was dying.

Kelly didn't respond and they lapsed back into uneasy silence.

They had such a comfortable rapport since they'd come back into each other's lives. The only tension between them had been the good kind—sexual. But now, they were making inane small talk as if they were strangers, instead of people who'd made mind-blowing love in the shower together that very morning.

He knew it was for the best. To protect Kelly he had to get the hell out of her life. The realization had hit him like a lightning bolt on the drive to Bill and Grace's house this morning, and it had taken root in his mind during the afternoon. He knew what had to be done, and for Kelly's sake he'd be brave enough to do it, but that didn't mean it wouldn't hurt like a knife in his gut. And the pervading sense of discomfort in the car was the first strike. It made him miserable.

Desperate for something to fill the void, James turned up the radio and didn't turn it down until they approached the parking garage.

As they got closer to home, he noticed Kelly shift uneasily in her seat. This was it. Once they got out of this car, it would be over. The laughter, the closeness, the love—all over.

"I don't see anyone by the parking entrance, but I think a couple of reporters are up on the corner," James observed.

Kelly ducked her head, but peered to the front of her apartment building. "You're right. Hopefully, Bill's car will do the trick and throw them off our scent."

They both heaved sighs of relief when they pulled into the fluorescent lights of the garage. James pulled Bill's sedan into Kelly's spot.

"We made it."

They got out of the car, and Kelly hesitated before speaking, and he fought against the hope that warmed his chest, when he thought she was going to invite him up, because in his gut he knew it would be easier for both of them if they made a clean break.

Instead, she held out her hand for the car keys. "Thanks for driving. I'll get these back to Bill when we make our swap."

James knew a firm dismissal when he heard one, and Kelly was definitely dismissing him. What he didn't understand was why it hurt so damned much when it was what he wanted in the first place. Kelly's life would be better James-free—it just would have been a little less painful if she seemed to want him in it just a little bit. Instead, he felt like he was getting the bum's rush out of her life.

He put the keys in her outstretched palm, and fought the overwhelming urge to take her hand in his and pull her into his arms for a passionate kiss, "Right. I'll head back to my place." A part of him still hoped for an argument from Kelly, but none was forthcoming.

"Okay. Good night." She looked down, which prevented him from seeing if her eyes mirrored the pain he knew was in his own.

James took a hesitant step toward Kelly as if he couldn't control the movement, but she was already walking toward the elevator. He listened to her footsteps echo in the garage until he heard the hum of the elevator taking her up and out of his life, and then ducked his head and jogged across the street to his own building's garage. He didn't feel up to facing the reporters camped at the front door just yet. He might give in to his baser urges and deck one of them, and that wouldn't help the situation at all. It was safer all around to go up the elevator from the garage to his condo.

****

Mildred watched Kelly come into her condo. Her shoulders were slumped and she sniffed back tears. Mildred felt nothing but glee. She followed Kelly into her bathroom and laughed at the choked sob she heard when the woman spotted James' shaving kit on her counter.

But her pleasure faded as she listened in on Kelly's thoughts and realized she was considering calling James to come over to get his things. That wouldn't do at all. They were both still too much in love and too close to getting back together for Mildred to allow them to see each other again tonight. She watched with trepidation as Kelly went into her bedroom and picked up the telephone to call him.

Okay, she had to do something fast to stop her from calling. She decided Kelly's insecurities might be another weapon in her arsenal. If Kelly's instincts to protect James from harm weren't enough to hold her back, Millie could just plant a few other thoughts in her mind to dissuade her.

Kelly wiped her eyes. This was ridiculous. If James wanted his things, he would have asked for them. He hadn't made any move to come up to her condo with her, maybe he realized he could do better than Kelly. She remembered the group of young, glamorous women at the charity exhibit. Why would he want a shy, thirty-five year old woman when he had a harem like that waiting for him? She shook her head and firmly placed the phone back on the nightstand. Nope. She would show some pride. If he wanted the stuff he left here, he could call to make arrangements to get it.

Mildred had a sudden fear that James might do just that, and she decided to pop over to his place to make sure that he didn't.

Kelly continued to get ready for bed, but realized she wouldn't be able to sleep. She'd just lie in bed and feel sorry for herself and that wouldn't help anything. Better to get some work done. She switched off the light and walked into the living room to start in on the revisions her editor had suggested.

****

James leaned on the railing of his balcony across the street and watched the light go out in the window of the room he now knew was Kelly's bedroom. He sighed. It looked like she was going to bed. Guess she wasn't having any trouble sleeping. He was the only one who was.

Mildred watched from the shadows and expanded on that train of thought and placed some more doubts in James' mind. She could tell he'd been tempted to go to Kelly until he saw the light go out in her bedroom. She had to drive the wedge between them even more firmly.

James suddenly wondered what Kelly could possibly see in him. From all accounts her late husband had been well on his way to sainthood when his life was cut tragically short. Everyone who knew him said Michael was smart, funny, and thoughtful. The perfect man for Kelly. And what did James have to offer her? A sketchy romantic past with a lying ex-wife out to stir up trouble and a long line of bimbos? For a short time, she had made him feel like a better man, but he knew the truth. Kelly deserved better than James, and she wouldn't get it with him hanging onto her like a pathetic limpet.

But, God, did he want her in his life. He was so selfish. See—further proof that she was better off without him.

He knew sleep would elude him tonight, so he went inside and to his studio. Might as well get some work done if he was going to be awake anyway.

Mildred smirked with satisfaction. Really, these two were so easy. All their noble urges and ridiculous insecurities made it so easy to manipulate them.

"What no good are you stirring up now, Millie? Why don't you just vamoose and leave Kelly and James alone already?"

The cowboy's low, threatening voice made Mildred jump three feet in the air. She unfurled her wings and flapped back to the ground.

Zane's face was shadowed by the night and his black cowboy hat. He looked more menacing than Mildred could ever hope to appear. He was a most unusual good guy, and she hoped she'd be able to come away from this assignment unscathed.

There was no use letting him see her fear, though. She cocked a plump hip, planted a hand on it and spoke with a confidence she was far from feeling, "Now why would I want to do that? Especially when they're both so heartbroken. All this sorrow is intoxicating to a fallen angel like me."

"I'd think at some point your self-preservation instinct would kick in. I'm an angel of limited patience, and I'm just about at my limit."

She gulped, but strove to put on a brave face. "You don't scare me, cowpoke."

Zane smiled, but with his icy eyes it was somehow more terrifying to her than his usual stone-faced expression. "I should, Millie. If you had a lick of common sense, I would scare you."

She pointedly looked around the balcony. "Where's your partner in crime tonight? Mooning around Kelly, I suppose. It's really lame how he still hangs around trying to help her when she's boinking another man."

"Michael's a better man than folks like you and me could ever understand."

"Where is he?" Her tone was belligerent.

Zane chewed on a toothpick and clenched it between his teeth to reply. "He has an idea how to undo some of the damage you've done. He's a smart guy. Always thinking. With his brain and my muscle and un-angelic lack of ethics, you're in big trouble, Millie, old girl."

He winked at her and flashed away from the balcony.

Mildred stood for a moment to get her emotions under control. Zane really did frighten her. She didn't understand him—he had so much darkness in his soul, he could rule among the fallen angels. Yet he chose to work on the side of good. She didn't know how to fight someone like him.

She peered in the window at James in his studio. He was working like a man possessed, as if he could somehow exorcise his personal demons through paint. He looked good and miserable, so she should be feeling more satisfied, but the cowboy's words made her think. Just where *was* Michael and what could he possibly do to reverse the damage to James and Kelly's relationship?

Chapter 19

The next morning found Mildred back in the living room of Tracy's suite. The fallen angel sipped a Bloody Mary and smacked her lips with obvious relish. She was in much better spirits today than she'd been in the night before. A little distance from Zane had helped to break the spell of uneasiness he'd woven around her.

Michael and he could try to undo the damage she'd already done, but they didn't realize she wasn't finished yet. She just had to wait for Tracy to finally emerge from her morning *toilette* to put the next stage of her plan into action.

What could the woman possibly be doing to take this long to get ready? Tracy really did bring the concept of high maintenance to a new level.

The bedroom door opened and Tracy strutted out in a barely there candy-apple red bikini and gold sandals with mile-high heels. Her platinum blonde hair was fluffed up and her face was fully made up.

"Morning Millie," she trilled.

"Why aren't you dressed?"

Tracy glanced down at her body. "I am dressed—for the pool. What's the problem?"

Mildred felt irritated with the shallow woman before her. "We've got an appointment with that lawyer I told you about. To discuss your alienation of affection suit against Kelly Lynch."

Tracy raised one golden shoulder in a dismissive shrug. "We can always reschedule. I need to work on my tan while I'm in California, and maybe I'll meet a man at the pool. Arnold hasn't exactly run after me to bring me home, and James made it crystal clear he doesn't want me, so I need to hook up with another meal ticket. Pronto."

Mildred took a deep breath and worked to keep the impatience she felt out of her expression. When she finally spoke, her voice revealed nothing but patience and sympathy for what Tracy considered her dire position, "That's what this lawsuit is supposed to do for you. Kelly and James are both rich, and you deserve some of that money. Then you won't have to marry another rich, old guy. You can find yourself a hot, young stud if you've got your own money."

Tracy's shoulders slumped, and she bit her bottom lip, "I know you've done so much for me, and I appreciate it, Millie, I really do, but I think it would be easier for me to just snag another sugar daddy."

Mildred looked at the woman's surgically enhanced, gravity defying boobs, which were barely contained by two triangles of fabric, held in place by a golden ring doing yeoman's service. "It's true. You'd have no trouble finding a man, but wouldn't you rather have your own cash? Then you wouldn't have to depend on some rich man's whims. I mean, look at what's happening with Arnold—you can't count on a man sticking around."

Tracy lifted one shoulder and sighed. "I know. It just seems like so much work, and none of what I'm claiming is really true. What lawyer would take on a case like that?"

Mildred grinned. "Trust me; the lawyer we're seeing today won't let a little thing like the truth stand in the way of a good case. He'll throw so much mud at Kelly and James, they'll be willing to pay you whatever you want just to have you go away and leave them alone."

"I still don't know, Millie." Tracy looked down at the gold sandal she scuffed on the floor. "I've already gotten my revenge on them. You said they broke up."

"Sure, but you deserve something for the time you were married to James. It's not your fault he was still poor when you divorced. He's rich now, beyond your wildest dreams, and you deserve a piece of that pie. You slaved away as a waitress when you were married so he could have the time to paint—he would never be where he was today if it wasn't for you."

"You have a point there."

Tracy's natural avarice seemed to be getting back in the driver's seat. Now to play on her abundant ego. "And doesn't that phony goody-goody Kelly Lynch get on your nerves? Acting all holier-than-thou. Thinking she's better than you."

Tracy's eyes flashed. "She is not better than me."

Mildred jumped on Tracy's rising anger. "Of course she's not. So, let's show the world what she's really like."

Tracy thought for a minute and then nodded. "Okay. You convinced me. Let me change out of this bikini, and we'll go see your lawyer."

****

Michael sat unseen in the smoking lounge of a swanky private club in Manhattan. He watched the paunchy man in the leather chair puff on a cigar as he read the Wall Street Journal.

He'd been following Arnold Blackburn since the day before, and the man truly was a toad, both in appearance and in character. If ever two people truly deserved each other, it was Tracy and Arnold Blackburn.

While observing Arnold in the hopes of determining the best way to bring him back to his wife's grasping arms, Michael had learned that Arnold wasn't overly interested in reuniting with Tracy. He had some twenty-one year old chippie to replace her.

But Michael had also determined that appearances and respect meant a lot to Blackburn. He wouldn't want to be a laughingstock among his cronies, and he definitely didn't subscribe to the school of thought that what's good for the goose is good for the gander. He might be screwing around with a girl young enough to be his granddaughter, but he'd lose a lot of face among his peers if his wife were doing the same thing.

Two men sat in chairs near Arnold, and Michael decided to use them to put his plan into effect. Hopefully, Uriel would understand what he was about to do, and wouldn't hold it against him. He had to get Arnold out to San Diego to take his trouble-making wife back, because if Tracy were back in the comfortable clover of Arnold's money she would leave Kelly and James alone.

He concentrated on the two men, and expanded on the unflattering thoughts about Arnold that already existed in their minds.

"Isn't that Arnold Blackburn?" one of them asked the other.

"Sure is. What a sucker—have you heard about his

wife?" his friend answered with a smirk.

"Who hasn't? She's out in California throwing herself at her first husband. She must be desperate to get away from Blackburn."

"Who could blame her?" his friend asked with distaste. "I mean look at him. He's old enough to be her father, and he's ugly as homemade sin."

The other man snorted with laughter. "And to listen to my wife and her friends, the first husband is just as rich, but young, handsome, and an artist. You know how broads go for that sensitive bullshit. Artists get so much ass, it's depressing."

"She's playing Blackburn for a fool all right. I bet she's out there on his money, banging the ex-husband." He grinned lasciviously. "And she looks like the kind of woman who could bang a man's brains out. You can see where an old guy who probably can't get it up wouldn't ring her bell."

Arnold had the cigar clenched between his capped teeth. His face had turned brick red, and Michael was afraid the man would die of a heart attack before he had the chance to reconcile him with Tracy.

"I almost feel sorry for the old guy."

"Not me. You know the saying 'there's no fool like an old fool'? Blackburn is living, breathing proof of it. Sitting here puffing on a stogie like he's the king of Manhattan while his wife is letting the world know she wishes she'd never divorced her first husband."

The other man nodded. "Rumor has it she left the first husband for Blackburn. I used to think old Arnold must have something going on to have such a hot wife, but now, it looks like she was using the poor sap."

"I tell you what I'd do if it were me—I'd go to

California and drag my wife back to New York by her hair."

****

Arnold crushed his cigar out in the ashtray and threw his newspaper down. How dare these two nobodies pity and scorn him? He was Arnold freakin' Blackburn. He was a captain of industry in the prime of his life, goddamit, and not some old man whose wife needed a young stud to get the job done for her. If people were thinking that kind of bullshit, he needed to do something to stop it.

Maybe he should have paid closer attention to what Tracy was doing. He'd been so relieved when she left town, he hadn't worried overly much about where she was and what she was doing. Clearly that had been a mistake.

He needed to get her back under control and by his side where she belonged. It wouldn't do to have investors and business associates thinking he was a spent force who couldn't hold on to his wife. These two schmos might be imbeciles, but they had made good sense on one point. Arnold stood and held his head high on his non-existent neck as he strode out of the room. He was going to take their advice and fly out to San Diego and drag Tracy back by her expensively bleached hair. He'd bought and paid for the woman, and he was going to get his money's worth out of her.

****

Thursday afternoon, and Kelly was in the exact same place she'd been since Tuesday night—she sat at her desk and peered at her computer screen. Her hair was pulled back in a messy ponytail, and she was in an ancient, faded red Boston University T-shirt and shorts.

297

She pushed her eyeglasses up on her nose as she picked up a pen and furiously scribbled notes on a pad of paper.

She'd thrown herself into her work, and had alternated between doing revisions to her manuscript and research for her next book. Right now she was in research mode, but both activities kept her brain fully engaged, and didn't leave any time to dwell on how much she missed James.

She frowned at the knock on her door and the sound of muffled female voices on the other side. She really didn't want to talk to anyone right now, but she couldn't very well ignore the knock. She cranked music when she worked, so they had to know she was home. She tossed her pen on the desk, turned down the music, and went to get the door.

Grace and Janie were on the other side, along with Daphne and Charlie.

"Come on in. I wasn't expecting you," Kelly said with less than her usual graciousness.

Janie patted her on the cheek as she passed by. "We know, sweetie, but what choice did we have? You're not answering your phone."

"Or texts, or email," added Grace as she swept into the condo.

"How did you get in the building?" Kelly asked.

"We ran into Mrs. Schwartz out front, and she let us in—she said to let you know she'll be by the pool later, if we wanted to join her."

Kelly clenched her jaw and made a mental note to pop up to the pool later and have a conversation with Mrs. Schwartz about the importance of security in the building, as it seemed like she was forever letting people in the front door.

"Now that you're here, would you like something to drink?" Kelly offered half-heartedly.

Grace grinned cheekily as she pulled a bottle of Chardonnay from the small wine refrigerator, built into the kitchen island. "Don't worry. We know where everything is."

Janie pulled four wine glasses out of the cupboard, and Grace opened a drawer to retrieve a corkscrew.

Charlie's round face was wreathed in smiles as he looked at Kelly and held out his chubby arms in open invitation to hold him.

Kelly smiled for the first time in two days, and took him from his mother. Daphne tossed the giant diaper bag she'd had slung over her shoulder onto the ground.

"I cannot wait until he's old enough that I don't have to lug around a bag the size of Texas full of baby supplies."

Grace handed Daphne a glass of wine. "Don't rush things. The time goes by so fast. It seems like my Lydia was just his age, and now she's eleven going on forty."

She shoved another glass at Kelly. "What have you been doing besides ignoring us?" She sniffed the air around her friend delicately. "Because you clearly haven't been spending the time on your personal hygiene."

Kelly plunked the glass of wine on the table and sat down. She bounced a gleeful Charlie on her knees. "I've been working. I guess I've been kind of caught up in it. Sorry, but you know what I'm like."

Janie's smile was gentle. "We do know that about you. We also know how you use work as an escape—

like you did after Michael died."

Kelly's face tightened, and she bounced Charlie a little more aggressively. The boy didn't mind, in fact his delighted chortles seemed to indicate he thought it was the best pony ride ever.

Daphne looked between the other women anxiously and said in a voice that seemed designed to diffuse the storm brewing in the room, "I don't know anything about your work habits, but I was worried. Neither you nor James will answer your phones. I do know James, and I've seen him cut himself off like this twice before—when Tracy left him, and again when his mom passed away."

Kelly widened her eyes. "You think James is unhappy? I thought his life would go back to normal without me in it."

"Ah ha!" Grace exclaimed like Perry Mason to a hostile witness. "I knew you had some cockamamie self-sacrificing motive for breaking up with him."

"Grace, remember we agreed—no judgment," Janie reprimanded in a quiet voice.

Daphne ignored them both and answered Kelly, "Steve and I haven't been able to get in touch with him. Steve's over at his place now to see how he's doing, but I think it's safe to say he's not happy, Kelly. He never isolates himself when he's happy, only when he's miserable. He was happy with you—happier than I've ever seen him, and I've known James for a long time."

Kelly wrinkled her forehead. "I thought without me around Tracy would back off, and he could go back to dating beautiful girls like the ones at the charity exhibit."

"Does it look like Tracy's backing off?" Grace

asked with one perfectly plucked and shaped eyebrow raised.

Kelly shook her head ruefully. "No. As a matter of fact she's not. My lawyer heard from Tracy's lawyer today, and she's going to file some frivolous alienation of affection lawsuit against me."

Daphne frowned and held up her index finger. "Hold on—we'll get back to this bogus lawsuit in a minute. I just want to emphasize to you James wasn't happy with any of those glamazons when he was dating them. He had nothing in common with them. With you, he wasn't afraid to be himself. And he's a great guy, although his finely honed defense system doesn't let many people see that about him. He's smart, funny, kind, and generous. James isn't just Charlie's godfather. It's in our will that he'd raise him for us if anything ever happened to Steve and me—that's how much we think of him. There's no one we'd trust more to take care of our son than James."

Janie frowned, and rubbed soothing circles on Kelly's back. "Back to the lawsuit. What are you going to do?"

"My lawyer thinks Tracy wants to intimidate me into settling out of court. He believes she'll keep dogging me in the press until I pay up, so he thinks I need to get my version of things…"

"You mean the actual, planet Earth version of things—not the out-there lies that bitch is telling?" Grace interrupted.

Kelly nodded. "Right. The truth My lawyer thinks it will help my case to be more visible and tell my story in a public forum. I spoke to the P.R. department of my publishing house, and they managed to set up an interview with Sarah Bennett tomorrow." She named a prestigious journalist who appeared on a well-respected weekly news program.

"That's good," Grace said with a sharp nod of approval.

"I suppose." Kelly shrugged. "I hate to talk about my personal life on national television, but I want to set the record straight about my marriage to Michael and about James and Tracy's divorce. I don't want those lies about us to go unanswered."

Grace took a healthy swig of her wine. "Please tell me you'll be showering before you go on television to make your case."

****

Steve leaned against the wall of glass in James' studio, and watched his friend flick gray, black, and red paint on a canvas. He took a long draw on his bottle of beer and observed, "That is one friggin' gloomy piece of shit you're working on. It looks like Jackson Pollack meets Tim Burton, and then they stop off for a beer with Herman Munster."

James scowled. "It's how I feel right now."

"I am really sorry to hear that, man." He gestured at the canvas with his beer bottle, "'Cause that—right there—is misery on an easel."

"Shouldn't you be at work on a Thursday afternoon?" James asked with a scowl.

Steve grinned. "That's the beauty of being the boss, my friend; I can duck out when a buddy needs me. It's a benefit I hadn't really considered when I started my own graphic design firm."

"A buddy needs you? Then you'd better be on your way," James suggested hopefully and made a shooing motion with his paint-splattered hands.

"Nice try, but you're the buddy in need. You don't call. You don't write. You're worrying Daffy."

James smiled at his friend in spite of his dark mood. "But I'm not worrying you."

"Hell no. There couldn't possibly be anything for me to worry about. The James I know wouldn't be enough of a douche bag to break up with the best thing that's ever happened to him, and certainly not for a reason as lame as his skanky witch of an ex-wife stirring up trouble in her cauldron."

"I guess you don't know me as well as you thought you did then, because Kelly and I are no more."

"And the reason for that would be…" Steve prompted.

"I'd think it's obvious—Kelly is better off without me. I've got to put her needs above my own, like her late husband would have done. Tracy is going after her like a rabid pit-bull. Take me out of the mix, and she'll leave Kelly alone."

"Yeah, but is she leaving you alone?"

James frowned and shook his head. "No. My lawyer called and told me she wants to pursue financial recompense for our time together."

Steve shook his head in disgust. "Money for the marital bed. Doesn't that officially make Tracy a hooker?"

James uttered a bark of humorless laughter. "I guess it does. About time she made it official—she's been dressing like one for years."

"She doesn't have a case though, right? What does your lawyer say to do?"

"He thinks I need to put my story out there. Try to

get public sympathy on my side, so Ellen set up an interview for me tonight with Sarah Bennett. This way I can tell the truth about my divorce and Kelly's marriage. Hopefully it will salvage a little of Kelly's reputation, which is currently in tatters thanks to me."

"Not you. Tracy. It's all her fault, dude. Don't blame yourself."

"But I'm the connection between Tracy and Kelly," James growled his response.

"Look, you know I don't like to butt into your business. It's against the guy code, but I can't just sit back and watch you fuck things up with Kelly. Tracy's betrayal left you bitter and suspicious of women. You wasted a lot of years on women not fit to shine your shoes, because of that pitiful excuse for a woman. Don't let her wreck a single day more of your life. You were happy with Kelly, and she's one hell of a woman. You two could have what Daffy and I have together, and I want that for you, man. Don't let Tracy have any more of you. Don't let her win. Go get Kelly back."

Chapter 20

"And just who is this Mildred woman anyway?" Arnold roared as he paced the living room of Tracy's suite like a caged lion.

Tracy jutted out her chin and said with spirit, "Millie's my friend."

"Since when? You never mentioned her to me before, and does she ever stink like rotten eggs! I can still smell her in here even though she went back to her own room five minutes ago."

Mildred tried to tone down her scent. She might be non-corporeal but Arnold's tirade had her so angry the natural aroma of a fallen angel grew stronger. Her eyes darted around as she tamped down her sulfurous odor. The man made her frightened on top of angry. She had a lot riding on her scheme with Tracy, and the woman's pain-in-the-ass husband was about to blow it all sky high.

Tracy shrugged. "So her perfume's a little strong. She's been a good friend to me during a difficult time."

Arnold scoffed. "A little strong? What the hell is it called—*Eau de Brimstone*?" He glared at his wife, "And you want to talk to me about a difficult time? The way you're making a spectacle out of yourself over your ex-husband—you're turning me into a laughingstock back in New York."

Mildred could tell that Tracy had been intimidated

by her husband's anger since he'd blown into San Diego that morning like a storm cloud, but now she was good and mad—more like the Tracy Mildred had gotten to know over the past few days. The Brooklyn accent Mildred suspected Tracy worked hard to suppress, in her effort to present herself to the world as a Manhattan society lady, became more pronounced as her anger grew.

"That's rich! You were a laughingstock? Good! Now you know how I've been feeling while everyone in Manhattan knows you've been banging some slut young enough to be your granddaughter. All the phony concern I've been getting from my so-called friends, when they're really snickering at me from behind their perfectly manicured hands. Fuck you and your humiliation! It seems like turnabout is fair play to me, you two-timing old bastard!"

"Nice mouth on you Tracy," he said with disdain.

She narrowed her eyes and clenched her fists until Mildred feared she'd draw blood as her long red nails cut half-moons into the palms of her hands. "You never used to have any complaints about my mouth—in or out of the bedroom, not until you decided to parade your underage strumpet around like a trophy."

Arnold waved a pudgy finger at her. "Amber is not underage. I was very careful about that."

She laughed bitterly. "Well doesn't that just make you a friggin' saint? Why the hell did you fly three thousand miles just to yell at me? Couldn't you have done it over the phone? Then at least I could have had the supreme pleasure of hanging the hell up on you!"

Arnold took a deep breath and composed himself. He adjusted the knot of his silk tie at his thick neck, and adjusted the cuffs of his custom-made suit. "I didn't come here just to fight with you. I came to try to reach some sort of mutually beneficial agreement between us."

Tracy raised an eyebrow at his conciliatory tone. "In other words—you need me."

Arnold cleared his throat. "What I'm saying is there's no reason we can't hammer out a solution that suits us both."

A sly smile spread across Tracy's face. "Your business associates were willing to turn a blind eye to you cheating on me, but when you're the cuckold it started to hurt the bottom line, huh?"

"Cuckold is an ugly word."

"But it's what you're being called, isn't it? And you don't like it. Which brings me back to my original point. You. Need. Me." She pointed to her ample bosom, which threatened to fall out of the red and gold short kimono-style robe she wore. She'd been getting ready to go to dinner with Mildred when Arnold had almost knocked the door to her suite down.

Arnold's jowls quivered in exasperation. "Fine. I need you. Happy? I need you in Manhattan giving every appearance of being a happy, well-satisfied wife, but you need me, too—at least financially." His beady eyes narrowed in the folds of fat, which surrounded them on his face.

Tracy inclined her head. "What do you propose?"

Arnold breathed a sigh of relief. "You'll come back to New York with me and will act adoringly to me in public. In return, I would also give a public appearance of being a faithful, loving husband. In private, we would go our separate ways. As long as they were handled with the utmost discretion, we could both pursue extramarital activities."

"Sounds like you'd be having your cake and eating it, too. What's in it for me?"

"You would have access to my money…"

"Our money," Tracy interrupted.

"Fine. You would have access to our money. All those society bitches you're always sniffing around would think I was a model husband. And as long as there is never a whisper of scandal, you can 'eat cake', too."

Tracy pursed her plump lips as she considered his offer. Her eyes grew shrewd as she said, "I have conditions. I want to be protected in case you ever get it into your head again to leave me. I want my financial position clarified in a legally binding document."

Arnold's face turned even redder than its normal hue as he thought over her condition. He finally replied tersely, "All right. But in said document, I want it stated that if you behave the way you have been lately, all bets are off. You get nothing if you publically chase after your ex-husband—or any other man—again."

Mildred frowned as she could tell Tracy only pretended to consider his counter-offer.

"I guess that's fine," Tracy said with a great show of reluctance that was completely phony.

"One last thing. I want to squelch all the supposition about your relationship with James Flynn. I've set up an interview with Sarah Bennett before we leave San Diego. You'll appear on her show with me, and we'll tell the world our recent behavior has all been geared toward getting each other's attention. You'll state you don't love Flynn. Only me. And you'll clear up any rumors you've started about him and that mousy-looking egghead he's dating."

Tracy hesitated. She was afraid she'd look like a complete fool if she went on television and admitted she'd bent the truth about James and Kelly.

Arnold sensed her hesitation and said with quiet determination, "It's a deal-breaker, Trace. I won't have people thinking I'm your second choice. Take it or leave it. But remember, if you leave it, you walk away with nothing. And don't think it will be easy for you to find another man like me to support you. No man in Manhattan is going to want my sloppy, middle-aged seconds—and that's what you are, Trace."

Mildred almost screamed in frustration—he was speaking Tracy's language, and there was no way the aging tramp was going to refuse his offer.

Tracy pouted and her words confirmed Mildred's worst fears. "Fine. I'll take it."

Mildred buried her face in her hands. All her well-laid plans were about to go to hell in a hand basket. And so, she feared, would she. Quite literally.

****

Kelly leaned her head on the back of the chair and heaved a sigh of relief. Her interview with Sarah Bennett was over and it had gone as well as could be expected. She lifted her head and waved at David who had watched the whole thing from behind the cameraman, on the other side of the swanky hotel suite where it had taken place. He grinned at her and flashed the thumbs-up sign.

A member of the crew approached and helped Kelly remove the microphone from her celery green dress. She smiled her thanks and stood. She tried in vain to smooth the wrinkles from it and wondered what had possessed her to wear linen.

Her lawyer, an older gentleman with abundant white hair, who was dressed in a well-tailored suit walked up to her. "Good job, Kelly. This interview will go a long way toward repairing the damage to your reputation. You did good, kid." His phone buzzed in his jacket pocket, and he pulled it out to answer it. "Excuse me for one moment."

He stepped away to take the call, and Kelly strolled across the room to David's side. She smiled at her friend and the cameraman to whom he was speaking. "Bit of a busman's holiday for you, huh, David?"

Sarah Bennett's cameraman laughed. "I was just saying the same thing to him."

David gave Kelly a quick hug. "You came across really well. Now the rest of the world will get to see the fabulousness that is my best friend."

Her shoulders slumped. "I'd settle for the rest of the world realizing your best friend isn't a two-timing ho."

David looked around at the crew packing up their equipment and at Sarah Bennett who was deep in conversation with her producer. "I think we can probably head out now, Kel."

She nodded. "Let me grab my purse and tell Mr. Davis we're leaving."

Kelly retrieved her bag from the table where she'd stashed it and gestured to her attorney that she was leaving. He nodded and held up his index finger to indicate he wanted her to wait a moment for him.

As she turned to go back to David, Sarah Bennett quickly finished up her conversation and hurried to

Kelly's side. She rested her hand on Kelly's arm.

"I won't keep you long; I just wanted to speak to you quickly before you leave."

Kelly smiled and said sincerely, "Me, too. I wanted to thank you for treating me so respectfully during the interview."

The journalist's eyes widened in surprise at her statement. "How did you expect me to treat you?"

Kelly shrugged. "For the last several days I've had reporters camped out in front of my condo. Every time they catch a glimpse of me they shout questions that make me sound like the whore of Babylon. I guess it's lowered my expectations of the press."

Sarah scoffed. "Tabloid reporters and paparazzi. They're just looking for sensation, not the truth. I'm more interested in looking at a story from every angle to help the viewers form an opinion based on fact. I'm sure after this piece airs the public will see the real you, and the scandal mongers will leave you alone."

"I hope you're right. I'm grateful for the opportunity to set the record straight about my late husband and James."

"I was happy to provide you a forum to do so. I have to confess, I'm a huge fan of your Tony and Tessa mysteries."

"Thank you. The next one comes out in September; I'll be sure to send you a copy."

"That would be great!" Sarah hesitated and cocked her head. "Could I ask one more favor of you?"

"Sure." Kelly said.

"You strike me as a woman who is uncomfortable with publicity, and I suspect you have no intention of watching this piece on my show tomorrow night."

Kelly grimaced. "Seeing myself on television is right up there with root canal on my list of least favorite things to do."

Sarah peered intently into Kelly's eyes and said seriously, "Please promise me you'll watch. I've interviewed other people as well, and I think it would help you to see what they have to say."

Kelly's brow furrowed in confusion. "Okay. I promise I'll watch."

Sarah smiled and patted her arm. "Great! You won't regret it."

Mr. Davis approached. "Ready to roll, Kelly?"

Sarah had already moved away and was talking to her assistant and checking her phone. Kelly gestured to David, who said goodbye to the cameraman and came to her side. He squinted at the attorney. "You look like you just won a case in the Supreme Court. What's up?"

The lawyer ushered them both out of the suite and to the elevator. He pressed the down button and said, "I just had a call from Mrs. Blackburn's extremely disgruntled attorney. He was most unhappy to report she's dropping her cases against both you and Mr. Flynn."

Kelly's jaw dropped, and David whooped with pleasure.

"I don't mean to be a negative Nelly, but it seems almost too good to be true," she said.

The elevator doors slid open, and the lawyer gestured in a courtly manner for Kelly and David to precede him. "A piece of free advice—never look a gift horse in the mouth, Ms. Lynch."

****

James and Steve stepped out of the gym and onto

the busy city sidewalk. The strong summer sun had James swing his gym bag off his shoulder to find his sunglasses.

"Real men don't wear shades," Steve scoffed.

James rolled his eyes as he popped his sunglasses on his face. "Oh yeah? What do they do about this kind of glare?"

"We squint. Like Eastwood."

James noticed his cell phone in his bag. "Hold on a sec. I've got a couple of messages."

"Maybe one of them is Kelly," Steve suggested hopefully.

"Doubtful. I'm sure she's too busy enjoying the calm of her now James-free life to think about calling me."

Steve looked down as he scuffed the rubber toe of his sneaker on the sidewalk. "Daffy wouldn't want me to tell you this, but…"

James froze in the middle of retrieving his voice mail. "Tell me what? Is something the matter with Kelly? Is she okay?"

"Yes and no."

"What the hell does that mean?"

"She's not sick or injured or anything like that, so technically she's okay, but she's sad, man. She misses you."

James narrowed his eyes. "And you know this about her how?"

"Daffy, Grace, and Janie went to see Kelly on Thursday."

James couldn't prevent the hope, which he knew his old friend would see as it flared in his eyes. He tried to sound casual, "And she misses me?"

"Look—Daffy didn't want me to tell you. Female unity or some such bullshit. Don't make me say any more about it. If you're that interested in how Kelly's doing, maybe you should just friggin' call her."

James scowled at what he perceived as his friend's meddling and went back to checking his messages. He listened to the first with a quizzical expression, and the second caused his face to light up with happiness.

"I can only think of one thing that could put that shit-eating grin on your face—Kelly!"

"Indirectly. It wasn't her, though. It was my lawyer. He said Tracy dropped her bogus lawsuits against Kelly and me."

Steve whooped with delight and pulled James into the classic one-armed man hug. "Great news, buddy. With Tracy and her bullshit allegations out of the picture you can get things back on track with Kelly."

James tossed his phone back in his gym bag and walked to his car. Steve fell in step beside him.

"You are going to get back with Kelly now, right? I mean she's sad without you, and you're staying home and wallowing in your own personal gloom-a-palooza without her. I had to drag you out to the gym today. What's holding you back?"

James didn't answer right away. Finally he said, "She's too good for me. She might be sad now, but she'll get past it and realize she's better off without me."

Steve punched his friend's arm. Hard.

"Ouch! What the hell?" James rubbed his upper arm.

"That is the biggest, steamiest pile of bullshit I've ever heard in my life. B.S. is kind of my thing, so I know what I'm talking about."

James chuckled in spite of his sore arm and the situation with Kelly, which he viewed as hopeless despite his best friend's arguments to the contrary. He grinned at Steve and said, "If only the world knows what Daffy and I know about you. Under all that caveman B.S., you're a nice guy. I've even seen you tear up at that Sarah McLachlan commercial with the abused animals."

"Hey, you'd have to be made of stone not to let that ad get to you. That one-eyed Shih-Tzu with the matted fur..." His voice broke and he took a breath to compose himself. "But back to the matter at hand. I've known you my whole adult life. Aside from Daffy, you're the best person I know. You're good. Down to the ground. I trust you with my son, and that says a lot. Kelly's a hell of a woman—yes—but you're every bit as good as she is. You two have something special, and if you throw it away for such a half-assed reason, you're a hell of a lot more stupid than I think you are."

They walked the rest of the way to the car in silence, as James considered Steve's words. The certainty of the beliefs that had come into his head the last time he'd been with Kelly had him convinced without a shadow of a doubt Steve was wrong.

But that puzzled him; it wasn't like James to see the world in such black and white terms. Usually, he was someone who thought there was a lot more gray out there, but where Kelly was concerned he'd known since that moment in the car he had to get out of her life. For her. But it didn't mean he didn't appreciate Steve's support. No matter how misguided the new little voice in his head told him Steve was.

"Thanks for that, man. You're the best friend I've ever had."

"Of course I am," Steve acknowledged with a cocky grin. The caveman was clearly back in control. "Hey, what was your other message? It had you looking confused."

They reached the classic red-and-white sports car parallel parked on the street. James opened the door and tossed his gym bag in as he answered, "It was Sarah Bennett."

"That reporter you did the interview with yesterday? What did she want?"

"She asked me to be sure and watch the piece on her show tomorrow night. She said she talked to some other people, and I'd be very interested in what they say. I don't know who she could mean. Is it you? Did she talk to you and Daffy?"

Steve held up his hands and shook his head. "Not us, man."

They climbed into the car and James started it up. The engine roared to life, and James deftly maneuvered the Corvette into traffic.

"Do you, Daffy, and the kid want to come over tomorrow night to watch it with me? I'll grill steaks," he offered as an incentive.

"Make mine a porterhouse and we're there."

James grinned at his old friend. "You're so easy."

"Yep," Steve admitted with no shame. "Give me prime grade-A beef and a beer, and I'd follow you into hell."

Chapter 21

Enrique and Kelly carried glasses of soda to the sofa in front of the flat-screen television set mounted on the wall. David followed with a huge bowl of popcorn.

"Sorry to make you take time out of your weekend with David to watch the Sarah Bennett piece on the mess that is my love life, Enrique," Kelly apologized.

David flashed his perfect smile. "For all intents and purposes you're my family, Kelly, and I live in L.A. now, this is what we do when we're starting a new relationship. Come—meet my family and watch them air their dirty laundry on national television. It's totally Hollywood."

Enrique joked back in his sexy Mexican accent, "You're not fooling anyone, David." He grabbed a handful of popcorn and looked at Kelly. "He's hoping there will be more 'Love Triangle' talk. He kind of gets off on having his name romantically linked to James Flynn."

David sat in the center of the sofa with the bowl of popcorn on his lap. He patted the cushions on either side of him to indicate his companions should sit.

"Hell, yeah! Of course I do. What red-blooded gay American man wouldn't?"

Kelly grinned and rolled her eyes as she sat next to her old friend and tossed some popcorn in her mouth. She pointed at the TV and swallowed quickly.

"Shh…it's starting."

****

Across the street, James slid the balcony door open and entered his condo with a platter of delicious smelling grilled steaks.

Daphne placed her glass of red wine and two beer bottles on the table, which was set up in front of the television.

Steve snatched the platter from James. "Smells great! If I was a cartoon dog, I'd sprout little wings and fly after this smell as I sniffed the air."

Daphne took Charlie out of the high chair where she'd already fed him his dinner, and placed him in the rolling, bouncy seat James kept at his condo for his beloved godson.

"Nice visual, you meat-obsessed Neanderthal." She paused and wrinkled her nose as she pondered. "Did Neanderthals eat meat? I've got to look that up."

Steve put a filet on Daphne's plate and hoisted a Flintstone's sized porterhouse onto his own. "Smart chicks, man. They might insult you, but they're always going to be sure their slams are accurate."

Daphne made a shushing motion with her hands. "Quiet. The show's starting."

Sarah Bennett's face filled the screen. She sat at an anchor desk in a Los Angeles studio. Her golden hair was pulled into an elegant French twist. She spoke to the camera.

"Tonight's story isn't the sort you're used to seeing me report." She smiled and continued in a confidential tone, "In an effort for full disclosure, I must admit to being an admirer of the work of two of the people involved in this story. I own a painting by James

Flynn—a very small painting." She held her thumb and forefinger a tiny distance apart. "And I've always been a fan of K.M. Lynch's mystery stories, so when allegations about these two surfaced recently, I was frankly dubious about their truthfulness."

A grainy photograph of Kelly at Michael's funeral appeared on the screen. It was apparent a photographer had taken it with a telephoto lens during the graveside ceremony. Her lovely face was ravaged by grief, and she seemed to only be standing upright with the support of her father on one side and David on the other.

"God. Look at her. She's so shattered," James said, his voice rough with emotion.

Sarah Bennett's voice came in over the photo on the screen. "I remember seeing this picture in a magazine two years ago when Lynch's husband died. The sorrow so evident on her face broke my heart. I felt terrible that someone whose work brought me so much joy should be in such pain.

"When Tracy Blackburn came forward with her story last week I didn't believe this woman..." The camera zoomed in on Kelly's tear-streaked face in the funeral picture, "...could have been cheating on the husband she'd just buried.

"A little digging on my part produced the records of Blackburn's divorce from James Flynn, and they contradict her version of events. Tracy Blackburn began her relationship with industrialist Arnold Blackburn while still cohabitating with her first husband, James Flynn, who at the time was a poor, struggling artist. She became engaged to Blackburn before her divorce from Flynn was finalized, and was married again within three days of the final divorce decree."

A photograph of a beaming Arnold and Tracy at their lavish Manhattan wedding was shown on the screen. Tracy was in a poufy white ball gown, and Arnold wore a tuxedo. They laughed and held a white handkerchief between them, as their wedding guests hoisted their chairs in the air. Tracy's brilliant smile held enough wattage to light up Manhattan.

"This did not look to me like a woman who'd been heartbroken by her previous husband's love for another woman, but one thing I've learned in my years in this business is to never judge solely on appearances. So when I had the opportunity to speak to Mr. and Mrs. Blackburn this week, I jumped at it. Here's what they had to say."

Bennett's live commentary cut to a taped interview with Arnold and Tracy in their hotel suite.

Tracy blinked with wide-eyed innocence as she said, "I'd like to apologize for any trouble I've caused my ex-husband and his girlfriend. They never saw each other, even casually, during the time of my marriage to James, and they never had an extramarital sexual relationship. However, I did. When I met Arnold I knew he was the only man for me, even though I was still married to James. You just can't fight your destiny, y'know?"

She took her husband's hand and batted her lashes adoringly at him as he puffed up like a toad with pride.

"There's only one man I love and that's my Arnold. Everything I've done since I've been here in San Diego, I was doing just to get my husband's attention."

Arnold patted her hand. "And she got it. I'd been a little too absorbed in my work, but from now on, my wife is going to be my top priority."

The journalist frowned. "That's a lovely sentiment, but didn't either of you think about the innocent people getting caught up in your games?"

Daphne waved her hands dismissively at Tracy's face on the television screen. "You are so well rid of that woman."

"That's the truth, dude." Steve concurred.

James ground his molars together, and was so hot under the collar that he was surprised steam wasn't coming out of his ears. "You two are preaching to the choir. Tracy's poison. I just don't understand why she had to go after Kelly."

The image on the screen switched to James and the reporter in his condo. Bennett's voice-over said, "I also spoke to James Flynn this week. He gave me a tour of his studio, and I got to see the painting *Love Awakens*, which played a large role in Mrs. Blackburn's now admittedly false accusations."

****

David looked at Kelly and her eyes were wide with shock.

"I take it you didn't know she'd be interviewing Tracy or James?"

She shook her head mutely and pointed the remote to turn up the volume on the television.

James and Sarah Bennett stood in front of his fireplace and looked at the piece of art hanging above it.

"So this is *Love Awakens*."

James nodded. "Yes. It's Kelly in my parents' backyard the night I met her seventeen years ago."

"You two did meet and date at that time?"

"Briefly, yes, but then we went our separate ways. I'm not going to say I never thought of her again because that would be a lie."

The camera zoomed in for a close-up of his ruggedly handsome face as he shook his head once before answering with regret in his clear, green eyes. "My ex-wife was into material things, but Kelly isn't like that. She's always cared more about people and ideas, so when my marriage turned sour, yeah, I thought about the road not taken with Kelly."

"Did you ever act on those thoughts?"

"You mean get in touch with Kelly?" He shook his head and said with vehemence, "No. Not until very recently when I learned she lived here in San Diego, too. Certainly not during my marriage."

Lines formed around his mouth as it tightened, and he looked directly into the camera and said in a way that left no room for doubt, "Kelly Lynch is not the sort of woman to cheat. Not on anything—not on a test, not on her taxes, and most certainly not on her husband. On the other hand, Tracy is that sort of person, which is why she could never understand an honorable woman like Kelly."

"Tell us what kind of woman K.M. Lynch is so we can all understand."

His face softened as he thought of Kelly and the lines at the corners of his mouth eased. "Kelly's smart, funny, loyal. She's the kind of woman who would do anything for the people she loves. But she'll also go out of her way to help people she doesn't even know. And people sense how caring she is." He chuckled. "If you go somewhere with Kel, be prepared to learn the cashier's life story, or how the waitress is a student in creative writing and would love it if Kelly had any tips for her."

Bennett smiled. "And did she have advice for the waitress?"

"Oh yeah. They ended up exchanging email addresses, and Kelly's going to speak to her creative writing class next fall. She's the best. There's no one like her."

His voice broke and he coughed to try to hide his emotions before he continued. "And I was fortunate to have her in my life, even if it was just for a little while. The lies about Kelly and her marriage made me so angry. Thank you for the opportunity to tell the public the truth about Kelly Morrison Lynch."

The program went back to Sarah Bennett live in the studio. "When we come back, you'll hear Kelly Lynch talk about this week's events."

David and Enrique both swiped surreptitiously at their tears, while Kelly's flowed unchecked down her cheeks.

"Don't let him go, Kel. If you do, it will be the biggest mistake of your life," David said with the bluntness of a lifelong friend.

****

Daphne dabbed at her eyes with a tissue when the news magazine program returned with Kelly's interview.

"You hadn't seen James Flynn since you were eighteen?"

"No, not until this summer. I was very happily married to Michael. My husband," she added by way of explanation.

She blushed prettily. "I'm embarrassed to admit it,

but I don't really follow the art world, and I didn't have any idea how successful his work had become."

"Then you weren't the reason his marriage ended?"

Kelly's hair swung over her shoulders as she shook her head. "Gosh, no. My understanding is that Tracy was the one who asked for the divorce so she could marry another man."

The hint of a smile played around her lips. "I know after his divorce James was a bit of a ladies' man, but I know him well enough to know it didn't happen during his marriage. James would never cheat on a woman."

She laughed before she continued, "There might have been a lot of women in his life, but there's not a doubt in my mind he only dated them one at a time."

Bennett's smile was kind. "What makes you so confident in him?"

Kelly's eyes took on a dreamy, faraway look as she spoke. "James doesn't even remember the first time we met, but I do. I was in first grade and he was in fifth. He defended me from bullies on the playground. I can still see him running up to us, the sun shining on his golden hair, as he got them to stop picking on me. To me he'll always seem like Lochinvar."

"A chivalrous knight," the reporter clarified.

Kelly nodded. "James is a strong man, but he'd never use his strength against someone weaker. You should see him with his little godson. He loves and takes care of the people lucky enough to be in his inner circle, which is small because he'd been so betrayed by his ex-wife." She quirked a wry smile at Bennett. "He has some trust issues as a result, so it's ironic that of all people, Tracy is the one to make these allegations about James. He's a good man—not the type to be unfaithful.

It made me sick to hear these lies about him and know some people are going to believe them. My late husband and James Flynn are the two finest men I've ever known. I don't know what I've done to deserve the love of one such man, let alone two, in my lifetime. I did this interview to clear their names."

The picture faded to Sarah Bennett, back in the studio. Her face was serious as she said to the camera, "There you have it, two very private people who put themselves out there on national television. And each one did it to save the other's reputation, and to clear the memory of a dead man. Neither one was the least bit worried about clearing their own name; they were both only worried about the other. I've interviewed a lot of famous people in my career, but I've never been so humbled by my subjects before. The network brass and lawyers aren't going to like what I'm about to say, but it would be a crying shame if a selfish woman's unfounded allegations about them tore James Flynn and Kelly Lynch apart."

"You heard the woman," Steve said as his wife snuffled into her tissue. "Go get her, dude."

James pushed his chair back from the table and stood. He spoke with determination, "I'm going."

****

As the program went to commercial, Kelly swiped away her tears. "You're right, David."

She jumped up and looked around frantically for a pair of shoes.

"I usually am. About what this time, though?"

"It would be the biggest mistake of my life to give up on what James and I have together. I've got to go to him."

She spotted a pair of flip-flops under her desk and dove for them.

"In that outfit?" David wrinkled his nose.

She was dressed casually for a night in, watching TV with friends in a gauzy white tunic top and khaki shorts. "What's wrong with what I have on?"

"Nothing," Enrique said quickly and gave David a pointed shove to his back.

David got the hint. He didn't want to slow down Kelly's momentum with a wardrobe change. "Right. Nothing. You look great. Go!"

A smile lit up her face and she pushed her glasses up on her nose. "I'm going. Wish me luck"

Kelly sprinted for the door and David called after her, "I don't think you'll need luck. You've got love on your side."

She slammed the door behind her.

"This is the most romantic thing I've ever seen," Enrique stated.

David trotted for the door to the balcony and gestured for Enrique to come along. "Let's watch from up here. Her head is so in the clouds I want to make sure she gets safely across the street."

The two men, one fair and one dark, stood at the rail of the balcony and waited for Kelly to make her way down to street level.

"Just how far is she going to run? Where does James live?"

David pointed to the balcony parallel to theirs on the building to the right of Kelly's. "Over there. Small world, huh?"

Enrique flashed his even, white teeth. "Smaller than you think. Look, it's Steve, Daphne, and their kid on James' balcony." He squinted as he peered across. "And is Steve eating a giant steak?"

David looked over and saw Steve standing at the railing with a plate in his hands. He shoveled a piece of meat in his mouth and watched the activity on the street as if he were in the cheap seats at a ball game. Daphne stood a small distance back from the rail with Charlie in her arms. She saw them looking over and waved cheerfully with her free hand. He waved back with a puzzled look on his face. "Where's James? Kelly's about to charge over there to declare her love for him, and he's not even home?"

Enrique pointed down at the street. "There he is! I think he's got the same idea as Kelly."

David looked at the street below and saw James run out of his building in a dark green polo shirt and worn jeans. A pair of dock shoes was jammed on his sockless feet.

"This is like a movie," Enrique marveled. "You sure know how to show a guy a good time."

****

Kelly rushed off the elevator, through the lobby and out to the street. She shoved past the few diehard tabloid reporters who still waited outside her building in the hope of getting a scoop.

She turned to the right and ran like a gazelle in flip-flops toward the entrance to James' building. She looked up and paused as she saw the object of her mad dash as he jogged across the side street that separated their buildings.

A huge smile brightened her face as she sprinted the last few steps and launched herself at James, who laughed with pure joy and threw his arms open to catch her.

Laughing and crying at the same time, Kelly jumped into his waiting arms. She wrapped her legs around his narrow waist and her arms around his neck. His strong hands cupped her bottom to hold her in place.

"Does this mean you're willing to take me back?" James asked through his own laughter, his eyes suspiciously bright.

"If you'll have me," Kelly said with a huge smile as she blinked away her own happy tears.

The paparazzi chased Kelly and their cameras flashed around the couple. But they were so wrapped up in each other, both literally and figuratively, they were oblivious to the people around them.

"Oh, I'll have you, Kelly Morrison Lynch. Now and forever. I've been enough of an idiot to let you go twice. It's not happening a third time. I thought you'd be better off without me."

"So did I!"

At James' crestfallen expression, Kelly clarified her statement. "I mean I thought *you'd* be better off without *me*. I had all these crazy thoughts and insecurities in my head. I don't know where they were coming from, but seeing you on Sarah Bennett's show it was like a veil had been lifted and they're gone now."

"Me too! While I was watching you on television I felt like my head cleared and I saw things as they really are for the first time since we were driving out to Bill and Grace's house last week. And I know one thing to be absolutely true—I can't live without you, Kelly Morrison Lynch."

"You don't have to. I see it so clearly now; I don't

know how I ever lost my way and didn't see it before. We're better together."

He captured her smiling lips in a passionate kiss, which had the bystanders on the street, and their friends on the balconies above them, cheering.

Suddenly aware they had an audience, Kelly lowered her legs to the ground, but kept her arms around his neck. She peered through her eyelashes at the crowd and smiled shyly. James left his arms wrapped around Kelly, as he sheepishly surveyed the scene on the sidewalk.

"Maybe we should take this back to my place."

****

Hovering on their snowy wings between the two balconies, unseen by the humans, Zane and Michael bumped fists in triumph.

"Hey! Is that Mildred across the street?" Michael chortled.

"Damn right it is. In your face, Millie!" Zane called out in a decidedly un-angelic manner.

On the sidewalk across the street, Mildred's shoulders slumped in dejection. Her doughy face crumpled as she watched James and Kelly walk away together to their happily ever after.

A swirling black mass appeared only to her and the two angels. It floated above the street, and the dark cloud emitted puffs of sulfurous smoke. A deep voice boomed out of the malignant cloud.

"The boss wants to see you, and he is not pleased with this disgusting display of love and happiness."

Mildred sighed and braced herself for her punishment as the mass engulfed her and she disappeared with it from Zane and Michael's sight.

"Going down!" Zane intoned like an old-time elevator operator.

"I almost feel a little sorry for old Millie," Michael said.

"Really?" Zane asked with wonder in his voice.

"Nah," Michael replied with a wave of his hands. "Not even I'm that nice."

A golden light surrounded them as Uriel appeared between the two angels. He draped an arm around each of their shoulders.

"You're nice enough, Michael," he said with a fond smile. "As a matter of fact, you're so nice that it's time for you to move on to the next plane."

Zane fist-bumped his friend. "All right, Mike! Let me know if there are clouds and harps."

Michael laughed at the shared joke. "You'll find out for yourself soon enough. You're too good an angel not to move on soon."

"He is," Uriel agreed as he gave Zane's shoulder a brief squeeze. "But not quite yet. His actions on this case have bought him a little extra time working for me here on Earth. Tonight is your time, Michael. Are you ready?"

Michael took a deep breath and nodded. He beamed down at Kelly and James as they walked down the sidewalk with their arms wrapped around each other, and their faces lit up with smiles, staring into each other's eyes with wonder and happiness.

"My work here is done."

He looked seriously at Zane. "Thank you for all your help. I couldn't have done it without you. I'll miss you."

The cowboy's smile was a little wistful, but not at

all jealous. "You're not getting rid of me that easy. I'll get there someday, and you're the first angel I'll be looking for."

Uriel patted Zane on the back and glowed even brighter than he had before. He left his right arm around Michael's shoulder as he looked heavenward and they elevated a short distance before they vanished in a blink of light.

Epilogue

Four months later…

Zane popped into James' condo, where Uriel had asked to meet him. He looked around and whistled low between his teeth. At least he thought he was in the condo, right now it looked more like the floor display of a candle store.

He watched as James hurried around the living area of his loft and lit candles. A fire flickered in the fireplace, and there was champagne on ice.

Someone had big plans for the night.

Uriel appeared next to him.

"Good, you're here. I thought you'd want to see how this assignment turned out."

James brushed past them, unaware of their presence. He put his phone in the docking station and selected soft, romantic music.

Zane looked around the room with a wry grin. "At the risk of sounding immodest, it looks like everything turned out pretty damn good."

Uriel nodded in satisfaction. "It did. I'm so pleased with your work. Mildred's immediate superior had an ax to grind with me and wanted to irritate me by hurting the people involved in what he saw as a pet project of mine. You didn't let that happen, and I'm very grateful to you. I would hate for innocents to be injured because of me."

"I couldn't have done it without Michael," Zane said humbly.

"Ah, Michael. He sends his regards and asked me to pass along a message to you."

Zane was pleased the other angel remembered him. He counted Michael as one of the few friends he'd ever had. "He did?"

Uriel nodded. "He said to tell you to hurry up and get your butt to the next plane. He misses your ugly face. That was a direct quote, by the way, not my opinion of your appearance."

Zane laughed at the archangel's rare joke. "How's Mike doing?"

"He's wonderfully happy. He reunited with his parents, and he's met a lovely angel. She'd just employed the services of my Guardian Angel Corps to help her husband find love again in the same way Michael did for Kelly. Michael and she have been enjoying each other's company."

"Go Mike." Zane laughed. "I'm happy for him." The cowboy looked at his well-worn boots and cleared his throat. "Tell Mike I miss him, too."

"I will. Oh, and I wanted to tell you the big boss was very satisfied with your work on this project. So pleased, in fact, that he has you in mind for another assignment of a romantic nature."

Zane took off his hat and slapped it against his thigh. "Well, shoot. I'm really not comfortable with all this love stuff."

There was a knock on the door and James' face lit up. Uriel watched the human's happiness and said pointedly, "You may not like it, but you seem to have a knack for this love stuff. I'll be in touch soon with more details on your next assignment," And with that, he flashed out of the room and left Zane alone to observe.

****

James threw open the door. Kelly stood in the hallway, his smile mirrored on her face. She kissed him as she came in wheeling a suitcase behind her.

"I brought my luggage. This way we can just head to the airport from here in the morning. I've got to admit I'm a little nervous about spending Thanksgiving with both our families in New Hampshire."

He flashed a quick grin. "What are you nervous about? My father and Becky are so thrilled you're not Tracy, they'll probably roll out a red carpet for you. On the other hand, your father thinks I'm some sort of amoral artist getting ready to lead his baby girl down the path of sin and debauchery."

Kelly patted his cheek. "He's mostly over that now."

"That really puts my mind at ease. Thanks."

She looked around the room for the first time and her jaw dropped. "Wow! Look at all the candles. Soft music. And champagne! Hmm, seems like you might have a little debauchery on your mind after all."

As Kelly looked around at the scene he'd set, James patted nervously at something in the pocket of his jeans.

"I assure you, my intentions tonight are strictly honorable."

Kelly snapped her fingers in mock disappointment. "Darn, I was hoping for a smidgeon of debauchery to tide me over for the next few days. With you staying at your dad's house, and me staying with my parents. I'm going to miss you at night."

"Know I'm going to be missing you just as much, if not more," James said with heat in his gaze.

Kelly raised an eyebrow in a mischievous challenge. "Make with the debauchery already. Or are you all talk, Flynn?"

James laughed and stepped up behind her. He placed his hands on her shoulders and gently steered her to stand in front of the fireplace, "I think you know that I'm not all talk, and I plan on demonstrating it tonight, but first I wanted to show you what I've been working on before we leave town. I call it *Love Reawakens*."

Kelly stepped forward to look at the new painting, which James had hung next to the now infamous *Love Awakens*. It had the same dreamlike fantasy elements of the first, and Kelly was once again in the foreground in profile on a lawn that overlooked the ocean.

"Is it the Pacific this time?" she asked.

"It is. It's sort of a composite of the view from Grace and Bill's house, and the one from Steve and Daffy's new place—it's great they ended up buying in Grace and Bill's neighborhood."

Kelly continued to gaze at the oil painting in awe. The lawn around her was covered in the little, wild violets that Saul had compared her to, and she was looking up and smiling at something. She followed her gaze in the portrait to see at what.

"Is that Michael and the cowboy hovering in the upper left corner as angels?"

"Yep. I thought it was fitting to include our own personal guardian angels."

"I love it, James." She peered at the painting, and

saw that in it the wind appeared to have caught her hair and she held it off her face with her left hand.

"What's that ring on my hand? I don't have anything like it, but I wish I did. It's beautiful."

She heard James shift his position behind her, but he didn't say anything. She turned around to see what he was doing and gasped when she saw him on one knee. He held a white velvet jewelry box out to her like an offering. The top was open and in it rested the ring from the painting. It was a large, square cut emerald with two triangular diamonds on either side of it, set in platinum.

Kelly raised her hands to her flushed cheeks and happy tears glistened in her eyes.

James' eyes shone in the candlelight, and they appeared to be the same color as the emerald in the ring he held out to her.

"I love you, Kelly. I know I'm not nearly good enough for you, but you don't seem to agree with me, and I'm not dumb enough to argue with you about it. The luckiest day of my life was the day you came back into it. Before you, I was just going through the motions, and with you I'm a better man. I want to spend the rest of my life with you. Loving you. Treasuring you. Laughing with you. Making love with you at night, and waking up next to you in the morning. Watching you carry my babies and raising a family with you."

He paused and took a deep breath. "Kelly, would you do me the incredible honor of letting me be your husband?"

She dropped to her knees in front of him with tears of joy dampening her cheeks.

"Yes, James, yes! Nothing would make me happier

than being your wife."

He grinned as he took the ring from the box and slipped it on Kelly's finger.

She held out her hand to admire the ring, and twisted her arm so the gems flashed in the firelight. She laughed a little breathlessly.

"You're not just doing this so you can face my father with a clear conscience tomorrow, are you?"

He laughed. "No, Kelly. I'm not doing this just to make an honest woman out of you for your father's sake." He paused and inclined his head. "Although, come to think of it, it's not going to hurt my case with him, is it? Maybe Thanksgiving will be a little less terrifying than I thought it would be."

She chuckled and swatted his cashmere-clad arm. She murmured in appreciation as she rubbed his bicep. "Mmm...soft sweater, but all hard and muscley underneath. Wasn't there some talk of debauchery tonight?"

James cupped her face in his large hands and said roughly, "God, Kelly. I love you so much."

He pressed a fervent kiss to her lips, which quickly deepened to something more passionate. Kelly twined her arms around his neck and ran her fingers through his hair.

"I love you, too, James," she whispered against his lips.

He pulled her left hand down and pressed a kiss to her palm. He toyed with her engagement ring. "I've really been looking forward to seeing you in this ring."

She waggled her fingers playfully. "Well, here it is!"

He grinned and raised his eyebrows as he reached

for her cherry-red cardigan and pushed it off her shoulders. "I meant in the ring and nothing else."

As he began to put his words to action, Zane realized that was his cue to leave. He looked thoughtful as he flashed away to give the happy couple some privacy. Kelly and James were deliriously in love and about to embark on a wonderful life together. Maybe he did have a knack for this love thing after all.

A word from the author...

After years working in the business world, my love of reading led me to get my MLS, and I currently work part-time in a school library, a job which allows me lots of time to explore my other love—writing romance!

I live in Maryland, with my husband, who is my real-life romance hero. We both enjoy traveling to visit our far-flung family and friends, and spending time on the beach with an umbrella drink and a good book.

Thank you for purchasing
this publication of The Wild Rose Press, Inc.

If you enjoyed the story, we would appreciate your
letting others know by leaving a review.

For other wonderful stories,
please visit our on-line bookstore at
www.thewildrosepress.com.

For questions or more information
contact us at
info@thewildrosepress.com.

The Wild Rose Press, Inc.
www.thewildrosepress.com

Stay current with The Wild Rose Press, Inc.

Like us on Facebook

https://www.facebook.com/TheWildRosePress

And Follow us on Twitter
https://twitter.com/WildRosePress